Mystery Heiress

SUZANNE CAREY

Published by Silhouette Books

America's Publisher of Contemporary Romance

I'd like to dedicate this book to my editor at Silhouette Books, Lucia Macro, who has unfailingly offered warmth, creative latitude and good judgment for the many years we've worked together.

 SILHOUETTE BOOKS

MYSTERY HEIRESS

Copyright © 1997 by Harlequin Books S.A.

ISBN 0-373-50185-4

Special thanks and acknowledgment to Suzanne Carey for her contribution to the Fortune's Children series.

Removable book marker strip is covered under U.S. Reissue Patent No. 34,759.

Printed in U.S.A.

Kate Fortune's Journal Entry

My whole world is falling apart! Just when I thought things were going to settle down, the unraveling scandal has never been more destructive. Our whole life is an open book for the public to scrutinize. All our deep, dark secrets we thought long buried are coming out one by one.

I've just found out the most shocking news about my dearly departed husband, Ben. Apparently, he had an affair that produced an illegitimate heir! I have to believe he had a good reason for what he did. After all, I've done a few dishonest things out of desperation myself....

A LETTER FROM THE AUTHOR

Dear Reader,

Writing about an extended family like the Fortunes makes me think of my own family, which is scattered from Illinois and Northern Kentucky to Florida, where I, my spouse and stepmother live. Its members range in age from a lively ninety-two-year-old who wins money at bridge and still drives her own car, to the latest addition, a precious two-month-old baby.

Needless to say, we keep the phone company and the airlines busy, visiting back and forth and exchanging information across the miles as we continue to weave new strands in the rich web of our connectedness. Often our talk (both earthshaking and otherwise) is phrased in a kind of shorthand because we share the same history, the same context. In my opinion, it's one of the ways families most help us find our place in the world.

In the story you're about to read, the heroine, Jessica Holmes, arrives from England in the hope her long-lost relatives, the Fortunes, will be able to provide a bone-marrow transplant for her ailing daughter. Though the Fortunes are quite wealthy, she claims that's all she wants from them.

Yet she clearly wants more—not money, as she insists, but rather her share of the common history and web of connectedness I've been talking about. To me, the way she goes about getting it, and fitting in, is as interesting as her struggle to save her daughter's life and her romance with the handsome but troubled physician she learns to love.

Suzanne Carey

SUZANNE CAREY

A Phi Beta Kappa graduate of Lake Forest College, Lake Forest, Illinois, and a former reporter who covered politics and criminal courts as well as undertaking investigative assignments for several newspapers, Suzanne Carey has been writing novels for Silhouette Books since the early 1980s. Though she was born in Illinois, she has been a resident of Florida for many years. She and the man in her life, a clinical psychologist who is now a university professor, currently reside in Sarasota, on Florida's Gulf Coast.

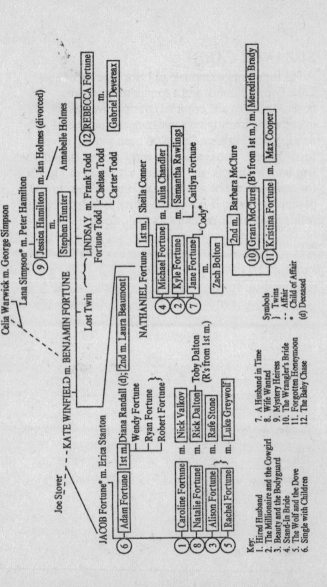

Joe Stover

Celia Warwick m. George Simpson

Lana Simpson* m. Peter Hamilton

(9) Jessica Hamilton m. Ian Holmes (divorced)

Annabelle Holmes

Stephen Hunter
m.

Lost Twin

LINDSAY m. Frank Todd — (12) REBECCA Fortune
Fortune Todd

Chelsea Todd
Carter Todd

Gabriel Devereax
m.

KATE WINFIELD m. BENJAMIN FORTUNE

NATHANIEL Fortune — 1st m. — Sheila Conner

Michael Fortune — m. — Julia Chandler
(4)

Kyle Fortune — m. — Samantha Rawlings
(2)

Jane Fortune — Caitlyn Fortune
(7) — Cody*

Zach Bolton

2nd m. — Barbara McClure

(10) Grant McClure (B's from 1st m.) m. Meredith Brady

(11) Kristina Fortune — m. — Max Cooper

JACOB Fortune* m. Erica Stanton

Adam Fortune — 1st m. — Diana Randall (d); 2nd m. Laura Beaumont
(6)

Wendy Fortune
Ryan Fortune
Robert Fortune

Toby Dalton
(R's from 1st m.)

Caroline Fortune — m. — Nick Valkov
(1)

Natalie Fortune — m. — Rick Dalton
(8)

Alison Fortune — m. — Rafe Stone
(3)

Rachel Fortune — m. — Luke Greywolf
(5)

Symbols
} Twins
-- Affair
* Child of Affair
• (d) Deceased

Key:
1. Hired Husband
2. The Millionaire and the Cowgirl
3. Beauty and the Bodyguard
4. Stand-In Bride
5. The Wolf and the Dove
6. Single with Children
7. A Husband in Time
8. Wife Wanted
9. Mystery Heiress
10. The Wrangler's Bride
11. Forgotten Honeymoon
12. The Baby Chase

F🦁RTUNE'S
Children

Meet the Fortunes—three generations of a family with a legacy of wealth, influence and power. As they unite to face an unknown enemy, shocking family secrets are revealed...and passionate new romances are ignited.

JESSICA HOLMES: The search for a donor to save her daughter's life and the discovery of her true heritage led Jessica to the Fortune family...and into the comforting arms of a man who can help her child.

STEPHEN HUNTER: Compassionate doctor. His strong shoulders are perfect for Jessica to lean on. But can he put aside the pain of his past to begin a new life with Jessica and her daughter, Annie?

MONICA MALONE: She was on the verge of achieving her lifelong dream of destroying the Fortune family...until she was mysteriously murdered. Is it too late for the Fortunes to stop the wheels of revenge Monica already put in motion?

GRANT McCLURE: Love doesn't come easy to a lonely cowboy who prefers his Wyoming ranch to the big city. Will he ever find a woman cut out for country living—and his special brand of loving?

LIZ JONES—
CELEBRITY GOSSIP

Illegitimate! Well, well, well. What do we have here? It seems that Jake is not the legitimate son of Ben Fortune after all! Apparently, the prim-and-proper matriarch of the family, Kate, wasn't a virgin bride! She was sleeping with another man and then tried to pass off to the world her unborn child as Ben's.

And one of the few people who knew the truth was Monica Malone. My sources tell me that Monica had been black-mailing Jake for quite some time, threatening to reveal the scandalous secret if he didn't sell her large shares of Fortune stock. If that isn't a motive for murder, I don't know what is! And if Jake isn't guilty, then why did he skip bail?

The Fortunes are on a sinking ship. And I for one don't see any chance of them staying afloat!

One

To some, he supposed, it must be an ideal summer day, bright and breezy if decidedly cool for the twenty-fifth of July—perfect for kicking over the traces and taking your kid to visit the lions, chimpanzees and zebras. But that wasn't how it felt to him. A pensive, solitary figure as he strolled the curving blacktopped paths of Como Park Zoo in St. Paul, Minnesota, thirty-six-year-old Stephen Hunter had no kid to delight with his undivided attention, no inquisitive, heartbreakingly courageous scrapegrace eight-year-old boy to whom he could explain that giraffes ate treetops for lunch and were strictly vegetarian.

To be gut-wrenchingly precise, he had no *David*. Instead of his cherished towheaded son, who'd succumbed to a rare form of bone cancer three years earlier, he had what felt like a gaping hole in his heart. To date, no one and nothing had begun to fill it. Or even come close.

Today was the anniversary of David's death. Having purposely kept his schedule light, in view of the depressed and angry feelings that were bound to surface, he'd been drawn to the zoo by loneliness, memories of better days, and the ache of a loss he believed would never fully leave him.

A dedicated physician who specialized in treating leukemia and other blood-related disorders at Minneapolis General Hospital, and knew a good deal about tumors, as well, he hadn't been able to stem the tide of David's downward progression or, in the end, keep the breath of life from deserting his child's wasted body.

Ultimately, the torrent of rage and helplessness that had followed in the wake of their son's death had driven Stephen and his ex-wife, the former Brenda Torgilson, apart. Immersed in those bleak, desperate days as deeply as he, Brenda had accused him of failing to be there for her. He realized in retrospect that her criticism was probably just. In his view, the emotional desertion had cut both ways. After David's loss, he'd snapped shut like a clamshell, living solely for his work and battling his grief in the keep of his own private fortress, while she'd gone to the opposite extreme, venting her tears and outrage on him.

Divorced now for the better part of a year, they rarely saw each other. Though Stephen regretted the breakup, viewing it as a personal black mark that could never be erased, he'd long since decided that in the final analysis, parting company was for the best. If they lived to be a hundred, he suspected, he and Brenda wouldn't be able to look into each other's eyes without seeing the pain of David's loss staring back at them.

Somehow, he needed to start fresh. Get a grip on himself. Live for real again, instead of simply going through the motions. He just wasn't sure how to start. Never the kind of guy to get involved in casual affairs, he didn't plan to take that path now. His son's memory deserved better of him. Yet he was paralyzed by the prospect of committing to anyone. Most single women his age who weren't already mothers deeply wanted a baby, while the thought of giving another hostage to fortune caused panic to grip him by the throat.

He, Brenda and David had come to the zoo as a family during David's final, painfully brief remission. Though they were living on borrowed time, the occasion had been marked by a kind of frantic, ephemeral happiness. The remembrance of that afternoon had been his reason for coming today. In a way that was irrational and would have been difficult to explain, he'd hoped to catch a sidelong glimpse of his beloved child, if only in memory and imagination.

Pausing to gaze at the gorillas and orangutans, which David had always loved, Stephen noticed a slim, attractive dark-haired woman and a rather frail-looking blond female child of approximately kindergarten age who were touring the zoo together. The woman's roses-and-cream complexion glowed as if it had been nourished by a cool but temperate climate.

Her naturally curly hair, worn short, framed her face in ringlets. Her clothes spoke of classic good taste and sufficient income to indulge it. She was wearing well-polished flat leather shoes, a hand-tailored beige wool skirt and a long-sleeved cashmere pullover in a flattering blue-violet shade. From what he could tell at that distance, the third finger of her left hand was innocent of a wedding ring.

The child was dressed a bit more warmly than her contemporaries at the zoo, in a plaid wool skirt, a cotton turtleneck and a red hand-knit cardigan with matching kneesocks and black patent Mary Janes. It was clear from the woman's demeanor, in particular her nurturing but vaguely worried air, like that of a fretful guardian angel, that she was the girl's mother and loved her very much.

Unfortunately, to Stephen's practiced eyes her little girl didn't look at all well. To begin with, she was too thin for her height. Her large, solemn eyes—he couldn't see their color, thanks to the distance that separated them—appeared too big for her face.

For some reason, when mother and child moved on toward the seal island and the aquatic animals, Stephen followed at a slight distance, keeping them in view. Ironic, isn't it? he thought, giving his head a wry mental shake. That today, of all days, you'd set eyes on a woman who could interest you. Really imagine, for the first time since David's funeral, how nice it would be to have a family again.

His emotional state being what it was, he supposed it was just as well that he and the woman were strangers and he didn't have an excuse to speak to her. The last thing she needed, if his assumption about her child was correct, was an emotionally crippled workaholic doctor cluttering up her life. She was probably married, anyway—a settled, if young and lovely, Minneapolis housewife with a doting, successful husband.

As it happened, the woman he was speculating about, twenty-five-year-old Jessica Holmes, a British investment analyst, had been widowed six months earlier, while she was in the process of obtaining a divorce from her philandering, well-to-do husband. She and her five-year-old daughter, Annabel, had arrived in the Minneapolis area just two days earlier, and were suffering from jet lag. Their tour of the zoo wasn't as brisk or cheerful as it might have been, in part because Annie, recently diagnosed with leukemia, was somewhat low on energy, and Jess was terribly worried about her.

Maybe the zoo hadn't been such a good idea, after all. Following their exhausting transatlantic flight, and a frantic day spent dragging her daughter to and fro as she tried to contact at least one member of the Twin

Cities' wealthy Fortune clan—as yet to no avail—she'd decided Annie needed a little fun for a change.

The expedition had proved to be only a modified success. Though she tried to tell herself she was just imagining things, Jess kept thinking she detected the harbingers of some ailment, a cold or the flu, that Annie's compromised immune system would fight inadequately at best. Even on "good" days, when Annie had a modicum of stamina, Jess couldn't seem to stop herself from hovering over the girl like a mother hen guarding a beloved and fragile chick. To her shame, Annie had picked up on her fears and, in her innocent, childish way, begun reassuring her.

I have a perfect right to be afraid, Jess thought, outwardly stiffening her spine and putting on her bravest face. Annie's form of leukemia is deadly. She needs a bone-marrow transplant, and soon. If she doesn't get it, I'm going to lose her. And that would be the end of both our worlds.

It was the need for matching bone marrow, a rare and precious commodity, that had brought them to Minneapolis. As Jess had quickly learned once Annie's condition was diagnosed, her child's best hope of finding a donor was among blood relatives. Unhappily, they'd already exhausted every possibility among Jess's scattered family members and the somewhat more prolific clan of her late husband, a prosperous but cavalier bank executive who'd been killed in an automobile crash, along with his most recent mistress, shortly after Jess initiated divorce proceedings.

Refusing to be immobilized by fear, she'd signed Annie up with a British bone-marrow registry and settled back to bite her nails when she ran across a letter, addressed to her grandmother, that had been among her recently deceased mother's possessions.

Specifically, the letter had been tucked in a volume of children's verses from which her mother had read to her every evening when she was Annie's age. Scrawled in a strong, masculine hand on yellowing, unlined paper, the letter had suggested that Benjamin Fortune, a legendary American entrepreneur who'd fought with the Allies in France during World War II, was her true maternal grandfather, not George Simpson, her grandmother's husband of many years.

In doing so, it had explained why some of the blood tests among her relatives had been so far off the mark, while opening up a whole new world of possibilities for Annie's salvation. There had been no reason to doubt that the letter was genuine. Making up her mind in an instant, she'd arranged for a leave of absence from her London investment-banking firm and carted Annie off to America in the hope that one of Benjamin Fortune's descendants could provide the help she so desperately sought.

So far, every door she'd tried to open remained closed in her face. True, after several minutes of impassioned pleading on her part, the formidable secretary who guarded the entrance to the executive offices of Fortune Industries in downtown Minneapolis like some kind of exquisitely coifed and made-up dragon at the gate had agreed to give Jacob Fortune, Benjamin's oldest son and the company's chief executive officer, her handwritten note when he returned to the office three days hence. But Jess doubted he'd bother to get in touch with her. From what she'd been able to glean from her hurried research into the family history, the Fortunes had been the target of numerous false claims on the family wealth over the years. Jacob Fortune could hardly be blamed if he regarded her plea as another swindle in the making.

Somehow, she'd have to convince him otherwise. None of the other Fortunes had turned out to be accessible. As she'd feared, most had unpublished phone numbers. International directory assistance had been able to give her just three subscribers with the Fortune surname in the Minneapolis–St. Paul metropolitan area when she phoned before leaving England.

The two she'd reached had turned out to be unrelated. She wasn't sure, yet, about the third. Phoning from her country cottage in Sussex several days before their departure, she'd twice managed to contact a certain Natalie Fortune's answering machine, which had played back a friendly greeting in a young woman's sweet, energetic voice. To her disappointment, though she'd left a message urging the unknown Natalie to phone her collect as soon as possible, no return call had been forthcoming.

A second call, made after they reached Minneapolis, had proved even less promising. This time, the answering machine had been switched off. Or unplugged. Maybe Natalie Fortune had moved, or something.

Whatever the case, Jess knew one thing for certain. She hadn't come to Minneapolis to fail. Unless a miracle occurred and Jacob Fortune returned her call without further prompting, she'd camp on his doorstep. I'll renew my quest tomorrow, she vowed, even if I have to leave Annie with a hotel-provided baby-sitter. It was a desperate attempt at pluck, coming from a devoted mother who hated to let her beloved, seriously ill child out of her sight for a single second.

Having looked their fill at the seals, polar bears and

penguins, Jess and Annie headed for the giraffes and the other hooved African animals, pausing at a vendor's cart on the way, so that Jess could buy her daughter a paper cone of raspberry-colored cotton candy. Her cheeks flushed from what Jess prayed was just excitement and not another bout of chills and fever to come, Annie took a bite of the spun-sugar confection, which colored her mouth a streaky hot pink, and ran ahead.

"Zebras, Mummy! *Zebras!*" she exclaimed.

Calling himself an idiot for maintaining his tenuous low-key pursuit of them, but intrigued by Jess's delicate good looks and what appeared to be the strong bond between her and her daughter, Stephen Hunter kept pace. As he watched, unable to intervene, Annie stumbled and fell to the pavement, skinning her left knee slightly.

Jess was beside her in a flash, inspecting the damage. "Are you all right, darling?" she demanded worriedly, sinking to her haunches so that she and Annie were at the same level as she attempted to brush every trace of dirt from the abrasion with a clean handkerchief.

Annie seemed willing to take the mishap in her stride. However, she complained, "My head feels hot, Mummy."

From what Jess could tell on closer inspection, her child's large green eyes were exceptionally bright, as if from a fever. When she tested Annie's forehead with the back of her wrist, she learned, to her dismay, that it was burning up. Her beloved child's deteriorating immune system had failed to protect her from yet another virus or bacterial infection.

"Oh, baby," Jess whispered, her heart sinking as she enveloped the girl in a guilty hug. "We've got to get you back to the hotel at once."

She wasn't aware of the tall blond man's approach. As a result, she almost jumped to find him towering over them.

"Excuse me, my name is Stephen, and I'm a doctor. Is there anything I can do to help?" he asked in his decidedly American accent.

He was tall and lean, with boyishly tousled, sun-bleached hair and penetrating blue eyes that hinted at the possibility of Nordic ancestry. His hands were neat and long-fingered. They looked capable. Jess's off-the-cuff impression was that he had a kind face. Despite everything she'd heard about crime in American cities, she was inclined to trust him. Instinct told her his claim to be a physician wasn't an empty boast.

Still, she wasn't accustomed to accepting medical advice from strangers on the sidewalk—especially not where Annie's welfare was concerned.

With a fluid motion that wasn't lost on him, she arose. "Thanks, but not really," she said in her cultivated British voice. "The abrasion on my daughter's knee isn't serious. However, she seems to have caught cold. I've decided to give up on the zoo for today...and return to our hotel."

Viewed at close range, she was stunning, in the fair-skinned, dark-haired way Stephen liked best. A young Elizabeth Taylor, as she'd looked when she starred in the classic version of *Father of the Bride,* he thought, ever the vintage-movie buff. Her accent betrayed that she was British—on holiday in the U.S., if her reference to a hotel was any indication. More than he could have said, he liked her natural air of refinement and her obvious devotion to her daughter.

After three wasted years spent imprisoned in the co-coon of his heartache and loneliness, he realized, the social man in him was on the verge of reaching out again. He had to admit, the idea was more than a little frightening. Meanwhile, in his practiced and usually infallible judgment, her daughter had contracted something more serious than a garden-variety upper respiratory infection.

With an unmistakable air of authority that swept past Jess's weakened defenses, Stephen crouched to lay his wrist against the child's forehead and feel her neck with strong but gently probing fingers. Brief though it was, the latter exam caused her to wince. And no wonder, Stephen thought with a slight shake of his head. She had swollen glands, and doubtless a sore throat. Though he couldn't be sure without a thermometer, he estimated her temperature at one hundred and one degrees Fahrenheit or thereabouts.

He made a production of examining her knee, as well. Producing a brightly colored stick-on bandage from the pocket of his tweed sport jacket, where he always carried them for his younger patients, he applied it to the child's injured knee as if it were a badge of honor before getting to his feet.

"Better?" he asked.

Distracted from her fever and the pain of her injury by the bandage's novelty, Annie managed a shy "I guess so" as she stared up at the tall, blond stranger. She quickly added a polite "Thank you," at Jess's prompting.

"Your daughter has swollen glands and a temperature," Stephen added, gazing directly into Jess's dark-fringed brown eyes. "Hadn't you better take her to a doctor?"

Tempted for a hot moment to abandon her us-against-the-world stance and let herself lean on this blond Viking of a physician who had invaded their privacy as if he owned it, Jess felt anger, tinged with panic, flow through her veins. What was he doing, exactly? Accusing her of negligence? Or attempting to secure a new patient?

"I would if we had one here in the U.S.," she snapped, then crumbled as Annie shivered slightly. "We just got here from England day before yesterday, and the weather's much chillier than I expected," she added almost apologetically, drawing her daughter close. "I'm afraid Annie's cardigan's not warm enough...."

Stephen didn't hesitate. "Here...take my coat," he insisted, shrugging off his tweed sport jacket and wrapping it warmly about Annie's shoulders. "Did you come by car?"

Jess nodded, overwhelmed by his take-charge manner and, now that she'd dropped her defenses, more than a little grateful for his intercession.

"Show me where it's parked," he offered. "I'll carry her."

With her mother at the tall stranger's side, evincing approval, Annie didn't protest when Stephen lifted her in his arms. Instead, she seemed to wrap her arms about the blond doctor's neck and nestle against his tan oxford-cloth shirt as if she belonged there, as if she appreciated his *fatherliness*.

It was just an illusion, of course, fostered by Jess's anxiety that she wouldn't be equal to managing Annie's medical crisis on her own, not to mention her residual pain over the fact that Annie's father had so seldom evinced an interest in the girl. Instead of reading stories and taking their precious five-year-old on outings, Ronald Holmes had spent most of his free time chasing other women and driving fast cars while under the influence.

As she led the way to the Wolf parking lot, where she'd left their cherry-red rented sedan with its unnerving left-hand drive, Jess reflected that her husband's untimely and undignified exit from their lives had become irrelevant. She and Annie were on their own, and in a sense they'd always been. Thanks to the fact that Ronald had died before the divorce was final, they had more than enough money at their disposal to pay for Annie's treatment. If they could just find a marrow donor...

Their little procession of three had reached her rental car and, squaring her shoulders, Jess fitted her key in the door on the passenger side. Taking Annie from his arms and placing her inside, she exchanged his jacket for the heavy woolen shawl she'd left on the seat and returned it to him.

"We'll be fine now," she told him, gazing up into his sky-colored eyes. "Thanks for your help."

Stephen shrugged off her gratitude with a polite murmur. Of his two chief emotions—a half-formed wish to see her again and his strong concern for her child—the latter took precedence. "Where are you staying?" he asked.

Again the multitude of news stories Jess had seen on the telly about the explosion of crime in American cities caused her to hesitate. Still, the man was a physician, if he was to be believed. And he seemed so kind, despite his pervasive air of loneliness.

"We're at the Radisson Plaza in downtown Minneapolis," she admitted impulsively.

Stephen nodded his approval. It was a first-rate hotel, with excellent service. Though he'd never slept in one of the rooms, he'd spent time there himself, at half a dozen medical conferences. She and her daughter were in good hands.

"In that case, you're just a short distance from Minneapolis General Hospital, which has a superb emergency room, as well as a topflight pediatric center. If you don't choose to consult the hotel doctor, you can take your daughter there. The concierge will be able to give you directions. In the meantime, aspirin, plenty of rest, fluids and a cold washcloth for her forehead should be fairly safe bets."

The prescriptive nature of his remarks was softened by a downward tug of smile, as if he were well aware that she hadn't asked for his advice and might not welcome it. Juxtaposed with his take-charge manner, the slight diffidence was charming. For half a second, Jess found herself tempted to ask his name and how to contact him.

It wouldn't do, of course. Annie had to be her first and only priority. Still, she couldn't help staring up at him in surprise. Imbued with wariness up to her eyeballs as a result of Ronald's infidelity, and totally preoccupied with Annie's welfare, she hadn't expected this rush of attraction and interest.

Thanking him again, she buckled Annie's seat belt and got behind the wheel. A moment later, she was driving away. Motionless in the parking lot, with its rows of automobiles and its scattering of potholes, Stephen stared after them. It isn't likely I'll run into them again in a metropolitan area this size, he thought, even if they stay awhile, unless she brings her daughter to Minn-Gen for treatment. Shrugging on his jacket again and thrusting his hands into its pockets as he strode toward his Mercedes, he told himself it was for the best. Yet he couldn't deny that his inner man regretted it.

* * *

The moment they reached their hotel, Jess escorted Annie upstairs to their suite, gave her a child-size aspirin with some orange juice from the minibar and tucked her into bed with the cold washcloth that Stephen had suggested on her forehead. "Try to take a little nap," she whispered, leaning over to kiss her daughter's cheek. "I'm sure that, when you wake up, you'll feel much better. We can watch a children's show together."

Unappeased, Annie clung to her. "It's a bore being sick all the time, Mummy," she said. "And I miss Herkie. Can't we just go home?"

The question tugged painfully at Jess's heartstrings. Herkie, short for Herkimer, was Annie's pet Scottish terrier, to whom she was extremely devoted. They'd been forced to leave the dog behind with Jess's cousin when they traveled to the U.S. The parting had left Annie desolate.

"I know, darling.... I miss Herkie, too," Jess agreed, attempting to comfort her. "But you know Cousin Amanda is taking especially good care of him. I promise...we'll go home to England just as soon as we can find somebody to give you that special treatment we talked about."

Her eyes bright with fever, Annie considered her mother's statement. "Will it really make me better?" she asked.

On occasion, bone-marrow transplants had been known to fail. However, the technology was improving by the minute. Jess wouldn't let herself entertain the possibility of defeat. The trick was to find a donor.

"Good as new," she promised. "Try to sleep a little, won't you, sweetheart?"

While Annie dozed beneath a blanket, with the hotel bedspread for added warmth, Jess curled up on a love seat in the adjoining sitting room and occupied herself by jotting down the phone numbers of several twenty-four-hour walk-in clinics. She also looked up the number for Minnesota General Hospital's emergency room. As she did so, images of the tall blond doctor who had befriended them at the zoo drifted through her head.

Annie was still awake when Jess checked on her, half an hour later. Though her fever had receded somewhat, it wasn't gone altogether. The thermometer Jess gently inserted in her ear continued to register a slight temperature. To her surprise, Annie was hungry.

"Can we get cheeseburgers, Mummy? Like we saw on the telly?" the five-year-old asked.

Against her better judgment, Jess ordered cheeseburgers and milk for two from room service. She wasn't surprised, just saddened, when Annie ate just several bites of her sandwich and pushed her plate aside. She tried to take comfort in the fact that the girl had drunk most of her milk and seemed ready to snuggle beneath the covers again.

Maybe she'd feel better in the morning. If so, Jess planned to head for the public library. Lacking phone numbers, she might be able to locate addresses for several of the Fortunes by poring through the Minneapolis city directory. Feathering a gentle kiss on Annie's cheek, she returned to the sitting room and switched on the television, adjusting the sound to a barely audible level.

Having stopped by his office to handle an emergency appointment after leaving the zoo and gone on to complete his late-afternoon rounds at Minn-Gen, Stephen was back behind the wheel of his sleek sedan, listening to light classical music on the radio as he drove toward his home on the wooded shore of Lake Travis, in the Minneapolis suburbs.

Some people would say I have everything—a medical degree, an expensive car, a striking contemporary house with a view of the water, he thought with a familiar tug of irony and loneliness as he turned off the two-lane highway that led into what was referred to locally as "the village" and crossed the rustic bridge that spanned the creek that fed the lake. Well, they'd be wrong. Though he cared deeply about each of his patients and genuinely loved his work, his son's death had eviscerated his personal life; for the past three years, it had been as empty as a discarded shell washed up on a beach, bereft of its former inhabitant.

Yet as he passed the former home of Benjamin and Kate Fortune, half-hidden behind its screen of mature firs and oaks, and proceeded the half mile or so along Forest Road to his own somewhat less imposing gateposts, he realized that a Rubicon of sorts had been crossed. Hesitant though he was to give his heart a second time to either child or woman, he'd allowed the mother and daughter he met at the zoo to open a chink in his armor. Into it had flowed an uncomfortable host of half-coveted possibilities.

No need to get bent out of shape just yet, he thought wryly. It isn't likely you'll see them again.

Set well back from the road, with its deck and its broad expanse of windows facing the lake, Stephen's cedar-sided house appeared somewhat closed and unwelcoming. Raising the garage door with his remote control, he drove inside and shut off the Mercedes's engine.

Each time he ascended the shallow quarry-tiled steps that led into the silent, empty kitchen, he experienced a moment of heartache that there was no David to greet him, no eight-year-old clamoring for his attention. Some evenings, he couldn't stop himself from going to the doorway of his son's former room and touching the toy cars, plastic action figures and stuffed animals that lined the built-in shelving in unnaturally neat rows.

Tonight, he switched on some music, popped a packet of frozen lasagna into the oven and poured himself a glass of Bardolino. At this time of year, the sun set around 7:30 p.m. Chelsea and Carter Todd, the young daughter and son of his next-door neighbors, were still playing outdoors, under the watchful eye of their sixtyish baby-sitter. Stepping out on the deck to sip his wine while the lasagna heated, Stephen stared at the blue expanse of water that fanned out from his pier and wondered if the laughter of another child, a different woman, would help to make him whole again.

In the sitting room area of her downtown hotel suite, Jess had drifted off to sleep. She awoke shortly after 10:00 p.m., stiff from the unnatural position in which she'd been slumbering on the love seat, and somewhat unsettled, thanks to a confusing dream. Annie was still asleep, her forehead warm and dry against the back of Jess's wrist, but not excessively feverish.

Deciding to let her sleep, Jess poured out a glass of mineral water and returned to the sitting room. The local news was on. Someone handed the sandy-haired anchorman a note as she retook her seat. It was clear from his facial expression as he scanned it that he considered the note to be of major importance, and she turned up the sound a little.

"This just in," the man was saying. "Former Hollywood leading lady and longtime Minneapolis resident Monica Malone was found dead this evening in her Summit Avenue mansion. We take you to Mary Ann Galvin, our reporter at the scene. Mary Ann..."

Positioned at the curb in front of the Malone mansion, which had clearly seen better days, the reporter gripped her microphone with barely disguised excitement. Several uniformed officers, the flashing lights of a police cruiser and a barrier of yellow crime-scene tape were visible behind her.

"Thank you, Jay," she said. "According to a spokesman for the Minneapolis Police Department, Miss Malone, thought to be in her midsixties, was found sprawled on her living room floor shortly after 10:00 p.m. She was pronounced dead at 10:15 p.m., when police arrived.

"Stating that the matter is under investigation, officers have declined to comment on the cause of death, or speculate as to whether foul play was involved. However, a tenant of one of Miss Malone's neighbors, who spoke on condition of anonymity, said he had heard she suffered a head injury...."

The name of the deceased former movie star rang a bell with Jess, and not just because of her films. I've seen it mentioned somewhere, and recently—I know it, she thought. Seconds later, she remembered where. Monica Malone's name had turned up in a long-outdated, somewhat sensationalized magazine article about Benjamin Fortune's career that she managed to dig up at a library near her home in England before leaving for America. Its author, who claimed to have known the Fortune patriarch personally, had suggested that he and Monica Malone had "conducted an off-and-on affair for years."

In part because of Ronald's infidelities during their marriage, Jess supposed, she strongly disapproved. Yet she couldn't have denied that she found every scrap of information she could accumulate about the man she now believed to have been her grandfather extremely fascinating.

When Jess awoke again, around 6:30 a.m., Annie was worse. Her temperature had soared to 103 degrees. She was coughing, shivering and whimpering. Terrified, Jess decided to take the advice of the tall blond doctor they'd met at the zoo and take her to Minnesota General Hospital's emergency room. However, she didn't think she could bear to see Annie carted off in an ambulance if it wasn't necessary. It would scare her to death and, incidentally, break Jess's heart.

Accordingly, she bundled the girl up in two sweaters and a raincoat, and wrapped her in one of the hotel blankets. A sympathetic bellhop helped her carry Annie downstairs and summoned a taxi for them.

"Mummy... Mummy...where are we going? You're coming with me...*aren't* you?" Annie asked in alarm as the bellhop settled her in the cab's back seat.

"Yes, of course I am. We're going to the hospital that nice doctor told us about yesterday," Jess said soothingly, unable to keep tears of consternation and panic from running down her cheeks as she got into the taxi beside her and drew her close. "You need better medicine than I can give you, darling. Plus some doctors and nurses to help make you better as soon as possible."

Both she and Annie were grim-faced, tense and more

than a little frightened as their cab drew up to Minn-Gen's emergency room entrance. Before Jess could get out and pay the driver, a nurse and an orderly were hurrying out to meet them. "You're Mrs. Holmes, right?" the nurse asked. "The doorman at your hotel phoned to let us know you were coming."

The next few minutes passed in a blur. While the nurse examined Annie and took her vital signs, one of the secretaries at the nursing station helped Jess fill out an admitting form. The latter didn't seem unduly concerned about Annie's condition until Jess wrote *leukemia* under the heading Known Medical Conditions. A quick conference between the secretary, a nurse and a male physician who was in the process of tending to an accident victim ensued.

"You'd better page Dr. Todd," the male physician decided, adding for Jess's benefit, "She's a pediatrician. I think I saw her come in earlier. She's probably still in-house."

With barely a skipped beat, the name of Dr. Lindsay Todd and the words "to the ER, stat" were being read over the hospital's public address system.

Jess barely had time to smooth Annie's forehead and whisper a few calming words to her before Dr. Todd appeared. Brown-haired, leggy, sweet-faced, in her mid-to-late thirties and decidedly feminine looking despite her white coat and stethoscope, she was crisp but extraordinarily kind and gentle as she gave Annie a thorough going-over and peppered Jess with questions.

The exam finished, Dr. Todd patted Annie's hand and turned to Jess with a concerned frown. "I'd like to run some tests...get her white-cell count, check on the number of immature cells, that sort of thing," she announced. "Or rather, I'd like to have an expert do it.

As it happens, we're in luck. Dr. Hunter's in the building.''

Jess knew what the tests were likely to show. Though she suddenly felt very far from home indeed, maybe it was for the best that Annie's crisis had occurred in Minneapolis. Maybe these energetic can-do Americans could keep Annie alive until she could find a donor.

"All right," she whispered.

"Good. You two hang in there."

Exiting Annie's cubicle, Dr. Todd pulled the curtain shut. At her request, the hospital operator paged Dr. Hunter. Called back to the hospital around 5:00 a.m., after a restless night, when an elderly patient suffering from polycythemia, a condition in which the body makes too many red blood cells, causing the blood to thicken excessively, had taken a turn for the worse, he'd barely had time to shave. His blue eyes were shadowed with fatigue as he strode into the emergency room.

"What can I do for you, Lin?" he asked.

The brown-haired pediatrician quickly filled him in on what she knew of Annie's condition. "The mother's been told she needs a bone-marrow transplant," she said.

Stephen nodded. "Let's have a look at her."

A moment later, with Lindsay Todd following closely in his wake, he was pushing aside the curtain that screened Annie's cubicle.

Jess's eyes widened as she glanced up at him. "You!" she exclaimed in surprise, unable to stop herself.

Two

Stephen's heart lurched with surprise, regret, and a strong sensation of déjà vu. On some deeper level, he supposed, he should have known the acute leukemia patient Lindsay had summoned him to examine would turn out to be the feverish blond child who'd skinned her knee at the zoo, accompanied by her lovely but worried dark-haired mother. The possibility likely would have occurred to him, if he hadn't been so gosh-darn tired and failed to scan the personal information on the child's chart, which almost certainly included a permanent address in England.

He did so now, with a quick downward glance.

"Hello again, uh, Mrs. Holmes…Annabel…" he said, extending his hand to Jess and lightly ruffling Annie's hair as he assumed his professional role like a coat of armor. "Under the circumstances, I won't say I'm happy to see you, though I'm pleased you decided to take my advice and come here. This is a very good hospital."

Aware of Lindsay's confusion, he added, "I met Mrs. Holmes and Annabel yesterday at Como Park Zoo."

"Oh," Lindsay murmured. "I see."

It was clear that she didn't—that she couldn't begin to imagine why, lacking a child to accompany him, he'd taken refuge from his busy but lonely life at a typical children's haunt. He wasn't in a position to explain. Nor would he have wished to, in any event.

"Let's see how this young lady's doing this morning," he proposed instead, picking up his stethoscope.

The exam, which included numerous questions and a great deal of gentle prodding and observation on Stephen's part, took several minutes. It wasn't difficult for him to see that Annie was very sick indeed. He could almost have guessed what her white-cell count would be. Her English doctors had been correct in stating that she needed a transplant as soon as possible.

Unfortunately, you couldn't just place an order for matching bone marrow as if it could be purchased from a catalogue. With just one in twenty thousand unrelated persons eligible to donate, from a genetic standpoint, and a paucity of registered and blood-typed volunteers, it could be difficult, bordering on impossible, to find a donor.

While they were searching, Annabel Holmes would likely need some form of chemotherapy as a stopgap measure. "No luck finding a donor for your daughter in England, I take it?" he asked Jess.

She shook her head. "That's why we came to the U.S."

Why Minneapolis in particular? he wondered. Does she have people here? There wasn't time to ask. He was being paged again. To him, the brief request to call the nursing station on 301 West was shorthand for the fact that Mrs. Munson, the elderly polycythemia patient, needed him again.

"I've got to run upstairs for a few minutes," he said. "In the meantime, Mrs. Holmes, I'd like to have the nurses here admit your daughter as my patient, with Dr. Todd as pediatric consultant, and assign her to a room.

I'll need your permission to run some tests so we can determine what her current status is...bone-marrow aspiration and biopsy, X rays, an electrocardiogram, blood and pulmonary-function tests, that sort of thing. I'll be in touch just as soon as her results are available. Okay? Naturally, we'll sign her up at once with every available U.S. registry.''

Annie's illness was rapidly approaching a crisis point, as Jess had already begun to sense. Her little girl would die or, if a miracle was in the offing, she'd get better. It was that simple, and that terrifying. Except for their quest to find a donor among Benjamin Fortune's descendents, her prospects weren't bright. Barely contained panic causing a lump to settle in her throat, she nodded without answering him.

A sensitive barometer to everything Jess was thinking and feeling, Annie picked up on her fear at once. "Do I have to stay here?'' she chimed in worriedly, gazing up at the tall blond doctor she'd trusted without hesitation the previous afternoon. "Can't I go back with Mummy to the hotel?''

"I'm afraid it's the hospital for you, sweetheart,'' Stephen said, smiling in an attempt to hide his own consternation over the likely severity of her case. "We need to have you handy, so we can do our best to make you better.''

She appeared to think over his explanation and accept it. "Well, could I have another of those cool bandages, then?'' she asked with five-year-old straightforwardness.

He didn't make a production of asking where it hurt—just produced the requested bounty from the pocket of his lab coat and solemnly affixed it to the back of her hand, as if it were a good-conduct medal.

A moment later, after ordering the tests he'd outlined, along with an antibiotic drip to help Annie's compromised immune system combat her current infection, he was gone.

Jess couldn't stop herself from shaking.

Lindsay rested a hand on her shoulder. "Dr. Hunter's the best hematologist around, bar none, and I'm not just saying that because we're friends and neighbors," she vowed. "Your daughter's in good hands."

West of the city, in the posh, handsomely appointed master bedroom where Erica Fortune, Jacob Fortune's estranged wife, slept alone, the bedside phone rang sharply. It was going on 7:40 a.m., a bit early for fifty-one-year-old Erica to be up in her previous incarnation as the pampered but increasingly unhappy mate of Fortune Industries' chief executive officer, who'd succeeded his widowed mother following her fatal light-plane crash in the Brazilian jungle.

These days, as a woman alone bent on finding herself, if not exactly thrilled that her husband had walked out on her, the sleek, silvery-blond Erica rose early. Nibbling on cinnamon toast and drinking black coffee as she dressed for a 9:00 a.m. Saturday class at Normandale Junior College in Bloomington, she reached for the receiver and murmured an absent hello.

Her green eyes widened when her caller identified himself as Lieutenant J. B. Rosczak, a detective with the Minneapolis Police Department.

"Is this the Jacob Fortune residence?" he asked.

She wasn't sure how to answer him. "Yes," she agreed tentatively, setting her coffee cup aside. "I mean, it *was,* until a few months ago. This is Mrs. Fortune. Jacob Fortune and I are separated. What's this about, anyway?''

Seemingly reluctant to discuss the matter with her in any detail, the police lieutenant ignored her question. "I take it he's not there, then, ma'am?" he said.

"No, he isn't," Erica confirmed.

"Any idea where we can contact him?"

It was beginning to sound as if Jake were in some kind of trouble. Standing there in her sheer panty hose, lacy undergarments and partially buttoned silk blouse, with her toes curling into the plush beige carpeting, Erica took a hurried moment to think. Should she answer in the negative, and try to reach Jake the moment her caller hung up the phone? Of course, that would mean telling an out-and-out falsehood. Though she continued to have protective feelings toward Jake—still loved him, in a guarded way, if she was willing to admit the truth, she didn't want to lie to the police on his account.

"Actually, he's been living in his late mother's house, up on Lake Travis, since our breakup," she said.

"We've already looked there," Detective Rosczak answered brusquely. "Any other ideas?"

Erica didn't have any. "Maybe one of our children would know," she speculated. "Or his secretary at Fortune Industries. Of course, she won't be in her office until Monday. *Please...* can't you tell me what's wrong? Though we're separated, I still care about him."

The line was empty of conversation for a moment, as Detective Rosczak apparently decided whether or not to answer her question. "He's wanted for questioning in the death of Monica Malone, ma'am," he admitted at last.

Erica gasped. "Monica...dead?" she repeated in astonishment. "Where? When? How did it happen?" A ghastly thought struck her. "Surely she wasn't murdered!"

It was clear from the detective's tone that he was more than ready for their conversation to end. "Maybe you should turn on the morning news, if you want that kind of information, Mrs. Fortune," he suggested.

Before saying goodbye, he made a point of giving her a number to call if Jake surfaced. "It would be better for him if he got in touch with us voluntarily," he advised. The implied threat was hard to miss.

Erica was stunned as she put down the phone. Her first impulse was to call Natalie—at twenty-seven, the third-oldest of the five children she'd had with Jake. Natalie lived in an aging farmhouse that had been converted into a duplex, directly across Lake Travis from the mansion that had once belonged to Ben and Kate Fortune—which also happened to be Jake's current residence. She and her father had always been close. Since he'd moved into his parents' home, following his split with Erica, Natalie had crossed the lake on a regular basis to visit him. Maybe she knew something.

About to punch the speed-dial button she'd programmed with Natalie's number, Erica ran one elegantly manicured hand through her silver-blond bob. It might be better to phone Sterling Foster, the family's longtime attorney and respected legal advisor, first. If Jake was in a bind and the police had become involved, Sterling would know how to handle it.

It was Saturday. He wouldn't be at his office so Erica rummaged in her desk drawer for her leather-bound address book. Finding it, she located Sterling's home number.

The attorney was just getting out of the shower. He hadn't read the morning paper yet. Or made contact with his first cup of coffee. He answered on the third ring, gruff because of the early call and the necessity of answering it wrapped in a bath towel.

"Hello?" he growled, adjusting the towel so that he wouldn't drip all over on the carpet.

She tried not to sound too worried, knowing he wouldn't like it. "Sterling?" she said. "Hi, it's Erica. Sorry to disturb you at home, especially on the weekend. But I just got a call from Detective Rosczak of the Minneapolis police. Monica Malone has died, and the police want to question Jake about it. They can't seem to find him. It's possible he might be in some kind of trouble."

Though he hadn't heard of Monica's death, Sterling didn't evince surprise. "Sounds like it," he answered dryly. "But then, when *hasn't* he been in some mess or another, lately?"

Erica was irritated at what she considered to be his cavalier attitude, and still ready to spring to the defense of the man who was still her husband. She didn't consider an inquiry from the police a laughing matter. "You have contacts in the department, don't you?" she asked, her soft, cultivated voice taking on a more strident note. "I want you to call them…find out what's going on. And find Jake! If he disappears when the police need to talk to him, he's bound to look guilty of something!"

Dropping the towel, which he no longer needed, Sterling reached for his bathrobe. "All right," he conceded. "I'll do what I can. Go back to bed and stop worrying. If you plan to go husband-hunting after all these years, you're going to need your beauty sleep."

Touchy on the subject of her breakup with Jake, not to mention her age, which, despite her still-youthful classic good looks, she didn't consider an asset, Erica considered the remark a put-down. It sent her through the roof. "Sorry to shatter one of your treasured clichés about me, but I'm getting ready for a Saturday-morning class!" she snapped, slamming down the receiver.

A tight sensation in her chest, she quickly called Natalie for emotional support. For his part, Sterling started to dial Kate, the spirited family matriarch whom he knew to be alive and well, though her family believed otherwise.

Seconds later, he changed his mind. Instead of phoning, he'd drive to her current hideaway, a penthouse apartment atop the renovated LaSalle building in downtown Minneapolis. She owed him breakfast, dammit. The last time she'd offered him brunch in conjunction with a business discussion, his ulcer had been kicking up. He hadn't been able to partake. Devoid of sympathy, she'd devoured her blintzes and strawberries under his nose with her typical gusto.

He decided to have a look at the morning paper first. Wincing slightly, he saw that Monica's death had made the front page, above the fold. Described as "still under investigation," it had been given a banner headline. A photo of the aging star, taken in better days, accompanied the text.

Scanning the story, which had been written by a reporter he considered competent, Sterling learned that Monica had been stabbed several times in the chest. She had also suffered an injury to her left temple. Signs of a struggle had been evident. Several of Monica's Summit Avenue neighbors had seen a man leaving her mansion shortly before her maid returned and found her body. No description of the caller seemed to be available, at least to journalists.

Damn, Sterling thought, tossing the paper aside. What was Jake doing there? The woman was poison. It's bad enough that Ben was fool enough to mess around with her. Reluctantly he admitted that Erica had a valid point. Kate's oldest son might turn out to be in some very hot water.

Though she'd probably heard the news of Monica's death by now, he doubted Kate had any inkling of her son's involvement. If she did, he reasoned, she'd have phoned him immediately. No, Jake's name hadn't appeared in the news. And Detective Rosczak, whoever he was, hadn't gotten in touch with her, because he didn't know of her existence.

She wouldn't have a clue.

It would be Sterling's job to break the news. Brushing his teeth, he shaved and put on a crisp white shirt, a maroon silk tie, gray sharkskin slacks and one of his expensive but conservative cardigan sweaters. A few minutes later, with his thick white hair impeccably combed and an unobtrusive Patek-Philippe watch adorning his left wrist, he was taking the elevator down to the basement garage of his condominium apartment building and striding purposefully toward his maroon Lincoln Town Car.

The LaSalle, a twelve-story brick-and-stone building dating from 1920, had been built in a style Sterling thought of as Mississippi River Valley Gothic. It had originally served as Minneapolis's YMCA. In recent years, its sturdy shell and somewhat decrepit interior had been exquisitely restored to contain thirty or so smallish, extremely private luxury apartments. You needed a key to operate the elevator. There were no nameplates—just numbers—beside the theft-proof mailboxes.

A child of the Depression era who'd grown up at a time when twelve stories constituted a fairly tall building, Sterling liked its cozy size, black-and-white terrazzo lobby, clubby woodwork and art deco details. He suspected Kate was similarly minded. Having moved around a great deal to avoid detection since she'd faked her death, she'd rented the LaSalle's top floor several months earlier. It was divided into two penthouse apartments. Hers, luxuriously carpeted and decorated, boasted several skylights, a small fireplace and a sweeping bird's-eye view of western Minneapolis and its adjacent suburbs.

As he backed his Lincoln into an empty space at the curb and went inside, Sterling thought about the strange set of circumstances that had prompted him and Kate to agree on the extraordinary step of letting her family believe she had perished. Had they done the right thing? Or were they fools to think their scheme would help them flush out a would-be kidnapper or murderer?

As yet, it had been spectacularly unsuccessful. For perhaps the thousandth time, he puzzled over the identity of the hijacker who had stowed away in Kate's plane on her solo trip to a remote Brazilian village in search of a key ingredient for the Secret Youth Formula she was trying to develop for Fortune Cosmetics, then appeared in midflight to hold a gun to her head. The plane had gone into a nosedive in the ensuing struggle. By some miracle, Kate had been thrown free, to fall through the dense undergrowth, moments before it crashed and burned.

In Sterling's opinion, her attacker had been a killer-for-hire, in the pay of some unknown enemy. It was fair to say he'd probably never be identified. His badly charred remains had been taken for those of Kate by the Brazilian authorities. Meanwhile, having suffered a concussion, multiple fractures and countless cuts and bruises, Kate had been found and nursed slowly back to health by the natives of a remote Amazon village.

Aware that someone had wanted her dead, and might try again if they realized they'd failed, she'd disguised herself when finally she was well enough to travel, and made her way back to Minneapolis with extreme caution. Sterling would never forget the morning she'd phoned, her husky voice laced with fear and umbrage as she whispered into the receiver, "I'm alive, Sterling. *I'm alive.* Don't tell anyone."

Though he had a key, Sterling knocked at Kate's apartment door instead of letting himself in, as he sometimes did, since he hadn't taken the trouble to call first. Kate let him in. Clad in a red Chinese-silk bathrobe that flattered her small, slim figure and complemented, rather than clashed with, her upswept silver-streaked auburn hair, she clutched a mug of black coffee in one diamond-studded fist as she led him to the living room and a breaking news program on the television.

"Sterling...come in! You're never going to believe this!" she commanded, waving him peremptorily to a chair.

The story that had captured her attention was the same one Jessica Holmes had caught the evening before and Sterling had scanned in his morning paper—expanded as more details and peripheral interviews became available. Unlike Jess, Kate had a strong personal interest in the case. Recruited by her many years earlier to act as a spokeswoman for Fortune Cosmetics, Monica had repaid the favor by conducting an illicit on-again, off-again affair with Kate's husband, Ben, for years. Or at least that was what Kate suspected. Further, she had long sensed Monica to be a deadly personal adversary.

"It's Monica Malone!" Kate added. "She's been stabbed to death!"

Given a cup of coffee by the maid, Sterling scowled as a news commentator recapped the story. But he couldn't hide his growing concern. If Jake was involved in some way, he'd find himself facing an extremely nasty situation.

Kate hadn't picked up on his worry yet. "So...what do you think of all this?" she asked, her color high, as the station took an advertising break. "You know I'm not the vindictive type...that I wouldn't wish a rattlesnake harm unless it was about to strike. But I can't help feeling that what happened to Monica is at least partly her own fault."

Sterling's mouth failed to twitch with his usual amusement at her inventive turn of phrase. "I think Jake may have been mixed up in it somehow," he answered.

"What on earth are you talking about?" she asked in alarm, turning her penetrating blue gaze full force on him.

As succinctly as possible, he described Erica's call. "I'm just guessing, of course," he said. "But it's conceivable Jake visited Monica yesterday evening, and that it was he whom her neighbors spotted leaving the house shortly before her body was discovered. Otherwise, why would the police be looking for him?"

Kate's brightly lacquered nails dug into the arms of her chair. "You're not saying he killed her, are you?" she exclaimed.

"You know better than that."

According to Sterling's retelling of his conversation

with Erica, Jake hadn't spent the night in the Lake Travis house, where he'd taken up residence after their split. Where was he, then? Had he made himself scarce for a reason? Kate didn't want to believe it. The Jake she knew couldn't possibly be guilty of harming anyone.

"There could be any number of reasons the police want to speak with him," she hedged.

"Give me one."

"I don't know…recent business dealings, maybe. He sold her that stock, remember, though God knows what his reasons were. No doubt there were meetings, phone calls. They're probably combing the woodwork, hoping someone can give them something."

Sterling shook his head. "I don't buy it. This feels like trouble to me…right down to the core."

It did to Kate, too. Her instincts in full flush, she was on her feet, pacing. "Damn that woman to hell…even if she's probably headed there already!" she erupted. "She had her hooks into Ben for years. Now, as her swan song, she's going to destroy my oldest child!"

From Sterling's perspective, it was incomprehensible that Ben had ever preferred Monica to Kate, even as a side dish. Despite her impoverished beginnings, Kate was a genuine thoroughbred. And full of fire still; he'd have bet his stock-market holdings on that.

"What do you want me to do?" he asked.

She wanted him to protect Jake. Run interference for him with the police. Keep him from doing something foolish. Much as she loved her son, she knew his weaknesses. If he realized he was being sought by the authorities, he might panic. Yet he couldn't call on her for support—he didn't know she was alive. And he was too proud to call Erica. But he might get in touch with

Sterling if he found himself in a jam. Maybe he'd tried to do so already.

"My dear, dear friend...*please*, go home and wait for him to call you," she begged. "Keep the line open, just in case. Let me know when you hear from him."

A bit grumpily, because he'd planned on having breakfast with her, Sterling arose. "As always, I'm at your service," he murmured.

"If he calls, you'll go with him to the police."

"Of course."

Though he doubted she'd make a habit of it, Kate surprised him with a swift, spontaneous hug before ushering him out the door.

Jake awoke in a run-down motel, with a sour taste in his mouth. He'd drunk to excess the night before—he knew that much. His stomach felt like crap, and his head was pounding. Seconds later, the painful throbbing of his injured shoulder brought back the whole frightening, humiliating scenario that had taken place. Groaning, he shut his eyes as the details of what he'd been running from invaded his memory and settled there. The argument with Monica. Her coming at him with a letter opener. A thrust of pain that had made him gasp. Him pushing her away, and her falling against the marble fireplace...

Like a fool, or some desperate kind of idiot, he'd gone to her house to confront her over the way she'd been blackmailing him—threatening to reveal to the world that his father was a poor slob of a foot soldier who'd died in World War II, not the self-made, illustrious Benjamin Fortune, who'd married his mother and placed a silver spoon in his mouth.

It was news his power-hungry half brother, Nate,

would glory in hearing, and Jake had been determined to keep it from him at all costs. He should have known Monica would refuse to return the stock he'd sold her under duress, or promise to keep his secret—that she'd try something crazy, like trying to kill or injure him.

Because of her insane and jealous machinations, he'd all but destroyed the company his family had taken a half century to build, and lost most of the respect he'd once had for himself. Now she was dead, a corpse discovered lying facedown on her living room floor, according to the news account he'd watched before bolting from his parents' former Lake Travis house the night before.

I didn't kill her! he thought frantically. I know I didn't! She was alive when I left. She'd regained consciousness, and I'd helped her to the sofa. I should have stuck around, I suppose. Phoned for help and stayed until it arrived. But she didn't seem to be hurt that badly. She was shouting gutter language at me, threatening to come at me again, and I wanted to get out of there as fast as I could.

Who had killed her then? Jake didn't have a clue, any more than he knew whether someone had seen him leave the house. If his departure *had* been observed, he might not have been recognized. Yet his fingerprints would be all over the scene. His blood, too, he guessed, would have dripped from the wound in his shoulder. Plus, she'd scratched him. Bits of his skin would be found beneath her long red fingernails. His DNA would be everywhere. If he'd been placed by someone at the property near the time of death, the police would be looking for him. He'd be facing a mountain of evidence.

Fear congealing like an undigested meal in his gut, he got out of bed and paid an overdue visit to the bathroom. He was still wearing the clothes he'd worn the night before—thankfully, the clean pullover and slacks he'd changed into following the shower he'd taken at his daughter Natalie's insistence, not the torn and blood-soaked shirt and soiled trousers he'd stuffed into an up-stairs bathroom hamper. Unfortunately, his breath still smelled of Scotch. And he didn't have any toothpaste.

He shook his head. What must Natalie have thought when she came across the lake and discovered him, wounded, drunk and babbling? Now that he'd disap-peared, she must be worried sick. Somehow, he'd have to make it up to her.

In the meantime, he'd concentrate on getting out of the mess he was in. For one thing, he didn't know pre-cisely where he was. He only knew that, after learning of Monica's death, he'd hit the road and driven for hours, stopping finally at a run-down motel somewhere in Wisconsin's north country.

A quick scan of the checkout card revealed that he'd spent the night at the Heart's Desire Motel on Round Lake, near the town of Hayward. It occurred to him that, under the circumstances, his out-of-state flight wouldn't look good. He might need legal representation.

Though it seemed like years since he'd run from Monica's house and sped away in his car, less than twenty-four hours had elapsed. It was Saturday. Sterling Foster wasn't likely to be in his office. Racking his brain, Jake managed to come up with his home number and dial it with trembling fingers.

After leaving Kate's apartment, Sterling had returned home. But he hadn't stayed put, the way he planned. Instead, a worried call from Natalie had propelled him to her house, across Lake Travis from the Fortune mansion. She had things to tell him about Jake's involvement with Monica the night before—things she didn't feel comfortable confiding over the telephone.

Annoyed that he had to go when Kate had suggested he remain at home and make himself available for Jake's call, he'd quickly decided the trip had been worth it when he heard Natalie's tale of an argument between Jake and Monica at her house, possibly over blackmail, Monica's fall and Jake's assertion that he'd cut his shoulder. According to the secondhand information he'd received from her, the aging star had been alive and ready to continue their argument when Jake left the house. As for his comments about blackmail, Jake hadn't been specific. In fact, he'd backed off from them.

His claim that Monica had been alive when he left had alleviated the lawyer's concern only a little. Coupled with the fact of her death, the circumstances Jake had described to his daughter spelled big trouble for him, in his opinion. Kate had thought so, too, when he reported to her on returning to his apartment shortly before 11:00 a.m.

When his phone shrilled just seconds after they finished their conversation, he picked up on the first ring. "At last!" he exclaimed in response to Jake's tentative utterance of his name. "Where in the hell *are* you? Monica Malone's murder is all over the newspapers and television. The Minneapolis Police are seeking you for questioning."

The bottom dropping out of his feeble hope that someone else had been caught and charged with Monica's murder, Jake told Sterling where he was. "You've got to believe me...I didn't kill Monica," he begged like a penitent child, "though we did have a run-in. She was alive when I left. Still, if the police are looking for me, I suppose I'm in a heap of trouble. I'm going to need your help.''

Sterling calculated that the motel where Jake had spent the night was roughly a two-and-a-half-hour drive from Minneapolis. An unannounced and unaccompanied return might not be wise. It was entirely possible that the police had alerted their fellow officers throughout Minnesota and the neighboring states to be on the lookout for him. If he was arrested on his way back, or even detained for questioning, he could protest all he wanted that he'd planned to turn himself in and still not be believed.

In Sterling's opinion, the best course of action he could take would be to drive to Wisconsin and bring Jake back, after notifying the authorities that the Fortune CEO would appear at police headquarters voluntarily that evening and answer all their questions. That way, he'd have a chance to hear the full story from Jake's mouth—ask whatever questions he deemed necessary, and help him settle on the official version—before the detectives got a crack at him.

For Jake, the silence on Sterling's end of the line was deafening. ''For God's sake,'' he pleaded, ''*say* something. Tell me what to do.''

Having decided how to handle the situation, Sterling was brisk. ''Don't go out,'' he ordered. ''Wait there for me. Talk to no one. I'll phone the police when I get to Hayward and tell them I'm coming in with you...that you'll answer their questions willingly. There's a young man in my building who can accompany me, and drive your car back for you.''

Abject in his fear that he'd be accused of a crime he hadn't committed, Jake quickly agreed to do whatever the attorney suggested. Breaking their connection,

Sterling took a deep breath and dialed Kate. "Your son just called," he said without preamble when she answered. "He's in Wisconsin. I'm on my way to bring him back. On my advice, he'll submit to questioning voluntarily. Naturally, I'll be by his side...."

There was a brief silence on Kate's end. "Do you think he'll be arrested?" she asked.

Sterling was anything but sure about how to answer her. He tried to be optimistic. "I shouldn't think so," he opined. "Of course, I'll know more after I talk with him in depth."

It was the best he could offer her at the moment. Her relief, mixed with a certain amount of dread over what the future would hold, was palpable. "Sterling, thank you!" she whispered. "Without you, the family would disintegrate. Whereas I..."

Time was of the essence, and she didn't finish the thought. "Call Erica before you go, will you, so she won't worry too much?" she added, changing her tack. "She can get in touch with the children. Naturally, you won't want to give her too many details."

At the hospital, Jess had remained by her daughter's bedside, desperately trying to think of ways to contact the Fortune family while waiting for the first of Annie's tests to come back from the lab. A nurse entered the room around 1:00 p.m. and noted that Annie was asleep. "You've been here all day, since early this morning, without rest or anything to eat, Mrs. Holmes," she pointed out. "It won't help your daughter if you get sick, too. We'll keep an eye on her, and Dr. Hunter will page you when the test results become available. Why don't you run down to the cafeteria and grab a bite?"

If they could pull it off, Annie's rehabilitation would

take months. The nurse's suggestion made sense. Realizing she was starved, Jess decided to take her up on it. She was seated in the brightly lit first-floor cafeteria, munching on a tuna-salad sandwich and drinking a cup of tea, when Stephen slid into the seat opposite her.

"Is something wrong?" she asked, the panic that lay just below the surface of her thoughts staring back at him.

She was so lovely. So distraught. And so alone in Minneapolis, unless he was very much mistaken. It was all he could do not to reach across the table and pat her shoulder. "Nothing we didn't expect," he replied.

"Then...the results are in?"

"Some of them are. Enough to know Annabel's white-cell count is severely out of whack, with a large number of immature, ineffective cells circulating in her bloodstream. She's going to need a transplant, and soon, to correct the situation. As an interim measure, until we can find a donor, I want to prescribe a mild form of chemotherapy. It'll make her fairly sick for a couple of days. But then she should have a brief remission. We'll have a respite in which to search."

Jess had dealt with the problem sufficiently by now to know they didn't have any other choice. Reluctantly, because anything calculated to make Annie sicker was like a dagger in her heart, she gave her permission.

"I've asked my office nurse to register Annabel with all known marrow sources, including one that's previously turned up several donors for us in Australia," he added. "It'll take a few weeks, maybe longer, to find out if there's an available match."

"And...if there isn't?"

"Unless her remission's far stronger than I expect, your daughter's not a good candidate for autologous donation, the process in which a portion of the patient's own marrow is removed, cleansed of cancer cells and replanted after the remaining cancer is killed off with chemotherapy,'' he said, his gaze unwavering though it was deeply sympathetic. ''We could try it, I suppose, if all else failed. But it would be risky in the extreme.''

Jess didn't answer. There wasn't much use in arguing the point. Annie's doctors in England had advised strongly against the process in her case, as well.

''Mind telling me why you decided to come to Minneapolis, of all places?'' he asked, changing the subject.

She supposed she might as well describe her possible connection with the Fortune family, though it hadn't been proven yet. ''When my family members—what few I have—were tested as possible donors for Annie,'' she said, ''those on my maternal grandfather's side turned out to be so extremely wide of the mark that her doctors found it puzzling.

''Shortly thereafter, I was going through some things that had belonged to my late mother. An old letter fell out of a book she'd read to me as a child. To my astonishment, it suggested that my true maternal grandfather wasn't a man named George Simpson, as I'd always believed, but rather Benjamin Fortune....''

She could tell from the look on Stephen's face that he was taken aback and highly skeptical. Doubtless he's convinced I'm grasping at straws, she thought. Or worse. ''I have the letter right here, in my purse. I'll be happy to show it to you,'' she offered, determined that he should believe her search was motivated by Annie's welfare, not greed, now that she'd opened up to him.

''I suppose it couldn't hurt.''

Silently she took it out and handed it to him.

From what Stephen could determine, the letter appeared to be genuine. It was entirely possible that the lovely, dark-haired Englishwoman seated opposite him was a long-lost Fortune relative. The physician in him leaped at the possibilities for his patient.

"During the short time we've been here, I've done everything I could to contact someone connected with the family, to no avail," Jess went on, when he didn't speak. "They all seem to have unlisted numbers. Jacob Fortune's secretary did promise she'd get a message to him. But I'm not holding my breath."

At that, Stephen regarded her quizzically. "I gather you didn't realize that Dr. Todd, your daughter's new pediatrician, is a Fortune," he remarked.

Caught by surprise, Jess could do little more than stare.

"As a matter of fact, she's Benjamin Fortune's daughter," he continued. "Granted, you wouldn't have guessed it from her name. She went by Lindsay Fortune-Todd for a while after marrying Frank Todd, another of our doctors here, then simply dropped her maiden name...."

For Jess, it was if a door had suddenly blown open on a host of possibilities. Twin spots of color blossomed in her cheeks. With a surge of excitement, she jumped to her feet. "Surely, if she knows of the connection, Dr. Todd will help us!" she exclaimed.

"Not so fast," Stephen advised, rising also. "Lindsay and the other Fortune children lost their mother, Kate—who, as you probably know, happened to be their only remaining parent—in a plane crash last year. To potential fortune hunters, the money they inherited is like a plum, ripe for the picking. At least one young woman whom most people regard as an imposter has turned up, claiming to be Lindsay's long-lost twin, who was kidnapped shortly after their birth, and demanding a share. Long-lost relatives of any sort are bound to be something of a sensitive issue, especially with her."

"But...but...I don't want *money*," Jess protested. "I want..."

Taking her hands in his, Stephen caused little ripples of awareness to flutter up her arms. "Take it easy. I believe you," he said. "Lindsay and I are friends, as well as colleagues, and next-door neighbors. I think it's fair to say she trusts me. Why don't you let me talk to her?"

Jess wanted to fling her arms around him. "Oh, Dr. Hunter...*would* you?" she asked.

"Call me Stephen," he said. "Thanks to Annabel, or Annie, as you call her, we're going to be seeing a lot of each other. C'mon, let's go upstairs and see how she's doing before I have to check out of here."

Pale and wraithlike as she slept beneath her hospital blanket, Annie looked like a little-girl ghost. Her control slipping, Jess wept softly as she gazed at her daughter. "I'm so worried about her," she confided. "She's all I've got. I don't want to lose her."

All too well, Stephen knew how she felt. A moment later, he'd taken her in his arms. Her tears were soaking into his hospital coat. An unplanned act, the move was meant simply to comfort her, or so he told himself.

To Jess, his arms offered a place of sanctuary and trust—and, incredibly, of nurturance. She wanted to lean on him. *Blend* with him. Burrow against the warmth of his neck. Despite her fear and worry over Annie, she realized it was a wake-up call to the lonely, loving woman in her—a woman who'd built a fortress around her heart when she learned of her late husband's faithlessness.

As their embrace held, Stephen found he didn't trust himself to move, or speak. By some alchemy he'd thought long extinct, he was holding a woman who filled his arms—one who, with her obvious refinement and strong capacity for love, might be able to fill his heart, as well.

A moment later, he was withdrawing from her. He was her daughter's hematologist, after all. Professional ethics forbade his getting involved with her, even if his track record as a comforter of women who stood to lose a child did not.

"Ummm...Mrs. Holmes, I'd better be going," he said awkwardly, when she didn't speak. "We'll have a chance to talk again tomorrow. Try to get some rest."

Settling in a chair by Annie's bed after he left, Jess pondered the fact that he wasn't wearing a wedding ring. By itself, of course, it didn't mean anything. Yet, coupled with the air of loneliness she'd noticed at the zoo and her persistent impression that he was a man who'd known sorrow, she thought it might.

She was aware their physical contact had embarrassed him. While her reaction to it had been quite a bit different, to say the least, she hoped it wouldn't interfere with his care of Annie. Or prompt him to forget his promise to talk to Lindsay Todd on her behalf.

Returning home to face an empty house and the remainder of a lonely, aimless Saturday afternoon, Stephen found himself going into David's room. On impulse, he opened David's toy box and picked up some plastic cowboys and Indians, complete with ponies, that his little boy had loved to play with. The ache in his heart was boundless.

Aside from bringing the impersonal cruelty of illness home to him in a very personal way, David's death had also taught him something about his fitness for a man-woman relationship, particularly one that might have to survive an emotional crisis. Or so he believed. As they'd dealt with the crushing blow of David's cancer and death, he and Brenda had failed each other.

"What are you doing even *thinking* about Jessica Holmes?" he asked himself.

Three

Sterling and his twenty-two-year-old companion, the son of a trusted neighbor, arrived at the Heart's Desire Motel on Round Lake shortly after 3:00 p.m. While the young man waited in Sterling's Lincoln, the attorney knocked at the door of Jake's motel unit and collected the keys to his Porsche. One glance was all it took to measure the Fortune CEO's physical and mental state. Crusty, experienced courtroom warrior that he was, it tugged at his heartstrings to see Kate's aristocratic-looking son so thoroughly leveled by the sordid situation in which he found himself.

Sympathy won't do him any good, he thought. What he needs is a good strong dose of tough-mindedness.

Reemerging, he instructed his assistant to drive the sports car back to Minneapolis and park it in a guest spot beneath their apartment building. Handing over the keys, he gave the young man a crisp hundred-dollar bill. "Put the keys in my mailbox," he said. "If you're stopped, you're returning the Porsche to Minneapolis as a favor for a friend. That's all you know. Call me on my mobile phone if the police give you any trouble."

Chosen for his cool head and his lack of curiosity about other people's business, the young man pocketed the money. "Will do, Mr. Foster," he said with his typical nonchalance.

As he drove off, gunning the Porsche's engine

slightly, Sterling returned to Jake. "Okay," he said, dusting off a somewhat grimy-looking chair and taking a seat, "let's have it from the beginning. Tell me everything that happened last night. And I do mean *everything.*"

Still wretched and worse for wear, but with his wits more coherently gathered about him, Jake admitted going to Monica's house and arguing with her over some stock he'd wanted to buy back from her.

"I was willing to pay a premium for it," he said, bitterness permeating his voice. "She refused, using some of the foulest language I've ever heard. Suddenly, she came at me with a letter opener, and managed to stab me in the shoulder. When I struggled with her in self-defense, forcing her to drop it, she scratched at me with her fingernails. I didn't actually push her until she picked it up and tried to stab me again.

"At that point...well, I did. I considered my life to be in danger. I guess I didn't know my own strength, because she fell backward, hitting her head against that stupid marble fireplace of hers, the one with the naked dancing cupids. She was knocked out cold, but she came around pretty fast, and I helped her over to the sofa. Once she'd gotten her bearings, she started working up another head of steam. I was afraid she'd come at me again, and I'd had enough. I left and drove home...to Lake Travis."

"Was anyone else in the house?"

Jake ran his fingers through his silver-brown hair. In that moment, the troubled edge he'd had for years showed very clearly. "Not that I know of," he vowed.

"Was she expecting anyone?"

"If so, she didn't tell me about it."

A moment's silence held as Sterling regarded him

with a penetrating stare. If Monica had been blackmailing him, as Natalie's account of their conversation seemed to suggest, he needed to know. He decided not to put the question directly. "Why'd you sell her the stock in the first place?" he asked.

Somehow, Jake had known the attorney would get around to posing that question. He wasn't the first. Nate had grilled him about the stock, too, as had several of Fortune Industries' directors. The fact that Monica had been amassing a sizable number of shares, with potentially serious ramifications for the company, hadn't gone unnoticed by anyone.

He couldn't afford for the real reason to get out. "With my separation from Erica, and divorce looming as a possibility, I, uh, needed the money," he prevaricated.

Sterling's weathered-lion features contorted in disgust. "Cut the crap," he ordered. "I want the truth."

Usually so erect of posture, Jake seemed to sag against the mattress. "Whatever I tell you is confidential, right?" he asked after a moment. "Attorney-client privilege?"

The lawyer nodded.

"Okay, then. Several months ago, Monica informed me that I'm not Ben Fortune's son. According to her, my real father was some poor stiff of a GI named Joe Stover, who got blown to pieces in World War II. She threatened to tell the world about my parentage if I didn't cooperate."

Sterling whistled. This was no clumsy attempt at dissembling on Jake's part, but rather the unvarnished truth. His pain and sorrow were all too evident. The lawyer realized that, if Monica's claim was true, the implications for Jake's struggle with Nate over the com-

pany would be far-reaching. For one thing, they gave
Jake an excellent motive for killing her.

"I take it you believed her," he said.

Jake looked down at his hands. "Not completely,"
he said. "At least, not at first. Dad's name was on my
birth certificate. Yet I'd always had my suspicions that
I differed from my siblings in some way where he was
concerned. I'm not saying he didn't love me. Or even
dote on me. But compared to the way he was with Nate,
Lindsay and Rebecca, we were never really close."

For years, Sterling had considered himself Kate's
closest confidant. Yet she'd never breathed a word of
anything like this to him. "I assume the old tart offered
you some sort of proof," he said, a trifle angrily.

"She'd hired an investigator, rounded up a bunch of
affidavits from people who knew Mom when she was
just a teenage waitress. According to them, she was already pregnant by Stover when Dad appeared on the
scene."

"You saw the affidavits?"

Jake nodded. "They seemed genuine."

"Where are they now?"

"I don't know. Monica claimed that, after showing
them to me, she'd put them in her safe-deposit box."

The lawyer winced. In all likelihood, the affidavits—
genuine or otherwise—would be found by the investigators probing Monica's death. Her son, Brandon, a
self-involved would-be actor and sometime errand boy
for his mother, would become their proprietor. Even if
he didn't choose to bandy them about, they'd become
part of the public record if Jake was tried as her murderer.

Somehow, Sterling had to keep that from happening.
If it did, Kate would be wounded to the quick. And the

family would be shaken to its foundations. Setting aside Jake's bombshell for the moment, he concentrated on another aspect of the problem that was troubling him.

"From the way you describe events unfolding, your fingerprints must be all over Monica's living room," he said. "Your DNA, too, in the form of blood drops and fingernail scrapings. But...think carefully...did you touch the letter opener she stabbed you with? It's likely to have been the murder weapon."

His expression pained and his brown eyes focused on a point in midair, just past Sterling's left shoulder, Jake tried to recall the details of the harrowing experience he'd had the night before. "I think so," he said at last. "I must have, at some point, when I tried to wrest it from her grasp."

Sterling stifled a groan. Jake was in hot water up to his eyebrows. True, there weren't any eyewitnesses to testify that he'd done Monica in, because the simple fact was that he hadn't. But there was more than enough damning physical evidence against him. If the police and the district attorney's office settled on him, and suspended their efforts to find the real killer, he might end up being convicted of Monica's murder.

He was going to need a crackerjack criminal attorney—preferably a team of them. As a lifelong practitioner of family and corporate law, Sterling wasn't qualified to manage his defense. But he'd do his utmost to help. Frowning, he weighed the pros and cons of getting someone else involved at once, and decided against it. Jake would appear at police headquarters as a pillar of the community who had been victimized by Monica and had left her recovering from her excesses—an innocent man willing to tell the authorities all he knew, who had brought his family attorney with him for moral support.

It was time to call the police. Before picking up the phone, Sterling set some parameters for Jake. The Fortune executive was to repeat his story to the authorities exactly as he'd told it to him, without embellishment.

"The blackmail, too?" Jake asked reluctantly. "If it gets out that I'm not Ben's son, Nate will sue to have me disinherited."

Sterling was torn over that issue. There was always the hope that the whole ugly story would remain hidden until the real murderer was found. But that possibility was exceedingly slim. Besides, it must be clear from the physical evidence that Monica and Jake had struggled. For that, there had to be a reason. If Jake didn't offer one, his story wouldn't hold together.

The attorney wished mightily that he could consult with Jake's yet-to-be-chosen defense attorney on that crucial issue. But it wasn't to be. With characteristic firmness, he came to a decision. "You'll have to tell them about it," he said. "Your story won't make sense if you don't. And it'll come out anyway. When it does, you'll be seen as withholding evidence. As for Nate, there's no way he can pull such a stunt. You're Kate's son, whoever your father was. And it was from Kate, not Ben, that you inherited."

Instead of contacting Detective Rosczak, and working from the bottom up, Sterling went straight to the top. Nels Petersen, the Minneapolis police commissioner, happened to be a personal friend. "I understand your boys want to talk with a client of mine, Jake Fortune, the CEO of Fortune Industries, in connection with the death of Monica Malone," he said forthrightly when Commissioner Petersen came on the line. "Mr. Fortune admits he visited Miss Malone yesterday evening. Though he had nothing whatever to do with her demise, he realizes the details of his exchange with her might prove helpful..."

Jake fretted visibly as Sterling listened to the police commissioner's reply. The lawyer didn't bother to enlighten him. "He's out of town just now, but he'll be back by dinnertime," he said at last. "All right if we meet with you and the detectives who are handling the case at the Government Center around 7:30 p.m.? You'll be there personally, I trust?"

It was a big favor to ask on a Saturday evening, when Commissioner Petersen doubtless had other plans. Yet the man agreed. Now, thought Sterling, all I have to do is drive Jake back to Minneapolis, see to it that he gets a shower, a shave and a hot meal, and help him firm up his story. At times, he reflected, lawyering was a lot like baby-sitting.

Jake's encounter with the police that evening at the Hennepin County Government Center went as well as could be expected. With Sterling and Commissioner Petersen present, Detective Rosczak and his partner, Detective Harbing, didn't try any tricky stuff. Yet they were hard-edged, skeptical, persistent. To Jake it felt as if they went over every point of his story a hundred times. Though both detectives seemed surprised, even taken aback, by his admission that Monica Malone had been blackmailing him, neither of them appeared to believe his version of what had taken place.

At last, Sterling called a halt. "We've been covering the same ground for the past three-quarters of an hour," he pointed out. "Either charge Mr. Fortune or let him go."

Though Jake's face expressed alarm at the suggestion, the lawyer knew that conclusive lab results in the case couldn't possibly be back yet. For the time being, the police didn't have sufficient evidence to do anything of the sort.

Reluctantly they agreed to end the session. However, they asked if Jake could come in to talk with them again in the morning.

"Give us a break!" Sterling exclaimed. "This is the weekend, for God's sake. You've heard what my client has to say...over and over again. He's telling you the truth and, in my opinion, he's been remarkably forthright and patient. Monday morning ought to be soon enough."

The detectives glanced at each other. "Monday morning it is," Detective Rosczak agreed. "We, uh, were wondering if, at that time, Mr. Fortune would be willing to take part in a lineup." It was the stuff of police shows on television, and Jake flung Sterling a wild-eyed look.

"I see no reason for anything of the sort," the lawyer said calmly. "Though he didn't kill her, my client has admitted to visiting Miss Malone yesterday evening. That being the case, it wouldn't be too surprising if someone saw him leave the property."

Detective Harbing had played the role of "good cop" throughout the proceedings. "We'd like to establish the time he left, that's all," he said nonthreateningly.

Though he refused the detectives' request, Sterling appeared to leave the door open a crack. A short time later, after driving Jake to his condominium garage so that the Fortune CEO could pick up his Porsche and then following him to the Lake Travis estate in order to discuss the matter of retaining a criminal attorney, the lawyer called Kate from the library phone to make a quick, surreptitious report. By the time Jake entered the room after changing into a bathrobe for comfort's sake, he was speaking to Erica.

The moment Jake's estranged wife heard his voice in the background, she demanded that Sterling put him on the phone. But she didn't get much out of him. "Just tell the kids I'm innocent, okay?" he muttered. "I can't talk right now. Sterling and I have important business to discuss. In the meantime, I need a drink. And something for a splitting headache."

After taking a taxi back to her hotel to shower and change clothes, Jess spent a restless, worried night at the hospital. It wasn't possible to get much sleep in the oversize lounge chair that had been positioned near Annie's bed, no matter how much she turned and twisted. Though her little girl seemed better, thanks to the antibiotic drip that flowed steadily into her bloodstream from a needle inserted into a vein in her left hand, she was still very weak. The prospect of how she'd react when her chemotherapy was administered was a nightmare Jess couldn't dismiss from her thoughts.

"You're all I have, darling, don't you know that?" she whispered with a lump in her throat around 3:00 a.m. as she gazed at her sleeping child. "You have to hold on until we can make you better. There's a whole wonderful life ahead of you, just waiting for you to live it...."

Annie was awake and complaining about the catheter in her hand by the time Stephen popped in around 7:00 a.m. Surprised to see him at all on a Sunday, Jess was thankful she'd taken a moment to comb her hair and put on fresh lipstick.

"What are you doing here?" she asked with a smile. "Don't you ever get a day off?"

Before entering Annie's room, Stephen had stopped to check Annie's chart at the nursing station. Calling himself every kind of idiot, on impulse he'd made a point of scanning that portion of her admission form which listed the names and addresses of her parents. In the box allocated for the name of Annie's father, Jessica Holmes had written *Deceased*. That didn't prove she was single, of course. She might have remarried. But he didn't think so. Her air of bearing up under the weight of Annie's illness alone argued against it.

Now, noting the shadows beneath her big, brown eyes and the temporary lines worry had etched in her lovely face, Stephen wished he could do something to comfort her. She was having a very tough time. Unfortunately, he could relate to it. He knew all too well what it was like to worry over a child that way.

It occurred to him that he hadn't answered her question. Since he'd lost David, Sunday had become the most difficult day of the week for him. He felt relief, instead of annoyance, if he was called upon to put in an appearance at the hospital.

He couldn't tell her that. "I have an elderly patient on three who isn't doing as well as I'd like," he explained instead, minimizing Mrs. Munson's condition, because it wouldn't do to speak to her of a patient he expected to lose. "Since I needed to check on her, I thought I'd visit Annie, as well."

He turned to the child. "I see you've been a good girl and kept your catheter in, even though it hurts a little," he said. "That deserves a medal. Or some sort of treat."

Annie's eyes brightened at once. "What do I get...another of those terrific bandages?" she asked.

Stephen shook his head. "Not this time. I brought you a real surprise."

Her curiosity turned to delight when he reached into his jacket pocket and brought forth one of David's small plastic cowboys, along with a matching Indian to keep him company and two miniature ponies for them to ride. "These are really for me?" she exclaimed. "I get to keep them?"

Stephen's smile broadened. "You most certainly do."

"Wow!" Annie was overwhelmed. "A cowboy and an Indian! Thanks a bunch!"

Jess was smiling too. "You didn't have to do that," she told him approvingly. "But the fact that you did was awfully sweet."

In the house next door to Stephen's on Forest Road, Lindsay Fortune-Todd was having breakfast with her husband, Frank, her seven-year-old daughter, Chelsea, and her six-year-old son, Carter. The blueberry pancakes she'd made were perfect, as was the orange juice her husband had squeezed and the hazelnut-flavored coffee he'd brewed. Outside, birds were chirping in the trees. The sun was crosshatching Lake Travis with diamonds.

Yet all was not right with her world. Despite the beautiful weather and her immediate family's happiness, a frown drew her delicate brows together. Calls from her younger sister, Rebecca, and her sister-in-law, Erica, earlier that morning had given her plenty to worry about. From what they'd related, it sounded as if Jake might be placed under arrest and tried for Monica Malone's murder.

Frank, a tall, sandy-haired internist whose practice

was situated next to hers in the Minn-Gen Professional Building, squeezed her hand as she stared out the breakfast room's bay window at a pair of racing sailboats without really seeing them. "It's going to be all right, Lin...I know it is," he reassured her. "Jake's innocent. The police will find the real killer in due course."

She tried to keep the worry out of her reply for the children's sake. "Not if they fasten on him and don't keep looking," she predicted.

Just then, the phone rang again.

"I'll get it," Frank offered. "You need to finish your breakfast, if you're going to the hospital."

Getting up from the table and walking into the kitchen proper, he removed the portable phone from its wall sconce. His back was turned to her as he said hello. She couldn't hear his part of the conversation that followed, just his tone of surprise and distaste.

A moment later, he returned to the table with obvious reluctance and handed the phone to her. "It's the police," he said incredulously. "I told them you knew nothing whatever about the Malone case. They insist on talking to you."

Lindsay stared at him in consternation. A moment later, she was speaking stiffly into the receiver. "This is Lindsay Todd...."

"Detective Tom Harbing with the Minneapolis Police Department here," a male voice replied. "Sorry to trouble you on a Sunday morning, Dr. Todd, but I need to ask you a quick question. It's in regard to Monica Malone's murder. I guess you probably heard about it."

She vouchsafed him an icy "Yes."

The detective cleared his throat. "Begging your pardon, ma'am, but we were wondering where you were between the hours of 9:00 and 10:15 p.m. Saturday night.''

Lindsay all but hit the roof. "Surely *I'm* not regarded as a suspect!" she exclaimed, causing Frank to grip her shoulder.

"I wouldn't go so far as to say that," Detective Harbing replied, neither confirming nor denying her statement. "However, a neighbor of the victim, who was walking her dog around 10:00 p.m., claims to have seen a woman answering to your description in the vicinity around that time. Is it possible that, like your brother, you paid a visit to Miss Malone Saturday evening?"

In an effort to keep from using words she didn't want her husband and children to hear issuing from her mouth, Lindsay took a deep breath. "I hate to disappoint you, Detective Harbing," she said. "But I have an airtight alibi. I was at Minneapolis General Hospital during the time in question, checking on a sick child and tending to a newborn who was on the critical list. At least a half-dozen pediatric nurses and technical staffers will corroborate my statement."

Dismissing the detective's perfunctory apology with a curt "Goodbye," Lindsay leaned into her husband, attempting to draw comfort from him.

"It'll be all right, honey…you'll see," he predicted, demonstrating his awareness that she wouldn't want to be quizzed over the details of the call in front of Carter and Chelsea.

"I hope so," she whispered. "Since Mom died, things have seemed to go from bad to worse."

A moment later, distraught over the way the tentacles of Monica Malone's murder were reaching deep into her family, she was disappearing into the den to phone Sterling and apprise him of the latest development.

* * *

Lindsay was still visibly upset when she arrived at the hospital and ran into Stephen in the doctor's lounge. *I wonder what the problem is,* he thought. *She usually has such an even disposition.*

"After you," he said pleasantly, ceding his place at the coffee urn.

When they'd each poured a cup, he invited her to take a break with him at one of the round mahogany tables. A bit impatiently, she shook her head. "I've got a lot to do."

It probably wasn't the best time to approach her about Jessica Holmes's bone-marrow quest, but he hated to postpone doing so. Given the seriousness of Annie's condition, there was little time to waste. If the Fortune family could supply the needed marrow...

"C'mon," he urged. "It's Sunday. Besides, I need to talk to you."

Shrugging, she took a seat.

"It's about Annabel Holmes," he said, taking an experimental sip of his steaming brew. "According to her mother, they came to Minneapolis for treatment because of a hitherto-unknown familial connection. She's hoping one of her newly discovered relatives, if that's what they turn out to be, will be able to supply the bone marrow Annie needs."

"But that's wonderful!" Lindsay exclaimed, momentarily carried out of her family troubles by concern for a patient. "The odds of finding a donor among blood relatives are so much better than they are among the general population...."

Stephen's expression told her she hadn't heard the whole story yet. "You might not think it's so great when I tell you it's your family she's trying to reach,'' he cautioned.

Lindsay thought she'd heard it all when Detective Harbing asked her to describe her whereabouts on the night of Monica Malone's murder. But apparently she hadn't. A woman who seldom swore, or even thought in scatological terms, she found herself stifling cuss words for the second time that morning. Jessica Holmes had seemed so nice! Yet she was turning out to be cut from the same cloth as the detestable Tracey Ducet, who—with her odious boyfriend's help—had tried to pass herself off as Lindsay's twin, who'd been kidnapped shortly after their birth.

"I hate to sound so hard-hearted, but I'm sick to death of fortune hunters," she proclaimed, jumping to her feet. "If Jessica Holmes's primary interest is securing a pipeline to riches, instead of help for her daughter, I think it best that another pediatrician be put on Annie's case."

"Hold on." Stephen laid a restraining hand on Lindsay's arm. "I may be a patsy for distraught mothers, but I don't think so. And I tend to believe her when she says it's strictly bone marrow, not money, that she wants. She has an old letter addressed to her maternal grandmother that seems to substantiate a possible relationship. For Annie's sake, why don't you talk to Mrs. Holmes about it before deciding her quest is a mercenary one?"

Jess sensed Lindsay's hostility at once when the latter paid a routine visit to Annie's room to check on the girl's general condition a short time later. I see Stephen—Dr. Hunter—has told her I'm trying to contact the Fortune family as possible bone-marrow donors, and she believes it's just a scam, she thought with a sinking feeling. If I can't convince her otherwise…

About to ask the brown-haired pediatrician if she'd mind stepping out in the hall so that they could talk privately, Jess was startled by a request to accompany Lindsay to the nearest doctor's transcription cubicle for the identical purpose. Tension was rife between them as Lindsay ushered her inside the cramped, glassed-in space, which was furnished with a counter, half a dozen chairs and a row of tape recorders, and shut the door.

"I won't mince words, Mrs. Holmes," Lindsay said. "Dr. Hunter has informed me you believe my family may be related to you in some way…that you brought your daughter to Minneapolis in the hope that the Fortunes could provide her with bone marrow for her much-needed transplant. While I'm highly skeptical of that possibility, as one who has seen more than one con artist appear on the scene in hopes of skimming some of the wealth from my parents' estate, I'm willing to look at the letter Dr. Hunter says you have in your possession. However, I warn you…if it appears to be a fraud, I plan to resign from your daughter's case."

Can she really believe I'd use Annie that way? Jess thought, sorely tempted to take umbrage. Somehow she managed to keep her cool. Not answering, out of concern that whatever she might say would appear inflammatory, she withdrew the letter from her purse and handed it to the woman she believed to be her great-aunt in the tangled web of relationships Benjamin Fortune's marital infidelity had produced.

Accepting it in the same vein, Lindsay unfolded it and spread it out on the counter. With a start, she recognized her father's handwriting. As distinctive as the man himself had been, with its slashing capitals and energetically scrawled lowercase letters, it would have been a nightmare for a forger to copy. There wasn't any doubt in her mind that the letter was genuine.

That being the case, she doubted Jessica Holmes had stolen it for dishonest purposes. She was willing to bet Jess could document her relationship to the unknown Celia of the salutation to a fare-thee-well.

A frown knitting her brows together, she read the letter twice from start to finish. From what she could gather, Ben had fathered a daughter named Lana with the addressee, an Englishwoman named Celia Warwick, during his World War II military service. Though it hurt to realize her father had abandoned his child, she realized it had happened long ago, during wartime. When he'd returned to Kate, they'd married and her mother had given birth to Jake.

Resolved not to agonize over something her mother had probably known nothing about, Lindsay focused on the letter's content. In essence, it was a heartfelt plea on Ben's part for a chance to have some sort of relationship, however tenuous, with the child he'd fathered in England. Several of the comments it contained led Lindsay to believe he'd steadfastly been denied that privilege.

You say my wife and your husband would be hurt by it. Well, I don't buy that, Celia. Neither of them would ever have to know—nor would what happened before we married matter. To begin with, there's an ocean between you and Kate. I travel to England from time to time on business, and—preoccupied as she is with her own life—she seldom accompanies me. As for your husband, George, you could introduce me as a long-lost American

cousin. It's true, as you point out, that I have other
children, who know me well and bring me great
delight. Yet, as a mother, you must surely realize—
a parent's heart is big enough to love every child
he or she has brought into the world.

There wasn't any date. Stunned to learn that she had
a half sister, Lindsay realized that the Lana of the letter
must be Jake's age. I want to meet her, she decided.
With Mom gone, there shouldn't be any obstacle.

Jess saw at once that Lindsay's attitude toward her
had changed when the brown-haired pediatrician raised
her eyes from the page. She waited breathlessly for
some sort of verdict.

"I take it you're Lana's daughter, from your claim
of relationship to my family," Lindsay said slowly,
scrutinizing Jess with fresh eyes.

Jess nodded.

"Where's your mother now? Still living in England,
I imagine."

Sadly Jess shook her head. "Mom died of a heart
ailment several years ago."

"I'm sorry."

A small silence rested between them. "I would have
liked very much to meet her," Lindsay added, her
mouth curving with a pensive warmth that was like the
sun slowly emerging from behind a cloud. "Sorry I was
so hard on you. I shouldn't have distrusted you the way
I did, when your concern for your daughter was so obviously genuine. It's just that there have been fortune
hunters, including one who claims to be my long-lost
twin...."

Jess was willing to forgive her the earth. "I understand completely," she replied in a shaky voice. "Any-

one in your position would be wary. Do I dare hope
you'll put me in touch with your family members, so I
can ask them to be tested? If we could find a donor for
Annie…''

Her voice breaking, she couldn't stop several tears
from spilling down her cheeks.

To her surprise, the brown-haired pediatrician who'd
seemed so unapproachable just a short time earlier
reached over and gave her a hug. "If you like, I'll approach them for you on Annie's behalf, starting with
the adults, including myself," she offered, giving new
life to Jess's hopes. "It would help tremendously if I
could show them a copy of this letter."

By now, Jess was smiling again, though her eyes
were still red-rimmed, and glittered with unshed tears.
"I'd be happy if you would," she said. "As it happens,
I made several photocopies.…''

Annie's temperature had registered as normal for almost eight hours by the time Stephen looked in on her
again before leaving the hospital. Though she still
seemed weak, in Jess's opinion, she was sitting up in
bed and playing with the plastic figures he'd given her
when he entered the room.

"Look, Dr. Hunter…my cowboy and Indian are having a shoot-out," she greeted him.

The look he threw Jess expressed pleasure in her live-
liness. "I hope nobody's getting too badly hurt," he
said as he lifted her wrist to take her pulse.

"Don't worry," she replied with an indulgent smile.
"It's just pretend, like at the cinema."

Lindsay, who'd been passing in the hall and dropped
in for a moment to assure Stephen that she'd do her
best to help find Annie a donor, couldn't help but notice
the warm glance he exchanged with Jess. Was it pos-

sible that her friend, who'd been referred to by the hospital's female staff as "tall, blond and unavailable" ever since his divorce, had at last developed an interest in someone?

An hour or so after Stephen left, Jess walked down to the nursing station to request some orange juice for Annie, who'd finally expressed a yen for something. On the way back to Annie's room, she overheard two nurse's aides gossiping about him. Intrigued, though she berated herself for her interest when her daughter was so sick, she made a point, later, of asking one of the women if he was married, or single.

"Divorced, I think," the woman replied with a grin. "But don't get your hopes up, honey. That one's out of reach."

Four

With Sterling at his side and very little restful sleep to his credit during what had remained of the weekend, Jake showed up at police headquarters shortly after 10:00 a.m. on Monday expecting another grilling. Embarrassed and chagrined at being subjected to what he considered an unmerited public humiliation, he could feel the department secretaries staring and whispering to each other as the desk sergeant led him and the attorney back to room 108, which housed the homicide division. For a man used to deference and first-class treatment, it was like being forced to run a gauntlet.

As before, Detectives Harbing and Rosczak were waiting for them. Thanking him for coming in, the two stony-faced detectives ushered them into an even smaller interview room, which contained just a battered table and four unmatched chairs. Two of the chairs had reclining backs and comfortable, padded seats. They were quickly appropriated by the officers. They motioned for him and Sterling to take the others, which were made of plain varnished wood.

Though Jake couldn't be sure, he was willing to bet the wall of what appeared to be frosted glass on one side of the room was in reality a one-way mirror that would allow higher-ups, possibly the police captain and an assistant county attorney, to observe the exchange that was about to take place. The thought of an unseen prosecutor scribbling notes as the two detectives tried to trip him up made him literally sick to his stomach.

"Okay," Detective Rosczak said. "Let's take this from the top. Tell us everything you can remember about the night Monica Malone was murdered...."

About to comply, feeling as he didn't have any other choice, Jake was peremptorily silenced by Sterling. "Not so fast," the lawyer snapped. "My client is the CEO of Fortune Industries. He enjoys an excellent reputation in this community. He came here in good faith to help with your investigation...not to be arrested for a crime he didn't commit because some minor detail of his account doesn't correspond with what he told you Saturday night. If he's a suspect, he wants to know it...*now,* so he can hire a criminal attorney to defend himself."

The detectives exchanged a look. "You might say he's a suspect," Tom Harbing admitted, causing Jake's heart to flutter. "Of course, if he can convince us of his innocence..."

Sterling's manner approached its most severe. "You know the score as well as I do," he said. "A man's innocent until proven guilty. And you'll have a hard time tagging Mr. Fortune with that label, because *he didn't kill Miss Malone.* We came here today in the expectation of answering additional questions that weren't put to Mr. Fortune on Saturday night, not hashing over the same ground endlessly. Since it appears you have the latter in mind, I'm advising him to keep his own counsel until such time as he may choose to testify under oath."

Again the detectives looked at each other, without speaking. All but quaking in his seat, Jake half expected Detective Harbing to jerk him to his feet and haul his hands behind his back while Detective Rosczak read him his rights and snapped on the handcuffs.

It didn't happen—at least not yet.

"Suit yourself," Detective Rosczak said, with an expressive shrug. "That time may come a lot sooner than you think. In the meantime, you'd do well to advise your client not to leave town without informing us of his destination."

Annie seemed better still when Lindsay dropped by shortly before noon with the news that she'd spoken with as many relatives as possible by phone. Though some were still mulling over the proposition, her sister, Rebecca, her nephew Adam and her niece Caroline had already agreed to be tested.

"In my opinion, most of the others will, too, once they've had time to get used to the idea," Lindsay prophesied. "As for myself, I plan to have blood drawn just as soon as I finish my rounds."

Because of her willingness to help and go to bat for Annie with her family, Jess's little girl stood a chance of beating the deadly disease that was ravaging her five-year-old body. On the verge of hugging her, Jess restrained herself. Though Lindsay had taken that liberty during their talk in the transcription room, she wasn't sure how the gesture would be received, coming from her. She didn't want to push her connection to the moneyed and wary Fortunes past their point of tolerance, or foist unwanted intimacy on them.

"Dr. Todd...I can't thank you enough," she whispered.

Lindsay's smile was positively beatific. "Don't mention it," she urged. "I consider it a start. We'll have to work on the others. Of course, I needn't tell you that the odds are still somewhat problematical. At a time like this, a person can't have too many relatives. I just wish my twin—the real one—hadn't been kidnapped. We were fraternal, and wherever he or she is today, my former womb-mate could have statistically improved Annie's chances.''

Jess was in full agreement. In seeking a donor for Annie, they'd need all the luck, and all the blood relatives, they could get.

''By the way,'' Lindsay added, ''I think it's time you stopped calling me 'Dr. Todd' and started using my given name. Just don't try putting an 'Aunt' in front of it....''

As the two women laughed, forging the first tentative bonds of what promised to become a warm cousinly friendship, Jake and Sterling were deep in conversation in the Fortune mansion's oak-paneled library, talking about Jake's life and the mess in which he found himself.

The attorney had returned to the Lake Travis house with him, not to baby-sit, philosophize or attempt to silence dire predictions of disaster, but rather to discuss the choice of a lead criminal attorney with him. He had two in mind: Eamon Walsh of Minneapolis, a brilliant, deceptively laid-back intellectual who did well with primarily white middle- and upper-class juries, and St. Paul native Aaron F. Silberman, a contentious bulldog of a bare-knuckle fighter who tended to sink his teeth into the prosecution's case and hang on until it had been reduced to tatters. Jurors of varying races and social backgrounds tended to be somewhat skeptical of his tough-guy stance at first. But they were quickly won over by his common touch, his expert questioning and persuasive arguments, and his strong air of conducting a dogged search for the truth on an innocent client's behalf.

Though in his opinion Jake would get on better with Walsh, Sterling had all but decided to recommend Silberman. The object was to keep the Fortune CEO out of jail and foil any attempt by the Hennepin County criminal justice system to pin Monica's murder on him, not to recruit a future golfing buddy.

Before getting down to brass tacks, he knew, he'd have to put in some time as father confessor and psychotherapist. It was a role he'd played for the Fortunes ever since signing on as Ben's and Kate's attorney of record, many years earlier. He only wished Jake would lay off the Scotch. It wasn't noon yet, and he'd already downed most of his second drink. He was going to need his wits and his sobriety about him in the days and weeks ahead.

From Jake's perspective, the selection of a criminal attorney and subsequent strategizing over a response to the murder charge that might soon be leveled against him were details he didn't want to face. To be honest, he was fed up with scheming and worrying in a futile attempt to deal with what had seemed an unending series of blows and crises in his personal and professional life. He wanted to go to ground somewhere. Fade into oblivion. Simply to drift, without engaging his thoughts.

The truth was, he'd never quite fitted the intrepid buoyancy of the Fortune mold. Yet as Ben's and Kate's oldest son—supposedly the child of both—he'd been groomed for the top job at Fortune Industries since college and been given it in due course. Yet he'd never really wanted it. As a youngster, he'd had a very different career in mind for himself. It was too late now to throw over the traces and change course, and it would be even if he weren't facing the fight of his life over Monica Malone's death. He was fifty-four years old, and the die had been cast. Yet that young Jake was still deep within him, craving peace, rest and a cessation of unwanted responsibility, and yearning after might-have-beens.

"You know," he told Sterling morosely, running long, tanned fingers through his silvering dark hair, "this is going to sound like alcohol talking. But none of this would have happened if I'd gone to medical school the way I'd hoped. I should have told Dad to stuff it...."

To Sterling, such maudlin musings were wholly beside the point. Whatever career Jake had pursued, Monica would have come after him if he had the stock she wanted and she possessed damning secret information to help her wring it out of him. Not for the first time, the lawyer wondered where she'd gotten it. Who had carried the tale of Jake's real parentage to her, inspiring her to dig into Kate's past for the necessary witnesses? In all his musings, he'd been able to come up with just one answer—her erstwhile lover, Ben Fortune, who'd had every reason to know the truth.

It was an answer that would devastate Kate's firstborn—and one Sterling was astonished he hadn't come up with on his own. "Why'd you hang on to the CEO position, then, if you didn't want it?" he asked, humoring him.

Jake shrugged, swirling what remained of the Scotch he'd poured into his Waterford-crystal tumbler. "Because Nate wanted it, I suppose," he answered, aware that his increasingly precarious position had caused him to dredge up some uncomfortable insights.

As the two men talked, closeted behind the library's massive double doors, they couldn't hear the buzzer go off in the kitchen that indicated someone was applying for entrance at the property's front gate. They weren't aware of Mrs. Laughlin, the sixtyish, somewhat severe-looking housekeeper Jake had recently hired, answering it. Neither had an inkling of heavier trouble descending until the unthinkable happened and she rapped against the double doors' heavy oak panels, disturbing them.

"Yes, Mrs. Laughlin…what is it?" Jake called warily.

She took his question as permission to enter. "The police are at the front gate, Mr. Fortune," she disclosed, her knobby fingers pleating the hem of her apron. "They demand to see you. What should I tell them?"

Tensing until he appeared to be carved from stone, Jake seemed incapable of answering her. "Ask them to come in," Sterling replied in his place. "They damn well better have a warrant," he added as the woman withdrew, "or we're going straight to the top with a formal complaint of harassment."

Jake hoped violently that the latter scenario would take place. Yet, in his heart, he knew better than to expect it. Since he'd gotten mixed up with Monica, it seemed, each unforeseeable step deeper into the muck of his connection with her had been preordained. "Time to hire a criminal attorney, I guess," he drawled, in an effort to tough out the moment. "I'll let you be the judge of whom to get."

Seconds later, the housekeeper was showing Detectives Harbing and Rosczak into the library. They didn't wait for her to leave the room, or mince any words before stating their business.

"Jacob Fortune, I'm placing you under arrest for the

murder of Monica Malone," Detective Harbing related as his partner tugged Jake's hands behind his back and snapped a pair of handcuffs about his wrists. "You have the right to remain silent. Anything you choose to say may be used against you. You have the right to an attorney…"

Powerless to prevent it from happening, Sterling watched, grim-faced. "I presume you goons have a warrant," he growled.

Detective Harbing looked as if he'd like to abandon his good-cop stance and punch the attorney in the mouth. "I have it right here, sir," he replied, proffering a crumpled document he'd been carrying in his inside jacket pocket.

Scanning the warrant, Sterling saw that everything was in order. It had been sworn out before a judge. He doubted it had been that difficult to get, given the preponderance of evidence. "Don't say anything, unless it's a request to go to the bathroom," he warned Jake. "No matter *how* understanding or accommodating they seem, don't talk to them!"

The Fortune CEO stared. "You're…not coming with me?" he croaked.

Regretfully Sterling shook his head. "I've got to retain a criminal attorney for you," he explained, wishing he'd done so earlier. "If I can get in touch with the man I want, and persuade him to represent you, it shouldn't take long."

After Jake and the police had gone, Sterling's first move was to phone Kate. "I have bad news, kitten," he announced, unconsciously reverting to the pet name he'd used once or twice when they were much younger and he was hopelessly in love with her.

She didn't answer for several seconds. Then she replied, "Give it to me straight," in her husky voice.

Beneath her silks, she was made of tempered steel. Though she might bend, if necessary, she'd never break. "Jake's been arrested for Monica's murder," he said, thanking God for her toughness and resilience. "As we speak, he's on his way to jail. I've told him to say nothing further to anyone until I can arrange for a top-notch criminal attorney to defend him."

Another silence rested between them. In it, Sterling imagined he could hear her unasked question: *Will Jake be convicted if the case goes to trial?* Aware that she was most protective of Jake among her children—that she'd grieve when, inevitably, the details of his parentage were bandied about—he didn't know how to answer her.

"Whom did you have in mind?" she said at last, letting him off the hook. When he mentioned Aaron Silberman, she reacted favorably. "I've seen him on television," she remarked. "He's a short, somewhat aggressive man, with energetic-looking hair and wire-rimmed glasses, isn't he? From what I could tell, he seems to know how to handle himself."

Sterling was pleased. "I'll get with him right away," he promised, resolving to take private detective Gabe Devereax off the ongoing investigation of Kate's crash and other Fortune mishaps and put him on the Malone case.

Her reply was terse but approving. "Don't let me keep you, then."

"I'll phone you this evening."

"Come by for a drink, if you're able."

Having spoken with Gabe and won a provisional commitment from Aaron Silberman to defend Jake,

Sterling headed for the jail to see what, if anything, he could do for his beleaguered client. No sooner had he found a parking place and stepped out of his Lincoln, however, than he was mobbed by members of the press, including several reporters with TV cameramen in tow.

The battery of questions they thrust at him had a common theme. Rumor had it Jake had been arrested for Monica Malone's murder. Was that accurate? What were the charges? Did Jake continue to profess his innocence?

To Sterling's way of thinking, barely enough time had passed for Harbing and Rosczak to file the arrest report. So where had these hyenas gotten their information? A tip from one of the illustrious detectives, perhaps?

"It seems to me," he said severely, "that hearsay isn't the best source of facts in a murder case. You'd do well to check the official record. As for Mr. Fortune, he maintains that Miss Malone was alive and well the last time he saw her. And I believe him. You may say that his family strongly believes in his innocence."

A call to the police commissioner got Jake out of the holding area and into a private cell within minutes of Sterling's arrival. They were joined by Aaron Silberman a short time later. Though Jake's initial reaction to the feisty, plainspoken attorney was one of scepticism bordering on distaste, he bit his lip and didn't argue against him. He wasn't in a position to do anything of the sort. Besides, if he'd learned anything over the years, it was that Sterling knew his job. If the family lawyer thought Aaron Silberman was the best man to help clear his name, that was good enough for him.

He found the necessity of going over and over the details of his visit to Monica on the night of her death painful in the extreme. Since repeating them to the police in Sterling's presence on Saturday evening, he'd tended to gloss over them in his head, softening the memory of his own stupidity in the process.

Now it was being brought home to him in full measure. What would Erica think when she heard he'd been arrested? His sisters? And his children? Would they stand by their belief in him?

At last, he couldn't think of a single detail they hadn't covered at least half a dozen times. "I've told you absolutely everything I can think of," he said wearily, cradling his aching head in his hands. "I *swear* to you that I didn't kill Monica, though I suppose I could easily have done so in self-defense. In my mind's eye, I can see her sitting there on the sofa, screaming gutter words at me as I went out the door, just as surely as I can see you sitting across the table. At that time, nobody had been stabbed with the letter opener that supposedly killed her but myself."

Aaron Silberman regarded him quietly for a moment. "Maybe I'm a nut," he said at last. "Or a patsy for the kind of story that skates so close to disaster it must be the truth. But I believe you. So...who's the guilty party?"

Jake was forced to admit he didn't have a clue. "Strange as it may seem, I barely knew the woman," he replied. "This whole mess got started months ago, when she came to me to discuss 'a matter of mutual interest.' As I've told you, that turned out to be the issue of my parentage. She showed me the affidavits I described, and swore that if I didn't sell her a sizable chunk of my stock in Fortune Industries at well below market value, she'd ruin me by making the information they contained public...."

"I take it that means you don't know who killed her," Silberman observed, tongue in cheek.

That evening, Jake's arrest was prominently featured on both the local and the national newscasts. Sterling had warned Erica what to expect. After an unsuccessful attempt to reach her estranged husband at the jail, she'd driven to her daughter Natalie's home to watch the news with her and architect Rick Dalton, her newly acquired fiancé. Several other family members—Natalie's sister Caroline, her brother, Adam, and his fiancée Laura—had gathered with them, as well. No one could believe what had happened, with the possible exception of Natalie, who had arrived at the Fortune mansion on the lake the night of Monica's murder in time to see her father's blood-spattered shirt and listen to his incoherent, drunken ramblings about what had taken place.

Like her siblings, however, Natalie was vociferously convinced of his innocence. "We have to call him...tell him we're behind him one hundred percent!" she exclaimed when the TV anchorman moved on to another topic.

The conversation she proposed wasn't to take place. A call to the jail's information desk yielded only the number of a pay phone in the male prisoners' dayroom, which continued to ring busy for several hours. Incredibly, the "pull" that had attached to being Fortunes in Minneapolis for as long as they could remember seemed to have evaporated just when they needed it most.

Five

To Jake's increasing sense of being at the vortex of a whirlpool that would drag him ever downward, severing him forever from the life he'd known, Aaron Silberman's attempt to win his release on bond at his arraignment the next morning failed. Sourly concurring with the assistant county attorney's argument that Jake was a poor risk because he'd left Minnesota the night of Monica Malone's murder, the judge issued a quick denial and banged his gavel, thundering, "Next case!"

The criminal attorney could offer but scant consolation. The arraignment judge, known to have come up from poverty the hard way and to harbor a strong resentment against society's more privileged members, wouldn't preside at Jake's preliminary hearing, several weeks hence. They could try again, with what Aaron Silberman predicted would be better results. "There's no reason to keep you behind bars, despite the seriousness of the charge," he said. "When asked, you went to the police of your own free will and told them what you knew of that night's events."

Visits with his grown children through a glass panel that didn't allow them to kiss or touch brought deep embarrassment and pain to him. When they were small, toddling about the house, and later, when they graduated from training wheels to ride their two-wheel bikes unaided around the neighborhood, he'd been like a god to them. He was mortified that, as adults, they should see him brought so low, so hollow-eyed from worry and lack of sleep, in his unpressed regulation-issue jail uniform.

At last he asked them not to come again. "The county jail's no place for you, any more than it is for me," he told them unequivocally. "For my part, it can't be helped. But I don't want your seeing me here to figure prominently in your memories of me someday."

Their protests that they'd never view him in that light in a million years didn't alter his opinion. "I'll be getting out of here just as soon as my preliminary hearing is held," he insisted, though secretly he wouldn't have bet money on it. "We'll be able to spend as much time as we want together then."

Somewhat dubiously, they agreed to do as he asked. On the way back to his cell after their last visit, he congratulated himself with a twist of irony that he'd been lucky in one respect. At least Erica hadn't insisted on visiting him, to carry away the image of how he'd looked at the nadir of his poise and self-respect.

Two weeks later, Jake was still behind bars. His preliminary hearing had been postponed at the county attorney's request, despite Aaron Silberman's objections. Meanwhile, at Minn-Gen, Annie's strength had improved sufficiently for her stopgap chemotherapy to get under way.

On the fateful morning, Jess was seated at her daughter's bedside in the special "clean air" room where Annie would reside until her bone marrow had regenerated sufficiently to offer some temporary protection from disease. She was smoothing the child's silky blond curls, with the aching realization that at least partial

baldness would result from her treatment, when Stephen
entered with a slim redheaded nurse-specialist in tow.
The latter was carrying an IV stand and several plastic
pouches of the clear, sick-making fluid needed to begin
her treatment.

It was time. A bit shakily, Jess got to her feet. With
all the fierce motherly protectiveness she possessed, she
wanted to scream that she'd changed her mind and order
them out of the room. No one was to touch Annie. Or
give her harsh chemicals to make her retch. There
would be time enough for that to happen when a donor
was found.

Stephen's heart went out to her when he saw the
trapped and terrified look on her face, just as it did to
his small patient, who would soon be sick to her stomach and vomiting into a metal basin as a result of his
prescribed treatment.

In the weeks that followed his gift to Annie of the
plastic cowboy and Indian that had once belonged to
his son, he and Jess hadn't so much as touched again.
But that hadn't kept him from imagining how it would
feel to take her in his arms and press his mouth against
her softly parted lips. He hadn't been able to stop thinking of her at night, and imagining what it would be like
to have her warm beneath the covers with him. Again
and again he asked himself if he had the courage to care
for another woman in her vulnerable and unenviable
position. If he took that leap and failed with her, too,
he'd have a second emotional catastrophe to his credit.

And if he didn't take the risk? What would he lose
by his cowardice? Just the chance to weave a life so
gauzy and bright with love in its everyday moments that
the inevitable tragedies of my profession might lose
some of their power to hurt me, he thought. To hear a

precious child laughing in the next room and know that, in a moment, she would scramble up into my lap and demand a story with blissful assurance…to kiss the soft nape of a beloved woman's neck beneath steam-dampened ringlets as she stirred something aromatic on the rangetop… What wouldn't I give for these simple but deeply satisfying things, if only I dared to reach out for them?

So far, he hadn't taken the most tentative step in that direction. Still, the weeks of Annie's hospitalization had propelled him and Jess from the formalities of ''Dr.'' and ''Mrs.'' to a first-name basis. Their almost daily meetings and their mutual concern for Annie had nurtured a camaraderie of sorts that could, he sensed, segue into something stellar, satisfying and, to his commitment-apprehensive soul, infinitely dangerous.

''We don't have any other choice, Jess,'' he said, deliberately resting a hand on her shoulder. ''Harsh as this course of treatment may seem, Annie needs this chance for a temporary remission so we can buy time to find a donor.''

He was right, of course. The IV nurse asked her to step back, so as not to impede the procedure that was about to take place, and she did so reluctantly. She all but held her breath as, after carefully preparing Annie's hand, the woman inserted the necessary catheter in her vein, causing the girl to cry out in pain and distress.

''Mummy…it hurts!''

The catheter wasn't wholly secured yet. Suppressing a corresponding outburst, Jess turned and hid her face against Stephen's lab coat. Seconds later, she'd realized her error and stepped back to tough out the moment. ''I know you're right,'' she said in a small voice, not quite meeting his eyes. "It's just that I'd give anything to bear this treatment for her...."

Stephen knew the feeling all too well. There wasn't a child he treated for leukemia or some other life-threatening blood disease who didn't bring David's illness back to him, with all its accompanying rage and helplessness. Unfortunately, his relationship with Annie was far more complicated than any other he'd had with a youthful patient since his son's death. During their brief association, the frail blond girl, with her plucky spirit and adorable British accent, had wormed her way into his affections in a way that, so far, none of his other charges had been able to do.

In part, he knew, that was because of his feelings for her mother, which neither reason nor the memory of his unhappy breakup with Brenda had seemed able to curb.

"We aren't giving her a full load," he answered, hating himself for the need to be so matter-of-fact with her. "In just a few days, she should be feeling better and taking nourishment. I have every expectation that, once her bone marrow regenerates, she'll be able to go home from the hospital for a while, until we're ready to do her transplant."

He makes it sound as if the transplant's a sure thing, though we don't have a donor yet, Jess thought. Like me, he's probably counting on the Fortunes to come through, since the initial reports from the marrow banks he contacted for us have been uniformly negative.

By now, Jess knew that attempting to match bone marrow was a much more difficult and complicated process than obtaining compatible blood types for a transfusion. For a successful transplant to take place, donor and recipient had to share at least three, and preferably

more, of the six markers, called human leukocyte antigens found on every human bone-marrow cell.

The first to be drawn and analyzed, Lindsay's blood
had indicated compatibility with only two of Annie's
six antigens. But there was still hope. Rebecca, Adam
and Caroline had appeared on schedule for their blood
tests, despite worries over Jacob Fortune, who was facing murder charges. The reports on those tests would
be back soon. And, thanks to Lindsay, others were in
the works.

Meanwhile, Jess would hug the prospect of taking
Annie home for a while—even if that home had to be
a hotel room. "I'll try to remember that tonight, and
tomorrow, when she's so sick," she whispered.

After what seemed infinite adjustments and calibra-
tions, the IV nurse had completed her task. Jess was
free to rejoin her daughter. Violating the rule that forbade family members and approved visitors sitting on
a patient's bed in one of the special "clean rooms," she
snuggled close to Annie on the side opposite the catheter and put both arms around her. Unfortunately, like
Stephen and the IV nurse, she was wearing a mask to
prevent infection, and she couldn't kiss the girl's cheek.

"It hurts, Mummy," Annie complained, nestling
against her. "I want to go home to England, and see
Herkie. Why do we have to do this?"

Jess knew instinctively that a glib explanation
wouldn't cut it. "I realize this is nasty medicine, and
that it hurts a lot, sweetheart," she said. "I wish I could
take it for you. But the truth is, it has some good things
about it, too. In a few days, you'll be feeling better, and
soon after that you'll get to leave the hospital for a
while, until we can find that very special medicine I
told you about. Once you take it, you won't be tired

and sick all the time. We'll be able to do lots of fun things together.''

Annie remained skeptical. ''I miss Herkie so much,'' she whimpered. ''Seeing him again would make me feel better, too, don't you think?''

Stephen remembered the girl mentioning someone named Herkie once before. I wonder who he is? he thought. Someone Jess is fond of, too? With other patients to see, he didn't have time to ask.

''You hang in there, okay?'' he urged, lifting Annie's chin with one gloved finger. ''I'll be back to check on you in a little while. You know, there are more cowboys and Indians where the first ones came from. I wouldn't be surprised if they turned up in your room one of these days.''

As morning wore on into afternoon, Annie got progressively sicker. Holding the basin under her chin when she threw up and wiping her face with a damp towel, Jess worried that she'd get the dry heaves. But she was only moderately successful in getting her wretched, unhappy child to take an occasional sip of water. Though Stephen checked back as promised, around noon and again about 5:00 p.m., each time he could only stay a minute.

Shortly after his departure, the last of Annie's retching stopped. She fell into a fitful sleep. Stiff from maintaining a sitting position for most of the day, Jess got to her feet and strolled over to the window for a change of scene. She was just in time to see Stephen leave the building in dress slacks and a sport coat and get into a silver-gray Miata convertible where a slim woman with shoulder-length ash-blond hair had been waiting for him. To her dismay, he and the woman exchanged a quick embrace before the little sportster shot out of its illegal parking space near the hospital entrance and joined the flow of cars out of the parking lot.

Her first reaction was a stunning sense of loss—one that brought home to her just how far her fantasies about him had flown. I should have known better than to believe that nurse's aide when she intimated that he wasn't dating anyone, she thought, the bottom dropping out of a place inside her that had cautiously begun to dream again. A man like that might play hard to get. But he'd be in constant demand nonetheless. What a fool he must think me, mooning over him! She wanted to die when she remembered how, just a few hours earlier, she'd rested her cheek against his lab coat, seeking comfort.

He could be sure it wouldn't happen again. As she sank into the Leatherette lounger beside her daughter's bed, she reflected that an endless parade of single mothers with sick children must develop crushes on him, unaware that his kindness and concern were strictly professional and humanitarian. Face it, she told herself bitterly. You and Annie are alone in the world, locked in the battle of her life. And it's likely to remain that way. You need to put blinders on where romance is concerned.

Arriving at a nearby restaurant with his dinner date, a friend of his ex-wife's who had recently undergone a divorce herself, Stephen scolded himself for being an easy mark. When the woman had phoned out of the blue to tell him about her newly single state and confessed her overwhelming loneliness, he'd done his awkward best to sympathize. She'd quickly responded by asking him out to dinner. Though he'd squirmed and struggled to think of an appropriate excuse to beg off, there had been no getting out of it. She'd been available "most any night."

He was in for a boring, frustrating evening, he guessed. From what he could remember of Gloria, she talked of nothing but golf scores, bridge, her poodle, Muppet, the spoils from her most recent shopping trip and the latest dirt circulating in his ex-wife's social set.

His current experience of her didn't turn out to be very far off the mark. For a while, as they ate their mesclun salads and pasta fresca with sun-dried tomatoes, he found he could uphold his end of the evening's bargain by simply nodding, smiling and posing a negligent question now and then. Still, it was uncomfortably clear that the former Gloria Denham had serious designs on him.

I can't wait for her to drop me off so I can run upstairs—to check on Jess and Annie one more time before I head home to Lake Travis, he realized. Their welfare has begun to mean a lot to me on a very personal level.

After interminable small talk over coffee and dessert, and several hints on his part that he had early rounds the following morning, Gloria murmured at last that perhaps she'd better drive him back to the hospital. "That is, unless you'd rather..." she added, her voice trailing off in embarrassment at the startled look he gave her.

Stephen quickly filled the awkward silence that followed by thanking her for being so understanding. "It's not everyone who's willing to sympathize with the demands of a busy physician's schedule," he said.

He considered himself fortunate to escape with soothing reassurances and a brotherly kiss on the cheek when she halted her Miata in front of Minn-Gen's main entrance a short time later. Before her taillights had disappeared down the circular drive, he was striding toward the elevator. Somehow, the evening with Gloria had made him doubly eager to see Jess.

Donning a surgical gown over his street clothes and slipping on a mask and a pair of gloves at the nursing station, he entered Annie's room. During his absence, dusk had fallen. Yet Jess hadn't bothered to switch on a lamp. In the half-light from the hall, he could see that Annie was sleeping—if not altogether peacefully, at least without a great deal of restlessness.

The pretty, dark-haired Brit he'd compared so favorably with his ex-wife's friend had spent the past several hours staring into space from the Leatherette lounger beside her daughter's bed, alternately contemplating what she believed would be a loveless future and worrying that they wouldn't have found a matching donor when all the Fortunes had been tested. Now, at Stephen's light step, she turned and got to her feet.

"How's Annie been doing?" he asked in a husky whisper, approaching to stand a little too close.

She couldn't see his mouth, just his Viking-blue eyes and the expression they contained. From what she could tell, it was as deceptively warm as usual—maybe even a little warmer, out of sympathy for their current plight. Thanks to the tableau she'd witnessed from her fourth-floor vantage point, she had a fair idea just how far that warmth could be expected to carry her. Exactly nowhere, she told herself. Thank God I woke up to my silly daydreams before I thoroughly embarrassed myself.

"About as well as can be expected, I guess," she answered.

Was he imagining it, or was her precise British

intonation a little cool? He tried again. "How about you, then? Have you had any dinner?"

She shook her head.

"You have to eat, Jess. If you don't want to leave Annie's side long enough to go to the cafeteria, let me run down to the snack bar and get you something."

He wasn't her brother. Or her keeper. Instead, he was her daughter's physician, a highly trained specialist with many patients to worry about—hardly the sort of person you dispatched to the nearest lunch counter to get you some fish and chips or an American hot dog.

"Thanks, but you needn't bother," she answered, without a crinkle of a smile in evidence. "One of the nurses offered me some yogurt from their unit kitchen. If I get hungry, I can take them up on it."

Well versed in detecting when a woman was displeased with him, thanks to his troubles with Brenda, Stephen could feel the chill. It's understandable, I suppose, he tried to tell himself. Her daughter's very sick, and I've made her sicker in the course of her treatment. At times like this, a parent isn't exactly rational. She's bound to feel some resentment.

Instinct argued that her reaction went deeper than that.

Murmuring a low-key good-night, coupled with a promise to check on Annie "first thing in the morning," he beat a strategic retreat. Yet he couldn't help feeling somewhat crestfallen as he headed for the elevators. His "date" with Gloria Denham, if that was what it had been, had filled him with mounting eagerness to be with Jess. He'd wanted to see her, touch her, listen to the music of her voice, just bask in her presence. To tell the truth, throughout most of the evening, he'd been teetering on the verge of doing something rash—namely, falling for her.

Saved by the deep freeze, he congratulated himself as he strolled to the physician's parking area and got into his Mercedes. Yet as he left the hospital campus behind and headed for his lonely Lake Travis residence, he couldn't get the concept of a narrow escape to stick. The fact was, he was too far gone in his admiration and longing for her to beat an easy retreat.

About the time he pulled into his garage and got out of his sleek, expensive car to face an empty house, Erica was returning home from a night class at the junior college she attended. Unceremoniously dropping her notebook, woven leather purse and cashmere cardigan on one of the Roche-Bobois chairs in her off-white living room, she headed straight for the kitchen for two aspirin and a glass of skim milk.

Her attempt to pay attention as her world-history instructor lectured on the fall of the Roman Empire while simultaneously worrying about Jake had given her a monstrous headache. It was only after downing the aspirin and thoroughly massaging the bridge of her nose that she noticed that the little red light on her answering machine was blinking.

There were two messages—one from Jake, and another from his sister Lindsay. Astonished to hear from her estranged husband, who'd let her know by default that he wanted her to have no part in his troubles with the police, she rewound the tape and played it again, listening carefully to every nuance of meaning and expression in his husky, somewhat self-deprecating voice.

She didn't glean much. Mumbling that he was sorry he'd missed her, he'd simply asked her to return his call and left an unfamiliar number, which she scrawled on the back of an envelope. Apparently he was still in jail. That meant phoning him in the men's dayroom. She'd heard from Adam and Caroline how difficult it was to get through there.

Kicking off her shoes, she padded on stocking feet to the bedroom where she and Jake had slept together before their breakup and dialed the number he'd given her. To her amazement, she got through on the first ring.

"I'd like to speak to Jacob Fortune, please," she told the somewhat gruff bailiff who answered. "This is his wife calling."

"I didn't know he had a wife," the man said. "Hang on a moment."

After what seemed an interminable delay, Jake came on the line. "Erica?" he asked.

"I'm here," she told him.

She couldn't know what it cost him to hear her voice. Lurking in its musical timbre were all the memories he'd tried to put from him—those of his courtship so many years ago of the leggy, gloriously good-looking model who, unaccountably, had preferred him to her other suitors; his treasured mental snapshot of the way she'd looked nursing Adam; the fragrant, heart-stopping sensation of holding her naked body in his arms.

It was a mistake to call her, he thought, his sudden longing for her intense. "I, uh, just phoned to see how you were," he managed. "And the kids. I suppose you heard... I told them to stay away for a while."

What would it have cost him to say he loved her, even if he didn't mean it? To say he craved her help and support in making it through the dreadful calamity that had befallen him? Listening and hoping for those things, though recent experience had taught her not to expect them, Erica was disappointed.

"I'm fine.... Keeping busy with my classes," she said without much expression. "The kids told me what you'd decided about their visits. I don't agree with it."

Jake's shoulders sagged a little as he slouched by the prisoners' pay phone. A couple of sentences exchanged, and already they were on opposite sides of the fence. "In my opinion, it's for the best," he asserted. "I don't want them to remember me in this kind of setting."

They're going to remember it anyway, Erica thought. What does it matter? They love you, just as I do. They want to help you through it, instead of being shut out.

"So...what can I do for you?" she asked.

You could hold me, Jake told her silently, if only in your thoughts. Forget all the crap I've dished out and offer to go forward, if I manage to beat this thing.

He couldn't bring himself to put his plea into words. "Just reassure the kids of my innocence, I guess," he said at last.

Don't you know I've done that already? she answered silently. "Of course I will," she promised. "But you needn't worry. They believe in you wholeheartedly. Anyone who knows you realizes you couldn't have committed the kind of crime they're accusing you of."

If she was stating her own confidence in him, she was doing so at a remove. It would have to do, he supposed. "Thanks. I appreciate it," he said. "I, uh, guess I'd better go. It's after hours. The bailiff did me a favor by letting me take your call."

There was no telling when she'd hear from him again. "If you must," she answered. "Keep well, okay?"

Briefly his voice lost its self-pity and defensiveness. "You, too, babe," he whispered. "Good night."

Erica decided she'd imagined the momentary lapse as she put down the receiver. Deeply hurt by the acrimony and increasingly separate lives that had driven them apart, she yearned for their old closeness. God, how it would help in our current situation, she thought. Apparently he didn't want it, though. Leaving Lindsay's message until morning, she took off her jewelry and stripped off her outer clothing. A moment later, she was facedown on her bed in her slip and panty hose, her sudden rush of tears wetting the bedspread's expensive moiré fabric.

The following morning, Annie was sick to her stomach again. Complaining that it made her want to throw up more, she began refusing to drink even a tiny sip of water. On Stephen's order, a second IV bag was hung on her stand, to make sure she got the fluids she needed and the electrolytes in her blood stayed balanced. By the time he returned to check on her around 3:15 p.m., Jess was beside herself.

"I don't know what to do for her," she said desperately, hugging herself. "She's my baby! And she's so miserable!"

Watching her suffer was too much for him. Maybe she'd seemed cool, even standoffish, the night before. Well, who could blame her? With a child so sick, her emotions were bound to fluctuate. He knew from personal experience how that felt.

Without pausing to consider where it might lead, he put both arms around her and crushed her close. "It'll be okay, Jess," he promised, his voice muffled by the mask he'd donned for Annie's sake as he spoke against her hair. "She'll soon be through the worst of this. And feeling better. There'll be time for candy apples and hopscotch and diving into piles of autumn leaves before she has to be readmitted so we can do her transplant."

Swept away by the immediacy of his embrace and his seeming certainty that a donor would be found, Jess loosened her hold on making things happen by force of will. She let herself believe, just a little, in the magic notion that it would be as he said. Concurrently, her memories of the blond woman who'd picked him up in her little sports car faded to little more than static. Instead of a highly trained specialist whose interest in them was purely professional, he became just Stephen, the kindly stranger who'd helped them at the zoo, a man she was beginning love.

"I don't know what I'd have done if you hadn't found us at Como Park and suggested we come here," she confessed. "It almost seems as if our meeting was meant..."

If they hadn't been wearing masks, Stephen would have kissed her on the mouth. From the depths of his soul, he wanted to—more than he'd wanted anything since David's death.

"Ah, Jess..." he said helplessly.

Lindsay chose that moment to walk in the door. Sizing up the situation, she pretended not to notice when they sprang apart. Wait until I tell Frank, she thought, bending over Annie. Our good friend and neighbor is about to choose life again. Let's hope he and I can help this darling little girl to make it.

By the end of the week, Annie had perked up more than Jess had dared hope. It would take a little time for her bone marrow to regenerate following her chemotherapy, but Jess realized they could look forward to a respite from the hospital, though they'd be paying frequent visits to Lindsay's and Stephen's respective offices.

Unfortunately, they still didn't have a donor. Though Rebecca's, Caroline's and Adam's tests had all come back, and the report from Stephen's inquiry to the Australian bone-marrow bank was in, as well, no one seemed able to supply the three or more matching antigens Annie required. If they couldn't find anyone, it would be just a matter of time until Annie was sick again. She'd need recurring doses of chemotherapy, which were bound to become less and less effective.

In Jess's opinion, which Stephen shared, the other untested or unanalyzed Fortune family members offered her daughter's best hope. Several of them, including Jake's and Erica's daughter Allie, a model and actress who made her home in southern California, and Allie's twin, Rocky, who owned and operated a rescue and tracking business in Clear Springs, Wyoming, had agreed to follow Lindsay's lead and have blood drawn at their local hospitals. The results would be forwarded to the lab at Minn-Gen.

The odds being what they were, however, Jess experienced hope like a shot of adrenaline one morning when, out of the blue, Natalie, the just-married daughter of Jacob and Erica, turned up in Annie's hospital room.

"Hi... I'm Natalie Dalton, Lindsay Todd's niece," she announced. "You must be Jessica. And you're Annie, of course. I understand we're cousins or something. You called me from England before coming to the U.S. I'm...er, sorry I didn't get back to you sooner. So much was going on in my life just then. I was in the somewhat bumpy process of acquiring a husband and an eight-year-old stepson...."

Above the mask that covered her pretty face, Natalie's eyes were smiling.

Jess had seen the brief wedding notice about her and architect Richard Dalton in the Minneapolis paper and guessed that, because of her father's troubles, it had been a quiet ceremony. She smiled, too. "Congratulations," she said. "It's nice when people are happy together. I've been looking forward to meeting you."

Plopping down her slender frame in the Leatherette lounger while her dark-haired hostess leaned against the windowsill, Natalie went on to relate that she planned to have her blood tested on Annie's behalf before leaving the hospital.

"Lindsay explained how critical it was," she explained. "I'd be absolutely delighted if I could be the one to provide the bone marrow Annie needs. Plus, I have something else you might be interested in...."

Digging in her oversize shoulder bag, Natalie produced what appeared to be several letters, yellowed by the passage of time and faintly moldy, as if they'd been stored in a damp place.

"From what I can tell, your grandmother wrote these to my grandfather," she said, offering them to Jess. "My stepson, Toby, found them beneath a loose board in our boathouse. I'd say that, even if the letter you showed Lindsay doesn't do the trick, these should document your relationship to us."

Lindsay then volunteered to contact Sterling in case any legal issues came up, and gave him a call.

Though the attorney was skeptical of yet another outsider claiming to be related to the Fortune family, he'd heard about Jessica and her sick daughter via the grapevine. He was well aware that she'd introduced herself as Ben Fortune's granddaughter—the product of a brief affair between him and her grandmother during the Second World War—and of her insistence that she didn't want a share in the Fortunes' wealth, just their help in saving her child.

"If you think the letters are worth looking at, she's free to bring them by my office on Friday around 11:00 a.m.," he suggested with an all-but-audible shrug. "We'll see if there's any way to make things easier with the hospital, or perhaps insurance."

Availing herself of the opportunity in Jess's place, Lindsay made the appointment for her new friend and cousin on the spot.

Sterling was pensive as he put down the phone. He hadn't mentioned anything about Jessica Holmes's claim to Kate. Given the necessity of keeping her survival a secret for the time being, he doubted she'd learned of it from any other source.

She'd have to be told now, with the story spreading through the family like wildfire and likely to become public knowledge at some point. Still, with Jake in jail, accused of murder, and all her concern focused on him, he questioned how she'd take such a revelation. While Lindsay, Natalie and the others might be charmed by the idea of meeting a hitherto-unknown cousin, Jessica's story was likely to reawaken bitter memories for Kate of her husband's cheating.

Then again, she might not give a damn. You never knew with her. Picking up the phone again, he dialed her unlisted number.

She answered herself, on the second ring.

"Any objection to fixing an old man a drink?" he asked.

He could almost see her wide smile—feel her little surge of pleasure at the knowledge that, for an hour or so, she'd have him to spar and worry with.

"None whatever, provided you watch your language," she retorted amicably. "The word *old* is strictly off-limits. I've stopped counting birthdays."

Six

Kate poured Sterling's Scotch—neat, the way he liked it, though she preferred hers with a little water. The lights of Minneapolis were beginning to wink on below her sweep of westward-facing windows as she handed it to him and waved him to a chair.

For a woman whose oldest son was in jail, accused of a crime he didn't commit, and who had been forced by circumstances beyond her control to go into hiding from the family she loved, she looked smashing. In black cigarette pants and a heavy white silk shirt that she'd knotted casually at her still-supple waist, with several jeweled "geisha" pins securing her Gibson-girl upsweep, she reminded him of Katherine Hepburn at her most glowing and self-confident. Sure, a few little laugh and worry lines were there in her face; he was her junior by a couple of years, after all. But they were insignificant. She still had great skin—as dewy and fresh as a rose. In his view of things, she continued to be the amazing girl Ben Fortune had married and hadn't always deserved.

"I have a story to tell you that you might not like very much," he admitted.

She leaned forward slightly, causing their knees to brush. "Let's have it, then."

As usual, he gave it to her straight. She listened without interrupting him. When he'd finished, she shook her head, a regretful but not wounded smile tugging at her mouth. "Ben Fortune was a randy old son of a she-goat, wasn't he?" she sighed. "You needn't worry, dear. His peccadilloes are water under the bridge to me now. I've sailed on past them, and hope to continue doing so for a long time yet. What, if anything, do you plan to do about this Jessica and her bone-marrow quest?"

Sterling's nod of approval for her élan was like a little salute. "Since a child's life is at stake, I thought I'd take a look at these letters of hers," he said. "Natalie found three of them, you know, at the old boathouse Ben used to visit. If they're genuine, I see no reason not to do what I can to help."

"When and where do you plan to meet with her?"

"Friday morning, in my office, if she can make it."

"Will anyone from the family be accompanying her?"

He guessed her plan at once. "Now, Kate..." he protested, foreseeing a raft of complications.

In a gesture she probably knew was death to his opposition, she covered his hands with hers. "Humor me in this," she begged. "No damage will be done. I guarantee it. Though she may have seen pictures of me, she thinks I'm dead. She's never seen your secretary. Besides, since getting mixed up with those kids from the St. Paul Laser Theater in my spare time, I've become adept at disguises. No one but you and I will ever be the wiser."

He wasn't the jocular sort. Yet it was all Sterling could do, on Friday, to keep from laughing in her face when Kate presented herself at his office in the flapper-era landmark Foushay Tower half an hour before Jess's expected arrival. In a way he found difficult to define, but which was remarkably, even devastatingly, effective, she seemed to have altered the shape of her features. Her lips were pursed, and the bridge of her nose was bumpy. She wasn't wearing any lipstick. Her smooth, silver-shot upsweep was hidden beneath a frumpy gray wig.

And that wasn't all. For the first time in the years he'd known her, Kate was dowdy. Her ill-fitting skirt and top had probably come from a consignment shop or the Laser Theater's costume department. Her shoes clumped.

"The glasses are a nice touch," he told her, knowing how strongly she preferred colored contacts.

"I *expected* high marks for my efforts," she answered complacently. "What do you say I take a letter, just to get in practice?"

Jess arrived a short time later, unaware that any subterfuge was afoot. Ushered into Sterling's presence by Kate, she quickly agreed that it would be all right if his secretary remained in the room to take notes.

Removing the letters from her purse, she handed them to the attorney. "The one on top is from Ben Fortune to my grandmother, Celia Warwick, who subsequently married George Simpson," she said. "I found it among my late mother's things after her death. Her name was Lana. If the information in the letter is correct, she was Ben's daughter. That makes me his granddaughter, and my daughter, Annabel, his great-granddaughter.

"As I'm sure Lindsay told you, Mr. Foster, the other three letters were written by Lana to Ben. Natalie Dalton's stepson, Toby, found them in the old boathouse across the lake from the Fortune estate."

Jess said nothing further as Sterling put on his reading glasses and read the letters without glancing at Kate, who had scribbled some notes on her stenographer's pad while Jess was speaking and now waited deferentially for further instructions from him.

The process took him several minutes. When at last he'd finished, he asked Jess if he could make copies. She quickly gave her permission.

"Miss...er, Johnson, could you oblige?" he requested, handing them to Kate.

Accepting them from his hands, she quickly left the room. She was gone a long time. Jess began to wonder if the copier was broken or out of order. Perhaps the secretary had been required to change the ink cartridge, and ducked into the loo afterward to wash up.

"My regular secretary's off today," Sterling explained, catching the drift of her musings. "Miss Johnson's a temp."

Shrugging faintly, Jess didn't press him for an opinion on the validity of her claim. At last Kate returned, to hand the original letters and her copies back to him. As she did so, with her back to Jess, he unobtrusively searched her face. Her slight nod confirmed that she'd found them authentic. He'd been given the go-ahead.

"Very well, Mrs. Holmes," he said, giving the originals back to Jess. "I may as well tell you...I consider your letters to be genuine. I'm told you're seeking bone marrow for your daughter...that you have no wish to press a financial claim against the Fortune family."

"That's correct," Jess replied, with a sudden catch in her throat. "Thanks to my late husband's broad range of investments, Annabel and I are financially very well-fixed. However, money can't buy bone marrow. And she's so ill...."

Despite her best efforts to maintain a serene facade throughout the interview, her eyes filled up with tears.

Though he'd been about to ask her to sign a disclaimer relinquishing any right she might have to the Fortune wealth before agreeing to help her, Sterling held his tongue as Kate handed her a tissue.

A moment later, she'd regained her self-control. "Sorry," she apologized in her cultivated British accent. "I'm just so worried about her, you see."

Since Kate approved, Sterling didn't have a problem with speaking to the family. In truth, he rather liked the pretty young Englishwoman, who hadn't been consulted about her grandparents' indiscretion prior to their committing it. "I'll be happy to do whatever I can to help, Mrs. Holmes," he said, bestowing what passed for a smile on her as he indicated by his body language that their session was at an end.

Thanking him profusely, Jess got to her feet.

"I like her," Kate said, relaxing once she was out of earshot. "She has spunk, coming all this way to a foreign country to save her daughter. I say we should do whatever we can to help."

A few days later, Stephen asked Jess out to dinner. Thanks to the gentle, almost affectionate way he'd treated her since they'd embraced during the height of Annie's reaction to her chemotherapy, she wasn't nonplussed. His tact in waiting until her daughter's condition had improved sufficiently for her to spend some time relaxing away from the hospital was very much appreciated.

"I'd be very happy to have dinner with you, Stephen," she replied, her brown eyes shining with an unaffected pleasure in his invitation that warmed his heart.

Neither of them had forgotten the spontaneous kiss they would have shared if they hadn't been wearing the necessary masks to guard against transmitting infection to Annie and Lindsay hadn't walked into her hospital room seconds after Stephen took Jess in his arms. Each of them guessed a more appropriate opportunity for kissing would arise during their evening together. They were both looking forward to it.

Instead of collecting her from the hospital, Stephen picked her up at her hotel. She'd arranged to meet him in the lobby, by its famous fountain, which featured a suspended marble sphere. Striding in via the main entrance to collect her, he caught his breath as, radiant in a red Valentino suit with a relatively short skirt that showed her shapely legs to advantage, she arose from the bench where she'd been sitting to greet him.

"You look absolutely lovely tonight...did you know that?" he asked in a low voice, drinking in a whiff of her perfume as he dared to place a light kiss on her cheek.

For Jess, the affectionate contact was electric. She could feel goose bumps skittering down her arms. At no time before or during her marriage to Ronald Holmes had her late husband ever snared her in such a dazzle of anticipation. She could only imagine what it would be like to make love to the tall, ruggedly good-looking blond doctor who—for that evening, at least—was definitely within her reach.

"Whereas you look very handsome in a sports coat and dress slacks instead of your hospital garb," she replied, declining to take a backward step.

His blue eyes glinted at her willingness to prolong their light embrace. While there was no guarantee anything more intimate would transpire between them that evening or in the future, he sensed that Jess wouldn't be averse to it. Since he'd met her, his every impression of her save one—that of the night when she'd been so worried about Annie—had hinted that she'd be both emotionally and physically affectionate.

"How would you like to leave the car here at the hotel and walk to the restaurant?" he suggested on the spur of the moment. "It's only a short distance. And the weather's beautiful."

The place he'd chosen, a French-style bistro with what she'd heard was legendary food, was situated on the ground floor of the Foushay Tower complex, where she'd visited Sterling Foster in his legal office. A secluded table with a leather banquette on one side had been reserved for them near one of the windows.

Jess liked his selection at once—the glittering bar, the echoing terrazzo floors and the thirties decor, even the exuberant din of conversation and the hurrying waiters in their long white aprons. Twin spots of color glowed in her cheeks as she and Stephen took their seats. She was only half listening as their server recited the plats du jour and invited them to draw on the paper tablecloth with the crayons provided while they sipped their drinks and waited for the food to arrive.

Dreamily leaning her chin on her hand, she asked Stephen to order for her when their server returned with pad and pencil. He did so with pleasure, choosing coq au vin, which was one of the bistro's better-known specialties. There was something about her that brought out his protective streak, even while he admired her courage and quiet strength in dealing with Annie's illness.

A shadow crossed his expansive mood as he considered that, despite his skill as a physician, his ability to protect her from the thing she most feared was only partial, at best. Though they'd tried everything known to science, he and the superb oncologist who'd been his son's primary physician hadn't been able to pull David back from the brink.

"So..." he said, willing his memories of loss to subside, so as not to color their evening. "You know something about me—what I do for a living, at least. Tell me about you, what your life was like in England."

Though Jess noticed he'd referred to that life as if it were firmly in the past, she gave no indication. Instead, she described growing up in a London suburb, her days at the university, her career to date as an investment banker at a London firm, and weekends at the Sussex cottage inherited from her mother, which she and Annie both loved, drawing little maps and cartoons on the paper tablecloth to illustrate.

The salads arrived, followed by the coq au vin, which was so tender it fell from the bones. At his prompting, she continued her monologue, touching briefly on her marriage to Ronald Holmes and the fact that he'd died in a car accident, without alluding to the infidelity that had marred their union almost from the first.

"That must have been difficult...losing your husband and, so soon afterward, learning of Annie's leukemia," Stephen remarked sympathetically.

He'll never know how difficult, Jess thought. She shrugged. "Life can be like that."

A brief silence ensued, in which he reflected that his curiosity about one aspect of her past, at least, hadn't been satisfied. He decided to seize the moment, and ask. "Who's Herkie?" he said.

Jess stared at him in surprise, then laughed, a dimple flashing beside her mouth. "Annie's Scots terrier, Herkimer McTavish III," she replied, unaware of how pleased he was to learn of the dog's existence. "They're great friends, and she misses him terribly. She has been going on about him a bit!"

For dessert, they had coffee and miniature chocolate éclairs. At last, given the early hour Stephen usually reported to the hospital, neither of them could come up with an excuse to linger.

They held hands as they strolled the four blocks or so that separated the little bistro from her hotel. As they did so, their shoulders brushed. Their eyes kept meeting. Their mouths curved with pleasure in each other's company. Yet both of them knew that the sudden deepening of their relationship—unexpected bliss that it was—was fragile still. One wrong word, a wrong move, could shatter it. Immersed though they were in the warm glow of a budding romance, each was posing unasked questions.

Before either was ready to do so, they'd reached the brightly lit hotel entrance. I should have kissed her good-night in the shadow of some darkened building, where we could have merged to our hearts' content without an audience, Stephen told himself as the uniformed doorman gave them the smile he reserved for lovers and held open one of the huge plate-glass doors for them.

Come home with me tonight, he longed to beg. I'm aching to make love to you. It was too soon for that, he knew. It was easy to see that Jess wasn't the kind of woman to conduct casual affairs. And they were still getting to know each other.

"Well…" he murmured, pausing by a potted palm as he debated whether to kiss her there in the lobby, or suggest seeing her to her room. Neither course of action appealed to him. If he chose the latter, she might feel pressured to ask him in for a nightcap.

He was going to say good-night with a peck on the cheek. Or, worse still, a handshake. That nurse's aide was right after all, Jess thought, tormenting herself. He *is* unavailable.

Though she was crestfallen and worried that their first date would be their last, she had the presence of mind to let her hands rest trustingly in his. "I've had a wonderful time with you this evening, Stephen," she said softly, her big brown eyes full of liking and acceptance as she gazed up at him. "Thank you so much for asking me...."

He'd be damned if he'd let the evening end like this. He was going to kiss her, at the very least—in a setting that would afford them a modicum of privacy. He couldn't survive another night without a taste.

"Mind stepping this way with me for a moment?" he said, tugging her toward a little-used lounge area off the lobby that was likely to be vacant at that hour.

To his relief, all the tables in the lounge area were empty. Just a single lamp had been left burning.

"What's...this about?" Jess asked, suddenly afraid he was going to tell her something negative about Annie's prospects.

She barely managed to get out the words before his mouth was descending on hers. His tongue parted her lips, so strenuous and loving that it almost broke her heart. Strong arms dragged her against a hard wall of muscle.

Imagined so many lonely evenings as she'd sat beside Annie's bed in a darkened hospital room, his kiss drew Jess into a maelstrom of passion and pleasure so intense she thought her bones would melt. She hadn't known so much feeling existed in the world. That at least half of it was flowing forth from her only made her discovery that much more earthshaking. Never before had a man made her want to give him everything—come out of hiding to share her private lusts, her deepest secrets, with him. It boggled her mind that one who'd seemed so self-contained and hesitant to get involved would be so Viking-fierce and precipitate in his lovemaking.

How delicious, how womanly, she felt! With a helpless little groan that acknowledged just how far his defenses had slipped, Stephen cupped the seat of her shapely red skirt and hauled her more tightly up against him. It was as if the drought of the past two years had ended in a cloudburst, a vast outpouring of need that met fertile ground instead of parched earth. From the depths of his being, he longed to ravish and protect.

In that intimate embrace, Jess could feel the rod of his desire pressing against her. Layers of clothing separated them. Yet her body responded, shuddering in a little explosion of need as she opened her deepest portals to his plundering.

Abruptly, it was over. A hotel employee armed with a vacuum and other cleaning equipment had wandered in, muttered a quick apology and left again, but not before they became aware of his presence. The slight distraction had been enough to bring Stephen to his senses.

"Jess...forgive me," he whispered, holding her now in a protective embrace. "I shouldn't have let things get so out of hand."

She gazed up at him, her pupils swallowing up her irises until they appeared fathomless. The palms of her hands continued to rest against his lapels. "It seems to me, Stephen," she said in her perfectly modulated British accent, "that we both did. As for whether we shouldn't have, that's a matter of opinion."

His passion subsiding, though it would have taken just the smallest spark to reignite it, Stephen felt gratitude and liking flow into its place. The corners of his mouth turned up. "Personally, I think what we just did together was pretty damn wonderful," he confessed, so emphatically that he had her smiling, too. "If you're willing, and you wouldn't consider it a conflict of interest with Annie in my care, I'd like us to see more of each other."

He wasn't going to withdraw from her. They would date. That being the case, she didn't have the slightest doubt that they'd become lovers, though in her heart of hearts she sensed there were barriers still to be erased.

"I'd like it, too," she answered.

"Then it's settled." Considering himself highly fortunate, he kissed her again with hard-won restraint. A moment later, he was stepping back to put an arm about her waist. "C'mon, darlin'," he added with a husky edge to his voice. "Since I don't trust myself to see you to your room, I'll walk you to the elevator."

Jake was in luck. The judge assigned to preside at his preliminary hearing had known Sterling for years. Though they weren't friends, they moved in the same social circles. At different times, he and the Fortune family lawyer had attended the same university, graduated from the same law school. He also knew Jake's reputation, and his ties to the community, firsthand.

It turned out that he knew Aaron Silberman, too—if not with the liking of friendship, at least with respect for his legal prowess. He listened with keen attention to the criminal attorney's contention that, by itself, the circumstantial evidence gathered by the state wasn't enough for the case to be bound over for trial, as well as his rationale that Jake had too much to lose by skipping town if he was granted bail—to wit, his close relationship with his children and his executive position with Fortune Industries.

As was his right, the assistant county attorney assigned to the case spoke in rebuttal, repeating the arguments he'd advanced at Jake's arraignment. Further, he proposed that a man who'd murdered once might be expected to do bodily harm again, and should be kept behind bars.

Finally it was the judge's turn to speak. He quickly ruled that the state had amassed sufficient evidence for a trial to take place. Somewhat reluctantly, given that evidence, he'd decided to accede to the defense attorney's plea for bond.

"I'm setting it at one million dollars," he warned Jake sternly. "You will be required to remain within the limits of Hennepin County until your trial. Any attempt to evade this jurisdiction will, in itself, be looked upon as a crime. You'll be returned to jail forthwith."

Stunned, Jake glanced from Aaron Silberman to Sterling. Was he really free to go? The family attorney nodded. A moment later, wearing street clothes for the first time since his arrest, Jake was brushing aside reporters' questions as he walked with the two men from the judge's chambers into an adjoining hall. His children and grandchildren were waiting for him. To his surprise, Erica was there, too, keeping somewhat in the background, as befitted their separation. He was both embarrassed and touched.

Natalie, the daughter who'd arrived at the family's lakefront estate on the night of the murder in time to

see his bloody, torn shirt, and had kept her promise
never to tell anyone—except Sterling—of what he'd
babbled in his drunken state about his confrontation
with Monica, threw herself into his arms.

They both blinked as several strobe lights flashed. "I
baked your favorite cookies, Dad," she informed him
with tears in her eyes, turning her face away from the
battery of cameras and microphones that were being
thrust at them. "Chocolate peanut-butter chip. They're
waiting for you at the house."

His other children followed. At last it was Erica's
turn. Coming forward somewhat hesitantly, she shielded
her face from the photos that were still being taken as
she offered Jake her hand. "I'm awfully glad you got
out," she said in a low voice as he took it and, for a
heartbeat, tightened his grip. "You didn't belong in that
place any more than the county attorney does. I...just
wanted to say that I believe strongly in your innocence.
If there's anything I can do to help, please don't hesitate
to ask."

Thanking her in a low tone, he drank in her familiar
scent, her much-loved face and her sleek blond loveli-
ness. How he'd missed her! They'd made a life, had
children together. Despite their troubles, which had
been legion, she was still everything he wanted in a
woman. Unfortunately, at the moment he had very little
to offer her.

It seemed she agreed with his assessment. During the
second or two it took him to answer a question put to
him by Aaron Silberman, he was aware of her slipping
away and heading unobtrusively for the exit. Apparently
she wouldn't be present at the welcome-home party
Caroline had informed him she, Adam, Natalie and their

respective mates planned to throw at the Lake Travis house.

Pleased as he was to be free of the confinement and humiliation of jail, he felt a twinge of regret. Without Erica, his life was empty at the heart. It didn't occur to him that she might be waiting for him to make some sort of move in her direction.

For her part, as she walked away, Erica thought she sensed a slight softening in Jake, toward her and their injured marriage. But she couldn't be sure. It turned out that she wasn't the only one to pick up those vibes from him. During a phone conversation with Adam that evening, her handsome oldest child told her he felt the same way.

"I know Dad doesn't show it, Mom, given the shame he feels over this whole mess," he said, in a voice that resonated uncannily like his father's in her ear. "But I'm convinced he's sorry the two of you split up. I honestly believe he'll try to make amends once he's managed to clear the slate. Added to the murder charges hanging over him, what happened with the two of you isn't much fun...for any of us. But I predict we'll come through intact as a family and be all the stronger for it."

The day after Jake's release from jail, Annie's hair began falling out in hunks. Though Jess had been warned that it would, and in fact had noticed an unusual amount of fine blond hairs clinging to her daughter's hairbrush, emotionally she hadn't been prepared for anything quite that drastic. Swallowing her own dismay, she put on a brave front, calmly preparing Annie to look in the mirror and see a bald head covered with blond baby fuzz instead of her shoulder-length curls.

More Fortunes had been tested, to no avail. Yet the news wasn't all depressing. To Jess's amazement, as well as Stephen's, Annie's bone marrow had regenerated much more quickly than he'd hoped. Though in time her leukemia could be expected to choke it again with a profusion of immature T-cells that would fail to protect her from infection, for a time she'd be well enough to play as ordinary children did. If everything went as expected, they could leave the hospital by the end of the week.

Stephen didn't mention it to her, but he was determined to solve a problem she hadn't tackled yet. She and Annie needed to remain in Minneapolis, close to him, Lindsay and Minn-Gen, until a match was found. But they didn't have to spend the period of Annie's remission in a hotel. With that in mind, he took the unauthorized step of seeking Lindsay's help in finding something more suitable for them.

Lindsay's suggestion that he ask Sterling if Jess and Annie could use the guest cottage on the Lake Travis estate suited him perfectly. If it could be arranged, they'd be staying just down the road from his house. "Do you really think it's possible?" he asked.

The two of them were standing in the doctor's lounge, where she'd reacted with suspicion when he told her of Jess's quest to save her daughter and asked for her help. This time, Lindsay was a dedicated ally. "I don't see why not," she answered slowly. "The cottage was built some distance from the house. Their presence shouldn't bother Jake."

"What about furniture?"

"Everything they'd need is in place, right down to dishes and silverware. The cottage is the perfect size for them—two bedrooms, a living room, bath and kitchenette. Of course, I'll have to ask...."

According to the terms of Kate's will, the Lake Travis property, which included the cottage, in addition to the main house, had been left to her children jointly. Sterling had been put in charge of its use. When Lindsay brought up the matter to him, the attorney didn't have a problem with it—provided Jake didn't object.

Immersed in the pain of his notoriety and his upcoming trial, Jake had remained more or less barricaded in the family mansion since his release, to avoid the predations of the media. He wasn't keen on the idea of having someone else live on the estate. However, he was basically a good person, one who'd do what he could for others who were less fortunate than himself, despite his troubles—provided it didn't cost him too much emotionally. After thinking it over for a day or two, he told Sterling he wouldn't object, if Jess kept her distance.

Naturally, the attorney checked with Kate, as well. He wasn't surprised when she granted her approval. Later that same day, Lindsay was able to offer the cottage to Jess.

"Do you really mean it?" Jess asked, her eyes lighting up. "A little house where we could live until Annie's transplant is over and she's back on her feet would be a godsend! I've been thinking I should look for one. But I didn't know where to start."

Lindsay smiled her sweet smile. "I've checked with the family attorney, and it's yours for no charge, as long as you want it," she confirmed. "Stephen has volunteered to drive you over for a look."

As Jess had long since turned in her rental car as an unneeded expense and begun using taxis to go back and

forth between her hotel and the hospital, a ride would
be necessary. When she told Stephen about Lindsay's
offer of the cottage later that afternoon, he repeated his
proposal in person.

"However, I'm starving," he said with a smile.
"Let's go out and get a bite to eat first. Afterward, I'll
drive you past my house, as well as Lindsay's. We live
on the lake, too...just down the road from the Fortune
place. When you move into the cottage, we'll be neighbors. I'll be able to keep an eye on you."

Like their dinner together at the French-style bistro,
the meal of *canh cua*, or crab-and-asparagus soup, followed by minced shrimp skewered on hunks of sugar-
cane, which he treated her to in a tiny Vietnamese restaurant near the hospital, was both delicious and
intimate. Their drive to the Lake Travis area afterward
took about half an hour.

They drove by his house first. From what Jess could
tell in the fading light as he slowed the car, it had an
oddly deserted look. Built in an angular contemporary
style, with lots of natural wood, it was large enough to
have at least four bedrooms.

Aware that he was divorced, she wondered suddenly
if children from his former marriage came to visit him
on weekends. "It just occurred to me that I don't know
much about your personal life," she said, turning to him
as they passed Lindsay's more traditional abode. "Giv-
en your rapport with Annie, I can't help wondering if
you have children of your own."

Though he'd been about to respond with a sharp
"No," Stephen held his tongue. What had happened to
his son had nothing to do with her. However, he
couldn't help feeling the old guilt Brenda had instilled
in him over the long hours he worked. While they

hadn't made David sick, they'd caused him to miss some precious moments with the boy—moments that could never be replaced.

"I'm sorry to say I don't," he admitted at last. "I guess you could say being childless is one of my life's greatest disappointments. However, I probably wouldn't make a very good dad, given my heavy schedule."

Though she begged to differ, something in his tone warned Jess not to pursue the subject.

By the time they reached the Fortune estate, letting themselves in the gate with the card Lindsay had provided, it was fully dark. My grandfather lived here, Jess thought, catching a glimpse of the big white house she'd only seen in pictures through the trees. And thought about my mother—the love child my grandmother wouldn't let him claim. How I'd love to see it, wander through its rooms in his footsteps.

It was not to be. Seconds later, following Lindsay's directions, they were taking the drive's left fork, away from the mansion Ben Fortune had built, through a stand of tall firs and gnarled, canopied oaks. Before long, they were parking in front of the white-painted cottage, which—with its bracketed eaves and hooded, paired windows—reflected the Italianate design of the main residence.

Stephen had the key. Their shoes crunched on pea-size gravel as they got out of the Mercedes and walked the few feet that separated them from the front porch.

The electricity hadn't been shut off at the circuit box, and they were able to switch on a lamp in the living room. Overstuffed furniture, wood floors strewn with faded Oriental rugs and a small brick fireplace with a framed Audubon print hanging above its mantel materialized out of the darkness. There were books. Throw pillows. Neatly stacked firewood.

"It's so cozy," Jess whispered as Stephen took off his sports jacket and slung it over one of the chairs. "Like a real home, all ready to move in. Annie's going to love it here...."

The lights in the kitchen worked, too. They revealed a black-and-white tiled floor, a somewhat antiquated refrigerator and stove, and white-painted wooden cupboards with clear leaded-glass doors on the upper tier. A table and chairs for four had been placed beneath a Tiffany-style lamp in the breakfast nook.

Their luck with illumination ran out in what Stephen guessed would become Jess's bedroom. Feeling his way through the darkened space, he managed to turn on a bedside lamp, only to have the bulb burn out with an audible *pop* from the slight surge of electricity.

"Maybe there's a spare inside the night table," Jess suggested from behind his left shoulder.

Instead of pulling out the drawer to feel for one, Stephen turned to face her. Their eyes met and held, gleaming in the faint glow from the hall. Seconds later, they were in each other's arms. His mouth was crushing hers

Seven

It was what she'd wanted since their kiss in an empty lounge at her hotel and, in a different sense, for most of her adult years, this wanton letting go, this helpless convergence with another's soul-deep craving. Yet, even as she gave herself over completely to Stephen's embrace, gasping with pleasure at his tongue's muscular seeking and the unyielding pressure of his need against her, Jess sensed there were barriers still to be erased. Unless he revealed them to her and they managed to deal with them, she might find herself going home to England without him when Annie was well again.

Maybe I'm riding for a fall, she thought fiercely, her humiliation at Ronald Holmes's hands still fresh in her memory, though she hoped it was no longer a factor in her decision-making. If so, I'll take my chances. Stephen's worth the risk.

For the lanky blond doctor who'd come to her aid that day at the zoo, the little sigh of delight and acceptance that escaped her as he deepened his kiss was like kerosene poured on a flame. Never in the years of his manhood, with their failed marriage and their deep, emotional yearnings, had he wanted a woman so much. Never had he longed with such heartfelt ambivalence to ravish and protect.

"Jess... Ah, Jess..." he groaned, his capable physician's hands fumbling like a schoolboy's at the buttons of her delicate sweater-blouse. "I'm crazy about you, don't you realize that? Stop me if you don't want what we're about to do. Because I won't be able to stop myself."

"Believe me, *I want it.*"

Wrung from her with such passion in her elegant British accent, the admission only intensified his hunger. His lips parted, his blue eyes hooded, he watched her undo the buttons herself, then helped her tug the soft garment from her shoulders.

The front clasp of her bra came next. A heartbeat later, it, too, had been cast aside, allowing her small but lushly formed breasts to spill into his hands. He groaned at the unbearable sweetness of it as her nipples puckered with arousal beneath his fingertips.

Somehow—she wasn't exactly sure of the manner in which it had come about—Jess found herself seated on the edge of the bed, with her skirt pushed up to her hips. Stephen knelt in front of her, cradled by her thighs. Bending his head, he took her left breast's peak in his mouth, to suck at it with lavish intensity.

Shuddering with pleasure at what she felt, Jess rested her cheek against his hair. He responded by teasing her other nipple to taut erectness. Currents of need knifed her to the quick. It was as if an erotic telegraph connected her aroused buds with the womanly depths where she wanted him most. She could feel them warming and opening, crying out for him to fill them.

"Take off your tie...your shirt, Stephen," she begged, working the tails of the latter garment free so that she could insert her hands beneath his belt. "I want to touch you...everywhere."

It had been a long time since he'd wanted anyone so much—longer still since sex and love had been knit up in it together. Though it was time he moved on, and learned to love again, David's death still studded the desert of his heart like a thorn-pricked monument. In the harsh light of that melancholy mind-set, learning to care for someone new, a woman whose child might be dying, as well, seemed the height of folly to him.

You're the doctor charged with saving Annie's life, he told himself. You know the odds, the crises that can erupt. If you fail with Annie, it will be partly your fault. Jess won't want to look at you again, even if she doesn't blame you for it.

In any event, she'll be going back to England....

Half-naked in his arms, Jess felt the change like a chill wind, an evil-looking bank of dirty gray clouds arriving to block out the sunlight. "What's wrong, Stephen?" she asked worriedly, resting her hands on his shoulders. "Is it something I did? Don't you want to make love to me?"

She deserves better, he realized. I wish I could give it to her. But I can't right now—not at this moment. Getting to his feet, he turned his back to give her a chance to cover herself.

Awash in humiliation, bafflement, and what was beginning to feel a lot like outrage, Jess hastily refastened her bra and put on her sweater. She stood also. "Aren't you going to explain?" she queried in a small voice.

"Don't think for a moment that I don't want you," he said at last. "I probably have since the day we met. But I was wrong to let this happen, especially now. Ethical constraints founded in my obligation to Annie stand in the way. I hope we can still be friends...have dinner again soon."

Like a mocking refrain, the word *unavailable* ricocheted through Jess's head. Retreating to the cool Brit-

ish demeanor that had been part and parcel of her up-
bringing, she smoothed her rumpled hair and picked up
her purse, preparatory to returning to her hotel.

"You're right, of course," she agreed, unknowingly
jabbing an additional sliver of pain into his heart. "It's
probably best that we don't get involved. I was wrong
to let anything or anyone divert my attention from Annie when she needs it so desperately."

Clad in a lapped-front red silk bodysuit that flattered
her petite figure, Kate was pacing in her penthouse
apartment. A week spent incognito in California, where
she'd swum in a private pool ringed by mountains, rid-
den a prize Appaloosa up Joshua tree–studded canyons
and flown a rented Piper Cub above the breakers at
Carmel hadn't cured her restlessness and frustration.
Her oldest son had been accused of murder. Ben's dealings with Monica were somehow involved.

Enough of working behind the scenes, she decided,
all but stamping one expensively shod foot for emphasis. I want to help from the forefront. Surely there's
evidence to be had—evidence *I* can find—that will lead
the police in the right direction.

Her mind made up, she dialed Sterling's number. "I
need to talk to you," she said, in a tone that brooked
no contradiction.

With a lengthy day under his belt and weariness in-
vading his sixty-four-year-old frame, the lawyer had just
finished taking a long, hot bath. He was lounging in his
bathrobe, with a cognac at his elbow. "Tonight?" he
asked, hoping against hope that morning would be soon
enough.

"As soon as possible."

He smothered a sigh. Since she'd faked her death,

with his cooperation and approval, he'd made a point of conferring with her in person, instead of using the phone.

"I'll be there in half an hour," he promised.

She was still stalking the confines of her skylit living room when he let himself in. "Thanks for coming, old dear," she exclaimed, catching him to her in a fond, somewhat relieved embrace.

A whiff of her perfume, an infusion of her famous energy, and he was less inclined to regret giving up the solitude of his easy chair. Unfortunately, he'd have to drive home when they finished their discussion. Despite their closeness, which had only continued to grow since her husband's death, he'd never chanced staying over.

"Don't mention it," he wisecracked with a trace of his native grumpiness, aware that she could see right through it. "I gather you're still on California time. Tell me what's bothering you."

To his chagrin, instead of a replacement for the cognac he'd poured out moments before her call, she offered him coffee, which was guaranteed to ravage his night's sleep.

"I'm sick of the whole damn thing," she responded when he declined, without proposing a substitute. "This *masquerade*. Jake's in jail. And I want to help."

She was considering a premature reappearance. Somehow, he had to put a stop to it. Monica was dead, and Jake hadn't killed her. Ergo, a murderer was on the loose—quite possibly the same one who'd masterminded Kate's plane crash in the Brazilian jungle. If he or she was to learn Kate hadn't died...

He shook his head. "What you're thinking about is just too dangerous. Whoever hired that hit man to take you out might be involved in this, as well."

She brushed his worry aside with a hand dripping the East Indian rubies Ben had given her to atone for some violation or other of their marriage compact. "My children need me," she vowed.

"Not at the expense of losing you for real," Sterling pointed out. "They're grown up, for God's sake. You said it yourself…they needed a nudge and enough rope to hang themselves or pull their lives together in ways they hadn't begun to contemplate. So far, nobody's gotten convicted of anything. Jake won't, either, if I have anything to say about it."

For once, she didn't interrupt.

"Strange as it may seem," he added, "I think this crisis will be the making of him. He's always been discontented with his lot, generous though it is. Now he's displeased with nature's choice of a father for him, as well. In my opinion, once he's weathered the storm, he'll know who he is and what he wants."

Kate gazed at the lawyer's gracefully aging, craggy-handsome features without replying for a moment. What a treasure he is! she thought. Like me, he's a senior player on the game board of life, high-stakes Fortune version. Except he has better sense. It occurred to her that they had a lot more in common with each other than they did with anyone else she knew. They even shared the same acerbic sense of humor.

"You're right, of course," she admitted, surprising him by capitulating without a fight. "Come sit with me on the sofa, and we'll talk about the good old days. I'll pour you that brandy you've been wishing for."

When Stephen and Jess met the next day at the hospital, it was awkward, to say the least. After having established a pattern of easy give-and-take and warm friendliness that only intensified since their initial dinner date, they were barely able to look each other in the face. A bit perfunctory in his examination, though he was as friendly and gentle with Annie as ever, he didn't stay long.

"Dr. Steve is acting funny," Annie observed in a chipper voice, giving Jess a puzzled look after he left the room. "Do you s'pose he's mad at us?"

Doubly embarrassed that her gamine, unnaturally balding five-year-old should notice that something had gone wrong with their relationship, Jess couldn't help picturing the scene at the Fortunes' guest cottage in which Stephen had rejected her. To her sorrow, it was hardly the first time she'd replayed that particular tape. The little tableau had unfolded over and over, like a film loop, in her mind's eye the previous night, as she tried to snatch some sleep at her hotel.

"I don't see why he would be, do you?" she asked, bending to administer a kiss to Annie's cheek.

The girl frowned as she considered the question. "Maybe he's getting sick, too, and he wants to be home in his bed," she speculated, drawing on her own most vivid personal experience for an explanation. "What happens when doctors get sick, Mummy? Do *they* have to sleep at the hospital like I do, and take lots of nasty medicine?"

"I should imagine so, if they're sick enough," Jess answered. "Doctors are just ordinary people who've studied hard for a long time so they can learn to make other people well."

Thankful Annie would be released at the end of the week and they wouldn't have to continue their daily contact with the man she loved, Jess rummaged in the tote bag of things she'd brought to keep Annie amused now that she had more energy, and pulled out an illustrated storybook to distract the girl. Yet as she read the classic tale of a young American girl growing up on a strawberry farm with her grandparents, she felt something akin to despair settle in her heart. Until Annie had cleared the hurdle of her transplant—assuming they could find a donor—she and Stephen would be forced to maintain a semblance of the friendship that had grown up between them. And the hollowness of it would tug at her heart.

I'm not sure I'll be able to stand it if we don't find someone quickly, she thought, picturing the waiting game they might have to endure as, one by one, the Fortunes' test results became available. For Annie's sake, of course, speed in locating a match was crucial. They'd have just a limited "window" of time in which to do a transplant before the benefits of her chemotherapy waned and her leukemia edged out of control again.

Meanwhile, she was wild about the tall blond doctor who'd courted and rejected her. In just the short interval since their dinner date at the French bistro at the Foushay Tower, she'd learned to care deeply for him—and count on his affectionate presence and support. Now that support was unavailable. It'll be like living with heaven just out of reach, she realized. Contrasted with the closeness I'd hoped for, the loneliness of it will be staggering.

There was still a great deal to hope about. Though the blood tests provided by the Fortune twins, Allie and Rocky, Natalie's younger sisters, had come back negative, Jess had finally managed to get in touch with Nate's son, Kyle, and his older daughter, Jane Bolton.

Both had been tested. The results would be available soon.

Though Jess couldn't know it, thanks to the front he put on, their daily contacts were tearing Stephen apart, as well. He couldn't look at her without wanting her and lamenting what he believed to have been his unforgivable cowardice in pulling back from the brink of their lovemaking. To make matters worse, his affection for her bright-eyed daughter continued to grow by leaps and bounds, threatening to erode his objectivity about her case. If I were to have a little girl, he thought, I'd want her to be just like Annie Holmes. Too easily, he could picture Annie and her mother installed in his lakefront home as his wife and adopted daughter—a family to come home to at night and love.

If only Annie's leukemia didn't stand in the way.

Each time such puerile, emotionally crippling thoughts flitted through his head, he wanted to kick himself. Neither Jess nor Annie could help the tragedy that had visited them. They hadn't brought it on themselves in any way. Instead, they were simply two wonderful human beings, perfect though flawed, blessed and unfortunate, who'd had a rotten run of luck. In the real world, he knew with his heart, if not his gut, you loved the people you couldn't do without and you took your chances. Guarantees of longevity and smooth sailing didn't enter into it.

It was just that he couldn't face the soul-wrenching agony of losing a child again, and proving inadequate to offer its mother comfort. If he were to marry Jess and she were to turn away from him under such crushing circumstances, he knew, the pain of his anguish would fill the universe. Yet he realized that, if he did nothing to make them his and Annie died, he'd grieve her death and Jess's departure from Minneapolis almost as much.

Still impaled on his dilemma two days before Annie was scheduled to be released from Minn-Gen, Stephen arranged for another specialist to fill in for him so that he could attend an all-day medical conference at a downtown hotel. He hoped a day away from the hospital would give him some perspective.

The conference organizers had chosen to hold the multitopic meeting at the Marriott City Center, directly across the street from the Radisson Plaza, from which—according to Lindsay—Jess would be moving that afternoon without his help. Just a glance at the Radisson's marquee and busy front entrance brought back memories of their passionate kiss in the empty lounge, not to mention their awkward leave-taking at the Fortune cottage the night he'd shrunk from making love to her.

Closeted in a seminar on the latest advances in the use of genetically engineered monoclonal antibodies to treat leukemia, a topic of critical importance to him and his patients, he found it difficult to keep his mind focused on the speaker's remarks. You've got to do something about this, he told himself. Either give them up, or bite the bullet—ask Jess for another chance and pray the dice fall in Annie's favor.

Except for a "lunch break" that consisted of tossed salad, sirloin tips and apple pie brought into the meeting rooms so that the busy physicians attending the conference wouldn't have to miss a beat, the highly technical sessions continued unabated until shortly after 5:00 p.m. His head teeming with new research findings and treatment protocols, Stephen was on the down escalator when he heard a familiar voice call out his name.

"Stephen...wait up!"

Pushing her way past several standees to his rear, his ex-wife, Brenda, materialized at his side. "How've you been?" she asked in a voice remarkably free of the accusatory tone he'd come to expect, taking his arm as they reached the mezzanine and lounge area opposite Gustino's Restaurant. "We hardly ever see each other."

Her red hair cut in a fluffy wedge that flattered her face and her green eyes gazing up at him from behind a pair of tortoise-rimmed glasses he didn't remember, Brenda appeared to have made substantial progress in getting over her grief since the last time they'd been together. It occurred to him that she might actually have achieved a degree of happiness.

"About the same," he answered. "I must say, *you're* looking well."

She gave him what for her was a shy smile. "Thanks. I appreciate the compliment. I'd like to have you believe I climbed up out of the quagmire I was in thanks to my own initiative. But I can't take full credit. The fact is, I've met someone...."

So *that's* why her eyes are shining and there's a new spring to her step, Stephen thought. He felt no jealousy—nothing but happiness for her and a measure of relief for himself. Thanks to her new heartthrob, whoever he was, he'd been absolved of some of the guilt he still felt for the part he'd played in her unhappiness.

"I'd like to have you meet him," Brenda went on, when he didn't speak. "Pass judgment, as it were. I always did value your opinion."

Unsure he was ready for that kind of responsibility, Stephen tried to demur. He had errands to run, and considerable catching up to do by phone on his patients at the hospital.

His attempt to escape was doomed to failure. "Here

he comes now," his ex-wife said, motioning to a balding, sandy-haired man with the muscular build of an
athlete.

Stephen recognized him as a fellow participant in
several of the day's seminars. "So...he's a doctor,
too," he commented.

Her cheeks took on a pinkish tint. "Guess I'm a
sucker for altruistic and talented authority figures," she
quipped, abandoning him to link arms with her new
beau. "Tom, this is my ex, Stephen Hunter. Stephen,
Tom McCaffrey. Tom's an internist in Wayzata. He
specializes in family medicine."

Taking each other's measure, the two men exchanged
a firm handshake. From what he could sense, Stephen
came to the provisional conclusion that Brenda was in
good hands.

"Have a drink with us," Tom McCaffrey said,
clearly pleased to find the new woman in his life on
friendly but unemotional terms with her former mate.

Unable to refuse the imploring look Brenda gave him,
despite his concern that the threesome might prove an
awkward one, Stephen agreed to accompany them into
Gustino's piano lounge for a quick cocktail. As he slid
into a chair across one of the low, round tables from
them, he braced himself, hoping David's name wouldn't
be mentioned.

It didn't come up right away. As they chatted amiably
about how Tom and Brenda had met, during a weekend
excursion for singles to Michigan's Mackinac Island, he
began to see the encounter as a positive event. Though
Brenda's company still called up painful memories of
their son's illness and death for him, he found he wasn't
hurting anymore about the breakup of his marriage to

her—just about the inadequacy as a spouse he believed it had brought out in him.

I hope Tom McCaffrey can make her happy, he thought.

Just then, the internist's beeper went off. "'Scuse me, folks," he said with a grin, reaching over to squeeze Brenda's hand as he got to his feet. "My cellular's on the fritz. Gotta find a public phone booth and call my service."

To Stephen's dismay, the moment they were alone together, Brenda gravitated to the topic of David's death, albeit approaching it from a perspective they'd never discussed. "I really hate to bring this up when we're getting along so well, but you're the only person who'd understand," she said, her green eyes taking on their shadowed look. "Tom and I are talking marriage. And I'm terrified of saying *yes*. He wants children. I'm not sure I could bear to have life catch fire in me again...carry another child beneath my heart for nine months and wonder if someday I'm going to lose him or her, the way we lost David...."

It was his dilemma, expressed from a woman's perspective. Her eyes bright with the tears he'd never been able to cry in her presence, Brenda was waiting for some kind of response from him—a dreaded confirmation that her fears were valid and should be heeded or, if he could muster it, a word of encouragement.

Bringing himself to offer the latter, he guessed, would serve as partial atonement. "This time last year, I never thought I'd be saying this," he admitted. "But life is meant to be lived. It's what David would want for us. In his place, I urge you to go for it."

Digesting his words, she was suddenly smiling at him.

As Tom McCaffrey returned to the table and he seized the opportunity to bid them goodbye, Stephen hoped he had the chutzpah to take his own advice. He guessed he'd better. His future happiness depended on it.

As he waited for an attendant to retrieve his Mercedes from the hotel garage, Lindsay was helping Jess move her things from the Radisson to the guest cottage on the Fortune estate. After loading up, the two women stopped at a supermarket so that Jess could stock her newly acquired larder with some of Annie's favorite groceries. As they strolled the aisles together like friends and the part-time homemakers they were, instead of an investment banker and her daughter's pediatrician who'd just learned they were related, Jess reflected that it was almost like having a sister—something she'd always wanted.

I'll be the luckiest woman in the world if our efforts to find a donor for Annie succeed and we manage to stay connected, she thought. A moment later, she revised her prognostication somewhat. Without Stephen in the picture, an important ingredient would be missing from her contentment.

Though she couldn't help reliving their aborted lovemaking and its aftermath as Lindsay parked her station wagon in front of the cottage and helped her carry her luggage and their purchases inside, she refused to dwell on it for the moment.

"Stay for a cup of coffee," she invited. "It'll be a housewarming of sorts."

It was almost time for the evening news. Addicted to watching since Jake had landed in hot water, Lindsay realized she wouldn't make it home in time to watch the program from the outset. Aware of her plans to assist Jess with the move, Frank had assured her he'd get there early. Their children's dinner wouldn't be delayed by much.

"Okay," she agreed, pleased to be Jess's first guest in her new place of residence. "But then I have to split. Mind if I turn on the television?"

Readily granted permission, she flicked on the set and sunk into one of the living room's lattice-printed couches as Jess ground the coffee beans. It turned out that she hadn't done so a moment too soon. Datelined Los Angeles, the evening's first report featured Monica Malone's adopted son, Brandon, holding forth for reporters on the damaging evidence revealed by a series of affidavits the Hennepin County attorney's office had requested he turn over to them. Until that moment, Lindsay hadn't been aware of their existence.

"The affidavits were in my mother's and my safe-deposit box, which I opened this morning in Minneapolis, as the executor of her estate," the late film star's suntanned heir recounted into a battery of microphones, raking a hand through his unkempt dirty-blond hair as if the gesture were a habit with him. "Naturally, I read them before turning them over to the authorities. When a person's mother has been brutally murdered..."

"Can you be more specific about what the documents contain?" one of the journalists asked.

"Why not?" Despite his loss, the would-be actor seemed to be enjoying his moment in the spotlight. "The affidavits contain testimony from several people who knew Jacob Fortune's mother, Kate, many years ago, when she was an unmarried waitress," he said. "In each of them, the witness claims she was pregnant with

Jacob Fortune before the man she married, Benjamin Fortune, came on the scene. In other words…''

Pausing, he invited his questioners to draw their own conclusions.

''Jacob Fortune isn't the preeminent heir to the family's power and financial assets, the way people have always assumed?'' one of them asked, putting words in his mouth.

''It would seem that way,'' he replied, a smirk of satisfaction lending character to his somewhat ordinary face.

''Sounds like, if it turns out to be genuine, the evidence your mother gathered about his past could constitute a motive for murder,'' a different reporter said. ''Do you agree with that assessment?''

Shrugging, Brandon Malone preened for the cameras. ''What do *you* think?'' he asked.

With the abruptness characteristic of network news programs, the scene shifted to New York, where the TV anchorman noted for the record that Jake had been released from jail on bond while awaiting trial, and moved on to an unrelated segment. Switching off the set in disgust, Lindsay accepted the mug of coffee Jess handed her and took a restorative sip.

''I suppose you heard,'' she remarked. ''According to the 'evidence' dredged up by Monica Malone's ne'er-do-well brat, Jake is my half brother…the son of a man none of us have ever met.''

Startled, Jess realized that, if the allegation was true, it would explain the lack of correlation between his offspring's antigen sites and her daughter's. However, she was too tactful to put her observation into words. ''Evidence, so-called, can be fabricated,'' she said. ''It wouldn't surprise me to learn that's what's happened in this case."

Hugging her in response to the positive words, Lindsay took a few additional sips of her coffee and bade her goodbye, promising to pick her up in the morning and drive her to the hospital. After watching the news segment about the Malone murder case, she was eager to hurry home and get her husband's take on the case's latest development. Yet as she drove the short distance that separated the Fortune estate and its guest cottage from her own lakefront residence, she found herself puzzling over something totally unrelated to the content of Brandon Malone's interview.

Though he'd spent quite a bit of time in Minneapolis as a youth, and visited his mother there regularly since leaving town to seek a Hollywood film career of his own, she and Monica's son had never met. Yet she had the oddest notion of knowing him. Or having run into him someplace—not just once, but on several occasions.

A moment later, she decided she knew whence it had sprung. Sadly lacking in refinement though he was, there'd been something about the way he smiled that reminded her of her father. Dad had little grooves like that beside his mouth, she remembered. And a similar way of shrugging when he didn't want to spell things out for you. With all her heart, she wished he and her mother hadn't died. If they were still around, the mess Jake's in would quickly be resolved in his favor, she told herself.

As he walked into Annie's room the following morning, Stephen realized he'd visit her in the hospital just one more time before she returned for her transplant. More pleased than he could have said that her temporary remission had taken such a firm hold, he couldn't help regretting the precipitous drop in the number of opportunities he'd have to see her and Jess. Of course, the dark-haired woman who'd so captivated his heart would be obliged to bring her daughter into his office for weekly checkups.

"One more day, and you're outa here," he told Annie with a smile, keeping Jess in his peripheral vision as he listened to the girl's heart with his stethoscope.

Annie giggled, having heard the American slang expression on television. "Mummy says we'll be living in a nice little cottage down the road from your house," she observed, dangling her skinny legs over the edge of her hospital bed as she gazed up at him. "Will you come to visit us?"

Ruffling the short blond fuzz that covered her beautifully shaped head, he stole a quick glance at her mother. "Of course I will, if you want me to," he promised.

He needn't say so unless he plans to follow through, Jess thought irritably, keeping her face expressionless. What's this overture of his about, anyway? Don't tell me the weather vane of his intentions is about to lurch in a new direction!

A few minutes later, Stephen found himself seated next to Lindsay in the transcription room on Annie's floor. Offering his sympathy with regard to the way her brother's case was going, he quickly switched the topic to Jess. "I understand you helped her move into the cottage yesterday," he said. "Everything go all right?"

Lindsay nodded, the lion's share of her attention absorbed by the chart she was updating. "Like I mentioned before, the place is perfect for them," she murmured distractedly. "The only problem is her need for a car. I gave her a ride to the hospital this morning, and I plan to drive her home. But I won't always be available.''

The casual remark posed an opportunity for him. To be around Jess is to want her, he acknowledged as he left the hospital after completing his paperwork and headed for some used-car lots he knew instead of pointing himself toward Lake Travis, as he usually did. Yet it's like I'm poised at the end of a diving board, longing for her but afraid to dive into the commitment of loving her. Something's got to give. If I don't reverse course, and soon, whatever chance I have left with her will be forever lost.

After his thickheaded pronouncements at the cottage on the night they'd almost made love, he wasn't sure what approach to take. There was a good possibility that she'd refuse to give him another chance whatever he said. At least I can help to solve her transportation problem, he thought. It would be a step in the right direction.

At the second lot he visited, an MG Midget in British racing green with a black convertible top was available at a minimal price. Though the car was old, and the model somewhat known for its eccentricity, the body appeared to be in good shape. By coincidence, he'd driven a similar car when he was in medical school, and done the mechanical work on it himself to save on expenses.

Removing his sport coat and rolling up his sleeves, he asked the salesman to turn the key and lift the hood. He got his hands extremely dirty checking everything out that could be checked with the car at a standstill. Though the engine could have benefited from a thorough steam cleaning, nothing obvious seemed to be amiss.

It was time to take the little convertible for a test-drive. Half an hour later, he was back at the lot, relatively satisfied. With a few minor adjustments, which he could make, the MG would be serviceable in the short run. Its English make meant it would also be somewhat familiar to Jess. The only thing that remained to be done was to introduce the two of them and see how they liked each other.

Given the fact that Lindsay usually worked late on Thursdays, Jess might still be at Minn-Gen. Taking out his cellular phone, he dialed the familiar number, requesting Annie's room when the hospital operator came on the line. Unused to receiving many calls, as she was relatively new in Minneapolis, Jess answered with a question in her voice.

"Hi, it's Stephen," he said offhandedly, as if their falling-out had never taken place. "I went for a little ride after my rounds this afternoon, and I've spotted the perfect car for you. It seems to me you'll need one if you plan to live on the Fortune estate for the next couple months. How would you like to leave Lindsay a note and come have a look?"

Silence greeted him as she assimilated his unexpected about-face. "I suppose you're right about me needing a car," she said at last, in a tone that wasn't particularly warm but wasn't as disparaging as he deserved. "I've been having similar thoughts myself. Lindsay just walked into the room, and she's eager to leave. I suppose I could go with you, instead, if you're free to take me home afterwards."

Suspended between elation and relief that she hadn't turned him down, Stephen decided it was the most he could expect.

Eight

Awash in conflicting emotions, Jess tried to stifle the scary but delicious feeling of letting Stephen look after her as he drove her to see the convertible he'd picked out. When they reached the used-car lot and got out of his Mercedes, she circled the MG warily, a skeptical expression on her face.

"Aren't they known for being somewhat idiosyncratic?" she asked with a frown, refusing to let him see the thrill of potential ownership she felt. "Best left to mechanics, I believe my uncle once said. The absolute last thing I need to deal with right now is car repairs."

Stephen shrugged, giving Jess her head. "Whatever you think," he murmured. "She's rather cute, though, in my opinion. I gave her a good going-over, and she's quite a bargain at the price. As for repairs, I used to own one. If a problem should crop up, I still have my metric wrenches."

Jess stared. He was saying he'd fix her car himself— a physician and a specialist! "I didn't realize you were a surgeon, in addition to being a hematologist," she deadpanned after a moment.

The burst of laughter they shared seemed to break the ice.

"C'mon," Stephen coaxed. "Let's take her for a spin. Aren't you curious to see how she responds to a new mistress?"

Enchanted with the little convertible after a lengthy drive that took them to Minnehaha Park, past the famous statue of its namesake and Hiawatha, and gave them a glimpse of the forty-foot waterfall that cascaded into a wooded glen there, Jess was determined to buy it. *Annie's absolutely going to love it!* she thought. *Of course, with so little hair on her head and the ever-present danger of catching cold, she'll have to wear a muffler and a stocking cap.*

Writing out a check backed by her credit card number when they returned to the car lot, she watched as Stephen attached her temporary tag and checked the gas gauge.

"Just in case there's something I overlooked, I'll follow you home," he offered, straightening.

Aware that their relationship was rife with fresh possibilities, she wasn't about to tell him no. It gave her a warm and cozy feeling to see him in her rearview mirror as she drove the increasingly familiar route to Lake Travis, shifting gears with the ease of a pro.

To her surprise, when she reached the Fortune gate and paused to get out her magnetic entry card, he stopped the Mercedes, as well, and walked over to speak to her. "You drive your new baby like a champ," he told her when she rolled down the window on the driver's side.

Jess smiled, causing his heart to race. "The Cortina I drive at home has a straight shift," she acknowledged. "It wasn't such a feat."

A moment of silence ensued in which they continued to gaze at each other. Unwilling to be parted from her with things so much improved between them, but afraid of inviting rejection if he asked himself in, Stephen was at a loss how to proceed.

"Look," he said, "it's late. And you're probably tired. Our most recent evening together didn't end particularly well, thanks to my stupidity. But the fact is, I've done a lot of thinking since then. And I realize I made a colossal mistake. I don't suppose you'd consider giving us another try, and have dinner with me tonight?"

Leaning her chin on her hand in a gesture he knew, she regarded him in silence for a moment. "No, I don't suppose I would," she said at last, keenly aware she'd be bringing Annie home from the hospital in the morning. "But I'd be willing to cook for us, if that would suit."

Now that it was September, the evenings had turned cool. To Stephen's relief and amazement, he found himself building a fire in the cottage's brick fireplace a few minutes later to help combat the chill. As he positioned the logs to create the proper draft and added kindling, Jess put the kettle on for tea. He had the cheerful blaze crackling by the time she was whipping up mixed greens and an incredible shepherd's pie—reconstituted mashed-potato crust fluffed atop carrots, onions and chunks of browned, cut-up lamb in a rich improvised gravy.

They ate off blue-willow ironstone at the kitchen table, in the mellow glow of the overhead Tiffany lamp. How utterly good it is just to be here, Stephen thought, watching Jess as she talked and ate, occasionally laughing at something he'd said in the helpless but refined way she had that had never failed to captivate him. Real food for my stomach and a balm for my loneliness, if not a total nepenthe for the grief I may never fully erase.

It occurred to him that, Annie's troubles aside, Jess, too, might have ghosts to bury in hallowed ground. Her

husband of at least six years had died in a fiery automobile crash shortly before Annie was diagnosed, if a
casual remark he'd overheard her make was any indication. Yet she'd been willing to take on the risk of
making love to him.

Maybe to her sex didn't equal commitment—at least
not at first, in the salad days of a new relationship.
Maybe he'd simply been *around,* an available man
caught up in the same perilous and trying situation that
was circumscribing her movements and claiming the
lion's share of her attention. But he doubted it. Everything about her suggested she was that much-prized
combination of principled, old-fashioned girl and sex-
ually awakened woman that most men dreamed of finding someday.

She was also the woman he wanted—so much that
peace of mind had eluded him since he'd walked out
on her. Though it meant taking a considerable risk,
given the affliction of his past and the precariousness
of Annie's current situation, he wouldn't burn his
bridges again.

Following the meal and a quick cleanup operation in
which they both rolled up their sleeves and participated,
they gravitated to the living room, to sit on one of the
overstuffed, lattice-printed couches in front of the fire.
With the lamps turned low and Jess's head resting on
Stephen's shoulder as they stared dreamily into the
flames, it wasn't long before they were nestled in each
other's arms.

Like love bites cunningly calculated to tantalize both
body and soul, the kisses with which they claimed each
other's mouths quickly got out of hand. "Let me stay
with you tonight," Stephen pleaded, coming up for air.

"Please, darlin'. I swear I won't leave you dangling again."

Could she trust him to keep his word, after what had happened on their first visit to the cottage together? Given the strength of her own wishes, she realized, the query was moot. From the depths of her womanliness, she needed him.

"If you do, I'll have to find a new doctor for Annie," she warned. "And I don't want to do that."

He didn't want it, either. Annie was his patient. He cared deeply about her. He was determined to make her well, somehow. "That's completely out of the question," he said, his hands finding their way under her gray cashmere pullover to caress her slender rib cage. "I swear to God, Jess. You won't have to do anything of the sort."

Her eyes bright with the lust he knew must be mirrored back at her from his own, she took off the sweater completely for him. "Let's make love right here on the living room floor," she suggested, causing his arousal to stiffen and jut forward like a cannon barrel primed for shot. "The fire will keep us warm. And there are plenty of pillows."

There wasn't any further need for words. Silhouetted against the fire's flickering red glow, they quickly stripped to the skin while watching each other with bated breath, then knelt on the pillows they'd arranged before it, thigh to thigh and mouth to mouth. I can't believe this is really happening, Jess thought, delirious over her intimate contact with the evidence of his desire. That I've found the man I was born to love, here in America. And he won't leave me till the morning light.

Cut adrift from his past, with one foot provisionally planted in the future, Stephen was reverently thumbing her nipples. She's like some exquisite lyre for the gods, allowing mortal man to touch her, he fantasized.

Coherent thought became impossible as he traced a feather's trajectory down her abdomen and slipped one hand into the velvet folds that guarded the apex of her longing. Stroking her gently, but with the inexorability of an avalanche videotaped in slow motion, he spurred his own heat as he awakened her to even more tumultuous craving.

She quickly realized that the force of what he was doing would sweep her away. "Stephen," she begged, her lower body pressed urgently against him. "Please...I want you inside me when it happens."

So precise and matter-of-fact when he was discussing courses of treatment with his patients, his rough-edged baritone became almost guttural. "We have all night for that," he said, nipping at the delicate curve of her shoulder as he continued his ministrations. "Let me please you this way first."

Though she'd been about to argue with him, Jess found she couldn't summon the necessary speech. Given her expanding and flowering physical vocabulary, the spoken word seemed beside the point. Moving headlong toward the brink and hovering there for an infinity that lasted several seconds, she abruptly journeyed past it, dissolving in a paroxym of pleasure that racked her to the soles of her feet.

Though she'd experienced that type of orgasm before, she'd never known one of such oblivion and intensity. It was as if a powerful electrical current had discharged within her body, freeing her of tension and anxiousness.

Only subliminally aware of the way she'd cried out

his name, adding the litany "Yes...yes...yes." She sagged against him and buried her face against his neck.

"Ah, Jess," he whispered, enfolding her and comforting her in her "little death" with the immediacy of his body. "You're as genuine as the earth, sweetheart...so utterly damn wonderful that it breaks my heart."

They started again when she'd quieted enough, with Stephen seated on a low hassock and Jess rocking astride his lap. Satisfied as she was, deep within her cells, she found herself soaring again as she watched his beautiful eyes glaze over with wanting her. Confounding the modest expectations her past had taught her, the massive discharge of erotic energy they produced together lifted her to a paradise inhabited by two, something she'd never before experienced.

As promised, her lanky blond lover lay tangled up with her beneath the woolen blanket that covered her double bed when morning came. Fortunately for the privacy of their newfound bliss, he was used to waking early.

"Jess...sweetheart...we forgot to phone Lindsay and tell her you bought a car," he whispered when she stirred and murmured something unintelligible against him. "I'd better be going, if we don't want her to find me here when she arrives to give you a lift. I'll see you when I show up in Annie's room to sign her out, okay? Try not to let on you notice if I nibble on your fingertips. Or take a surreptitious bite out of your pretty neck."

Released on schedule, Annie was delighted with the cottage and the roomful of creative playthings Jess had purchased in honor of her homecoming. She didn't

seem surprised, just happy to see him, when Stephen
dropped by for supper, bringing a homecoming present
of his own—a portable dollhouse with a resident family
of four and tiny, perfect furniture. Or think it odd that
he spent most of the weekend with them, departing for
his own home, a short distance away, only when bed-
time neared. On Monday, when he had to put in a full
day at the hospital again, she remarked with five-year-
old perspicacity that the cottage seemed awfully empty
without him.

Their unseen neighbor on the estate, Jake, chose
Monday to show up at his downtown office for the first
time since his arrest. The effort didn't begin well.
Somehow—perhaps they had him under surveillance?—
the Minneapolis police got wind of his movements and
an exchange regarding them was broadcast over the police radio. As a result, a pack of eager newshounds was
waiting for him when his chauffeur dropped him off at
the Fortune Building's main entrance.

Angrily brushing aside their questions, which cen-
tered on his parentage and the affidavits Monica had
been using to blackmail him, he shielded his face from
their whirring motor drives and brightly lit video cameras as he escaped into a key-operated express elevator
and shot to the building's top floor.

His longtime secretary, Joan Carmody, greeted him
with her usual deference. "Welcome back, Mr. Fortune," she said with a smile. "I promise not to belabor
the point. But I'd just like to say that all of us here are
convinced of your innocence."

Unable to hide his embarrassment over the situation
in which he found himself, he thanked her awkwardly
for her support.

"Your *Wall Street Journal* is on your desk," she

added. "I'll get your coffee right away. Let me know when you want to tackle the mail. As you might imagine, there's quite a stack of documents awaiting your approval and signature."

Perused with black coffee instead of the scotch Jake would have preferred, the business-oriented newspaper only confirmed that Fortune Industries stock continued to take a beating. Despite the company's assets, which were legion, it would soon be a takeover target, he guessed. If he didn't want to find himself attempting to beat back a hostile purchase offer with his right hand while quelling an internal revolt with his left, something would have to be done to stop the hemorrhaging in the share price before the fall stockholders' meeting.

An hour and a half later, after they'd plowed through perhaps a third of the most pressing matters that required his attention, he suggested Joan take her usual coffee break. It turned out to be an unfortunate move on his part. A new recruit, the assistant she left in charge of his outer office, didn't have the standing to deny Nate entrance to his inner sanctum without first consulting him.

"So...you're back in the driver's seat," his brother said sarcastically, bursting in and striding forward to plant himself squarely in front of Jake's desk. "Any crack-ups yet this morning? Or have you managed to stay out of hot water, on the theory that one murder charge hanging over your head—and the company, I might add—is enough?"

Since learning that he might not fully share Nate's privileged parentage, Jake had struggled with an inferiority complex where his brother was concerned. His unenviable position as an accused murderer, and his very real fears about what his future might hold, had

only exacerbated those feelings. Now the contents of
the affidavits Monica had been using to blackmail him
had been made public by her would-be actor son—and
on national television. Jake had little doubt Nate soon
would be in contact with Brandon Malone to learn the
details, if he hadn't phoned the little twit already.

"This is a private office," he declared, reining in his
temper with difficulty as he got to his feet. "I'd appreciate it if you'd leave, and come back when you have
an appointment. As you can see, I have work to do."

Nate stood his ground. "You're damn straight about
the work," he agreed with a curl of his lip. "If it were
solely up to you and that bottle of Scotch you keep so
handy, this company would be down the toilet. Fortunately, a lot of dedicated people, myself included, have
worked their tails off to keep it from happening. But
there's only so much we can do without the proper authority. If you care anything at all about saving the business our parents built, you should step down as CEO
and temporary board chairman…let go of the reins so
I can do what needs to be done, at least until this farce
has been adjudicated…."

Stung by his brother's harshly stated demands and
somewhat deserved recriminations, Jake didn't catch the
half-buried hint that Nate believed in his innocence.
"Don't you mean the business our mother and *your
father* built?" he shot back. "I'm sure you're aware of
the revelation Brandon Malone dished out to the press
on Friday. You probably cheered."

Nate was visibly taken aback by Jake's characteri-
zation of him. "Like hell I did!" he disputed. "You're
my damn brother, whoever your father was. I will admit
to being curious…"

Jake wasn't listening to anything but the sudden

throbbing at his temples. "No way in hell am I going to roll over and play dead just to please you," he said, rounding his desk and giving Nate a little shove. "Now get out of here. The next time you want to talk to me, you can call my secretary for an appointment!"

Reared in the same volatile household, with the same magnanimous but temperamental father figure on hand to help mold his character, Nate had a temper to match his. "Take your hands off me, you misguided baboon, unless you want me to punch your lights out!" he threatened.

Luckily for both their sakes, Joan Carmody chose that moment to return from her break. "Is something wrong, Mr. Fortune?" she inquired, directing her question to Jake as she opened the door that connected their offices partway.

Jake flushed that she should have surprised him and Nate on the verge of fisticuffs. "My brother was just leaving, Joan," he announced. "As for Kenwyn or Kendra or whatever that new girl's name is, tell her I don't want to be disturbed by unannounced visitors if you leave her in charge again."

With Nate gone, a couple of aspirin beginning to take effect, and Joan Carmody's help, Jake was able to clean up a considerable stack of backlogged work, winding down a little in the process. However, when the Swiss perpetual-motion clock on his credenza struck noon, he'd had enough. Swiveling his executive chair around so that he could contemplate the Minneapolis skyline, he tried to imagine something that would make him happy, or at least provide him with a modicum of comfort.

His first thought was of Erica. He hadn't seen her since the day of his release, outside the judge's cham-

bers. And he'd wanted to, if only for old times' sake.
Memories of the way he used to call her up and ask her
to meet him somewhere for lunch, away from the kids,
the household and his responsibilities to the firm,
brought a wistful smile to his face.

I wonder if she'd be willing to meet me today, he
asked himself. I'm clean, sober, dressed in a respectable
business suit. If we went somewhere out of the way,
where the regulars don't know me from Adam or a well-
heeled murder suspect, we might be able to talk in peace
like ordinary folk.

Impulsively he picked up the phone and dialed the
number that formerly had been his, as well. She answered on the fourth ring, sounding as if she were
somewhat out of breath.

"Well, *Jake*...what a surprise!" she murmured, her
words seemingly cool, but with an underlying warmth
that went a long way toward assuaging the emotional
pain he felt. "Is there something I can do for you?"

"You can have lunch with me," he answered. "The
way you used to do in the old days. Thanks to my newly
acquired notoriety, we'll have to pass on our favorite
spots and settle for some hole-in-the-wall."

Erica wanted to hug herself. Jake *missed* her. He'd
shaken free of his self-pitying stupor and sought her
out—acknowledged that they still had common favorites. "That could be arranged," she said, trying not to
sound too eager. "I know a place not far from the junior
college I attend. I'll need a few minutes to clean up. I
was outside, going over some things with the new gar-
dener. Jaime had a heart attack, you know."

Jake hadn't. It seemed that his former life was unfolding, reconfiguring, without him. "I'm sorry to hear

that," he responded after a moment. "If you see him, give him my best. Shall I pick you up at the house?"

About to agree, Erica regretfully asked if he could meet her at the restaurant instead. She had a class to attend afterward. Plus some books to return to the college library.

Though he'd been somewhat annoyed with her for deciding to earn a degree just when he was beginning to experience his second midlife crisis, he didn't mind. "Forty-five minutes?" he asked, grabbing a pen and a pad of notepaper so that she could give him the restaurant's name and address.

It really did turn out to be a hole-in-the-wall—a crowded, somewhat noisy burgers-and-pizza kind of place in a small commercial area overflowing with students, most of whom were younger than Allie and Rocky, his youngest children. Asking his chauffeur to return for him in an hour or so, he went inside. He didn't spot Erica right away. Then he saw her, looking about ten years younger than the sleek society matron who'd put in such a brief appearance at the courthouse.

She was wearing a gray cashmere twin set over a green-and-gray houndstooth-check miniskirt, with gray suede flats. Opaque tights called attention to her fabulous legs. The forward fall of her silvery-blond tresses was held back by a barrette.

"You look like one of the kids," he said with approval, sliding into a booth opposite her.

She smiled. "That sounds like a compliment. Tell me what's been happening."

A waitress brought menus, and they postponed the inevitable discussion of his case to order a salad for her and a California burger for him, with fries and extra guacamole. All too quickly, though, they were wading into the latest revelations, first and foremost among them Brandon Malone's press conference regarding his late mother's affidavits. To Erica, Jake seemed less concerned with their relevance as a motive for murder than he was with what they might reveal about his parentage.

"Do you think there's any truth to the claims of those witnesses Monica's detective interviewed?" she asked. "I was about to phone you Friday, to ask if you'd been tested yet as a possible bone-marrow donor for Jessica Holmes's daughter, when that segment came on the news. I realized that, if what the affidavits supposedly say is correct, there wouldn't be much use in your doing it. Any match between the two of you...or between Annabel Holmes and our children...would be a fluke."

The possibility, maybe even the likelihood, that he wasn't the son of Ben Fortune's loins didn't seem to bother her that much. Far from making him feel it was the man she cared about, not his inherited affluence or family tree—something that, by rights, should have cheered him—her attitude plunged him into depression again. If his estranged wife thought the information contained in Monica's affidavits was true, then it probably was. She'd always had exquisite judgment.

For her part, Erica could feel him slipping away as their food arrived and he picked at his burger, leaving the fries, which he usually devoured to the last morsel, mostly untouched. She was painfully aware that, descending from the plane of a meaningful exchange that had the potential of bringing them together, their conversation had deteriorated into his usual litany of begging her to urge their children to have faith in him, and her corresponding reassurances they didn't need reminding—they were behind him one hundred percent.

He didn't drop any hints about a desire on his part

to patch up their ailing marriage. Or ask her to have faith in him, as well. So hopeful when she'd received his call that things might be changing for the better despite the troubles they faced, she became increasingly despondent. As they parted, she decided with a heavy heart that it was probably all over between them but the shouting.

It was only when she'd gone, tooling off in her new Acura, and Jake was seated in his limousine, headed back to the safe confines of the Fortune estate, that he really focused on missing her. Since they'd parted, his nights had been long and lonely. He couldn't help imagining how good it would feel to have her in bed with him again. Soon, though, his thoughts were once more entangled in the intricacies of his case.

Meanwhile, at their huge, tastefully decorated home in one of Minneapolis's most elegant suburbs, Nate was unloading about Jake and his stubborn determination to bring the company down with him to his patient, ever-loving second wife, Barbara.

"I can't reach him, I tell you!" he exclaimed, pacing like a caged tiger on the exquisite Aubusson rug that decorated their living room. "If he hangs on...insists on staying at the helm while being tried for Monica Malone's murder...we're going to lose the company. It isn't fair to me, Lindsay or Rebecca, or the generation of Fortunes that comes after us. I wish to God our mother were still alive. *She'd* talk some sense into him!"

The following weekend, Jess had the Todds, their children and Stephen over for dinner. Both she and Lindsay were delighted with the way the latter's young-sters, particularly seven-year-old Chelsea, hit it off with

Annie. It was the first time since coming to America that Jess's desperately ill daughter had felt well enough to socialize—and the first she'd had friends close to her own age to do it with.

"I hope Annie and Chelsea will be able to spend more time together," Jess said as she wished Lindsay and Frank Todd good-night. "Carter, too, of course, though he isn't as fascinated with dolls and playing house as Annie and his big sister are."

Remaining after his neighbors had driven off, Stephen helped Jess do the dishes and sat on Annie's bed to read her several stories before Jess took over to kiss her and tuck her in for the night. He was waiting for Jess when she returned to the living room.

More than a week had passed since the night they'd made love in front of the fire and later enjoyed a reprise in Jess's bed. Since then, they'd wanted each other unceasingly, and it wasn't long before they were kissing, deep in each other's embrace.

At last, hunger overcoming his better judgment, Stephen begged Jess to let him stay long enough to make love to her. "Annie will never have to know," he argued.

"On the contrary, she's been something of a restless sleeper since becoming ill," Jess responded, gently extricating herself from his arms. "The truth is, she could wander in at any moment. And I don't want her scandalized."

Forced to agree, though it was a death knell for his hopes, Stephen apologized for his thoughtlessness. Yet he couldn't deny that his need for her was unabated.

They said good-night a few minutes later on her front porch.

"There's got to be a way for us to be together, sweet-

heart,'' he insisted, aware that love was the emotion he
felt as he crushed her to him in the faint glow from her
living room window.

Even as he said it, he doubted Jess would be willing
to leave her downy, precariously better chick with a
baby-sitter. The only other option open to them was
marriage. And he was too afraid of what would happen
if they couldn't find a donor for Annie, or her transplant
didn't go well, to take that step.

In the big house hidden behind the thick copse of
trees that screened their embrace from the road, Jake
was pouring himself another Scotch as he worried about
the stock he'd sold Monica to silence her assault on his
parentage. Thanks to that sale, which had taken place
in a series of transfers over the course of several
months, he'd lost most of his clout as a stockholder. If
Nate mounted a serious attempt to oust him as CEO and
enough disgruntled shareholders lent him their proxies,
he might get the boot.

The fact was, he *needed* that stock.

How to get it? Approaching Brandon Malone and
asking him to sell it back had seemed like a nonstarter
when he first contemplated it. As his mother's accused
murderer, Jake was unlikely to elicit much sympathy
from him. The dead movie star's son had little incentive
to give him what he wanted, no matter how astronomical the price he might offer for it.

A few more sips of his drink and he was thinking in
somewhat different terms. According to Gabriel Devereax, the detective Sterling Foster had put on the case,
Monica's estate wouldn't be settled for some time. Such
matters often took years to wend their way through the
courts. Further, with the exception of her decaying Min-

neapolis house and a similar California establishment where Brandon currently hung out, plus her Fortune stock and what Jake guessed would be a few hundred thousand in cash after the debts she'd accumulated during several decades of high living were paid, there wouldn't be much of an inheritance by Hollywood standards.

It was common knowledge in Minneapolis that Brandon longed to be recognized as an actor. Since his adopted mother's death, the thirty-seven-year-old had been negotiating to buy a production company on credit in the hope of showcasing his modest talents. Money in hand might tempt him.

The more Jake thought about it, the more the idea took on a madcap appeal. Strong men take drastic measures when the going gets rough, he told himself. Of course, the stock didn't belong to Brandon yet, as the estate hadn't been settled. But he could give Jake an option on it—deliver the shares when he inherited them.

With an option, Jake could vote the shares as if they'd never left his possession. Though it was currently trading at an all-time low, his former Fortune stock was still worth millions, enough to finance a low-budget film or get a production company rolling for the aspiring actor.

On impulse, Jake phoned Gabe Devereax for Brandon Malone's number and address. Reluctantly given it, he brushed off the detective's warning to stay clear of Monica's heir and dialed California with a fresh drink at his elbow.

A woman with a Filipino accent answered. At Jake's request, she called Brandon to the phone.

"Yeah?" the dissolute young man muttered impatiently into the receiver.

"Thish is Jake Fortune, of Minneapolish," Jake said, suddenly unable to keep from slurring his words. "I've got 'n offer for you that you can't refuse...."

According to the Hennepin County attorney, Jake Fortune had murdered Brandon's mother. Brandon tended to believe it. In his opinion, there'd been plenty of motive for the Fortune CEO to do so. "This is a joke, right?" he asked bitterly.

"Nah," Jake assured him. "I'm givin' it to you shtraight. Your mother blackmailed me outa most of my stock in Fortune Indushtries. And I wanna buy it back. I'll give you twenny percent more than it's sellin' for on Wall Street. You can use the money to start that produc'shun company you want...without waitin' for probate. You can give me opshuns...."

Coming to believe the caller was serious, and that he was indeed who he said he was, Brandon thought a moment. Was the Fortune Industries executive offering him a chance to avenge his mother's death? Giving himself a moment to think, he asked Jake to repeat the offer.

"So...whaddaya say?" Jake asked, after complying with the request. "Do we have a deal?"

Well aware that the terms of Jake's bond didn't allow him to leave Hennepin County, Brandon suggested he come out to the West Coast immediately to close the deal. "You're right in thinking I need the money," he acknowledged coyly. "The problem is, I need it *now,* not three days from now. Or next week. If you can come out right away, like tonight, I'll sell. Otherwise, you can forget it."

Floating as he was on a sea of Scotch, with his critical faculties dulled, Jake regarded Brandon's willingness to sell as the answer to his prayers. By his lights, he'd taken charge of the situation, in the process completing an end run around his brother.

"I'm on my way," he said. "See you when I get there."

Severing the connection, he phoned his favorite airline and reserved a first-class ticket for that evening with his credit card. It was too late to wake his chauffeur, whom he'd dismissed hours earlier, in any event. He decided to drive himself to the airport. Snatching up a sport coat and removing the checkbook for his reserve account from the library safe, he headed for his Porsche. You caught Nate with his pants down, he congratulated himself, roaring out of the garage and down the winding drive to the estate's electronic gate. No matter *whose* dad he was, ol' Ben Fortune would have been proud of you.

The way he bobbed and weaved through traffic on his way to the airport, it was nothing short of a miracle that he wasn't picked up for driving while intoxicated. Managing to pay for his ticket and find his gate, despite a few stumbles, he consumed more Scotch in first class, then snored for most of the journey, blissfully unaware that Brandon had phoned the authorities to report that he was in the process of jumping bail.

By the time the pilot turned on the seat-belt sign preparatory to landing at Los Angeles International Airport, he'd slept off some of the alcohol and begun to worry about flouting the terms of his bail. If he was caught in the act, he'd find himself behind bars until after his trial. His stomach going sour and his nerves tied up in knots, he realized he'd done a very foolish thing. However, he'd come too far to retreat. I'll buy the shares from the Malone brat as quickly as I can, he decided, and purchase another ticket home on the red-eye, under an assumed name.

He was more than a little nervous as the plane taxied to the gate. Yet at first, as he filed off the Boeing 757 behind a family with several young children, he thought he'd gotten away with his transgression. It was only after he cleared the gate and strolled into the broad concourse that connected it with the rest of the airport that his heart sank as someone clamped a firm hand on his shoulder.

''Jacob Fortune,'' a low voice said in his ear, ''you're under arrest for violating the terms of your bail. You have the right to remain silent...''

Vastly sobered as his fellow passengers and hundreds of other travelers who were passing through the busy airport gaped at him, Jake soon found himself on his way back to Minneapolis, handcuffed to a Los Angeles Police Department detective in compliance with an L.A. circuit judge's order.

Nine

As expected, Jake's bail was formally revoked the next morning by the judge who had granted it and would preside over his trial a few months hence. In addition to that crushing blow, he got a stern, embarrassing lecture, which was duly recorded for public consumption by a phalanx of TV and print reporters.

"Apparently you need reminding...all citizens of this great country are equal under the law, whether they come up the hard way or enjoy a privileged position in society, like yourself," the judge rebuked him. "When terms of bail are granted to anyone, rich or poor, socially prominent or otherwise, they're meant to be obeyed, not mocked. Since you chose to do the latter, you'll await trial in the county jail, no matter how long it takes. Don't think for a moment that this court can be prevailed upon to relent by further requests for lenience."

Thoroughly chastened and humiliated, Jake was at his lowest ebb as he was led back to his cell. Both Sterling and his celebrated defense attorney were furious with him. Plus, he'd ticked off the judge, who would make innumerable rulings during the course of his trial and the pretrial motions. As for Brandon Malone, he was probably laughing himself senseless. *The little twerp set a trap for me, and I walked right into it,* Jake acknowledged in despair as the door to his cell clanged shut, isolating him from his family, the company he was convinced his brother was trying to wrest from his control and the rest of the noncriminal world.

Yes, Brandon Malone had made a spectacular fool of him. A moment later, on sober and painful reflection, he realized he'd practically *invited* Monica's son to snooker him. The richly deserved dressing-down he'd received from the judge, Aaron Silberman and especially Sterling, when the family lawyer learned of his transgression, rang in his ears like a litany of accusations.

When she heard about the shambles Jake had made of things, Erica was almost unbelieving. Can this be the man I married, the father of my children? she wondered. Or has some impostor taken his place? The Jake I knew was far too savvy ever to torpedo himself this way. Yet even as these thoughts ran through her head, she remembered how, during their lunch at the little burger joint near the college, he'd degenerated from a semblance of his old self to the unhappy, self-involved man who'd pulled down their marriage as if it were a house of cards and set about destroying himself.

It would be so easy to blame what had happened on his misuse of alcohol. His problems with the company. Or Monica Malone's unprovoked attack on his parentage. Yet she realized those were essentially surface things—in the case of his drinking, just a symptom. In some deeply fundamental place within himself, she sensed, he felt an agonizing lack. Whatever its reason for being was, it had prompted him to become dissatisfied with the way his life had turned out, and the man that, now that he'd reached his fifties, he'd become.

He wouldn't want to see her, she guessed—not from the depths of his humiliation and probable anger at himself. Yet something in her wouldn't rest until she'd renewed her contact with him. About to dress for an unannounced visit in her usual expensive tailored separates, she recalled a news clip she'd seen of Jake in his jailhouse uniform and realized how sharply that kind of attire would delineate the gulf that separated them.

Her silvery-blond hair caught back in a ponytail and her face innocent of all but the most rudimentary makeup, she was sporting a gray cotton-knit sweatshirt, matching sweatpants and the sneakers she used to work in the yard when she arrived at the jail and joined the ragtag band of friends, relatives and lovers who were lining up to see the current crop of prisoners during visiting hours.

As she waited for a bailiff to bring Jake to the one of the visitors' windows, she thought her effort might come to naught. Yet, when she reached the head of the line, he shuffled out to meet her as requested, unshaven and wearing his most hangdog expression.

"Erica...I wish you wouldn't have come," he protested, sorrowfully meeting her gaze. "This is no place for you."

"We're still family, Jake," she answered. "We have children together. The truth is..." About to say she still loved him, she held her tongue. He wouldn't want to carry the added burden of her emotions. "I was wondering if there was anything I could do," she finished lamely. "You know...any business stuff I could pick up and deliver to you. Or errands I could run on your behalf."

He shook his head. Despite Nate's attempts to unseat him, the company would have to wait. "Just tell the kids to have faith in me, okay?" he asked. "That I'm innocent. And that I've given up alcohol for good. I swear to God I won't embarrass them this way again."

It was the usual refrain, calculated to shut her out. As dearly as she loved their children, Erica felt a moment's jealousy. Jake no longer gave a damn about *her*. To him, she was just a footnote.

It was all she could do to manage a few more minutes' banal conversation with him, and assure him that she'd do as he asked. Bidding him a pensive good-bye, she drove home and changed into one of her more typical outfits—a cranberry suede blazer and matching cashmere pullover, with a coordinating Donegal tweed skirt that ended several inches above her slender knees—to attend her humanities class. Deeply immersed in thoughts about Jake and what the future might hold for him, she was strolling toward the library afterward with some books she needed to return when one of the faculty members, a bearded history instructor who'd flirted with her since the beginning of the semester, fell into step with her.

"Doing anything special this evening?" he asked.

Usually adept at handling approaches from men, which she'd routinely fended off throughout her marriage, even during early pregnancy, Erica blinked in surprise.

True to form, she recovered quickly. "I thought I might start studying for my French exam," she answered with a smile.

The history instructor smiled, too. "There's a wonderful new singer on tap at the Dakota Bar and Grill in St. Paul," he said. "From the Cape Verde Islands. She sings in Portuguese. Any chance you'd like to go?"

Her ego stroked by the man's interest, which helped to assuage Jake's seeming lack of that quality when she'd visited him, Erica pondered the invitation for several seconds. But she never seriously considered it. There's such a thing as loyalty, she told herself, choosing to distance herself from her feelings by describing them in those terms. Jake's at his lowest ebb. Despite the fact that our marriage is on the rocks, if I dated someone else, I couldn't live with myself.

"Sorry, I can't…for personal reasons that have nothing to do with you," she answered. "But thanks for asking."

He didn't appear to be miffed. "No problem," he answered with a grin. "Maybe some other time."

As he said goodbye and headed for the parking lot, his friendliness and obvious admiration warmed Erica's heart. They gave her hope that, when Jake's troubles were resolved and he'd come to terms with himself, he'd find her desirable again. With characteristic stubbornness, she refused to think about the fact that her hopes might come to nothing if he was convicted of Monica's murder.

Distraught over the latest crisis to erupt in Jake's life, Lindsay stopped by the guest cottage on the Fortune estate on Saturday morning so that Chelsea and Annie could play together and she could have a cup of tea with Jess. Already fast friends, the two youngsters quickly settled down to play with the dollhouse Stephen had given Annie as a homecoming present. Though she smiled briefly at the beginning of what would likely prove a fast friendship, despite the three-year difference in their ages, Lindsay's usually smooth forehead was creased with a distracted frown as she took a seat at the kitchen table.

"I was so sorry to hear about what happened with

your brother," Jess said sympathetically with a shake of her head as she set the Earl Grey to steep in a blue-and-white china pot and popped a pair of crumpets into the toaster.

"It's incredible, isn't it?" Lindsay agreed. "You'd think he was in enough hot water, without jumping bail by running off to California on the spur of the moment! I can hardly believe he's the same big brother I used to look up to as a kind of surrogate parent when I was Chelsea's age. It's hard to imagine what he was thinking about."

In part because of his troubles, Jake was one of the few adult Fortunes who hadn't been tested for compatibility with Annie's bone marrow. Given his current situation, Jess imagined, it would be better not to point that out. Yet she ached to leave no stone unturned in finding help for her precious daughter.

Half afraid to ask, out of fear that the news wouldn't be good, she broached the subject after a few minutes' conversation about the effect of Jake's troubles on the Fortune family in general as she poured out the tea and placed the buttered crumpets on the table.

"I hate to sound like a one-issue person, but I was wondering if you'd heard anything more about Kyle's and Jane's blood tests," she murmured as Lindsay took a sip of the steaming beverage.

If possible, the brown-haired pediatrician's face took on a look of even greater distress. "Jess, I'm so sorry.... I should have told you the moment I walked in the door," she said. "Neither Kyle nor Jane have more than two matching antigens. As you know, that's not enough. Nate had one. Michael zero."

Jess's heart sank. What would become of Annie?

"I spoke to Kristina last night, and she's going to be

tested," Lindsay added, reaching across the tabletop to clasp her hand. "However, the odds being what they are, I think it's time we bite the bullet and have the children tested..."

Jess had been hoping with all her might that Lindsay would consider taking that step. Yet, as a mother herself, she could guess how little her friend enjoyed the prospect of Chelsea or Carter undergoing a donor procedure.

"I can't tell you how grateful I am, Lin," she said. "Naturally, I realize it's a tough decision for you. I'm sure if our positions were reversed, and Chelsea were in Annie's spot, I'd have qualms about Annie doing it."

Given Jess's well-founded worries over her sick child, Lindsay could appreciate the generosity of her statement. "You're right...I'm a little concerned about the pain that would be involved, though it's usually minimal," she agreed. "Not to mention the possibility that it might be frightening. Still, Frank and I want them to grow up as responsible members of their family and their community. Given the kind of people we hope they'll turn out to be someday, I know they'd never forgive me for failing to let them help if they were to grow up and learn that they could have made a difference."

A warm silence enveloped the two women as they gazed at each other like sisters. "You know I'd never let Annie die if I could do something to prevent it," Lindsay added. "Fortunately, Chelsea and Carter aren't our only possibilities. In addition to Kristina, there's also Jane's son, Cody, who's eight, and Kyle's daughter Caitlyn, who's ten. I suppose we could have Jake's grandchildren tested, as well, despite what appears to be a strong possibility that they're not your grandfather's true descendants.''

Jess nodded. Using information she'd picked up in bits and pieces from comments dropped by family members, she'd made a list of potential candidates herself. The only one Lindsay had failed to mention, aside from Jake himself, was Michael's new baby, who was too young to donate, in any event.

''Annie's illness aside, having you for a cousin and confidante has filled a deep need for me,'' she confided, her eyes glittering with unshed tears as the jumble of emotions she usually kept under wraps welled up in her throat. ''Coming from a big family with lots of interaction, as you do, you can't have any idea of how it's been for us. We have so few relatives on my grandmother's side, and when I learned the Simpsons weren't even kin, I felt as if we were alone in the world. Being accepted and helped by you and the rest of the Fortunes has been so wonderful....''

By now, Lindsay fully trusted that Jess didn't have ulterior motives where she and her family were concerned. Still, there was something she'd been wondering about. ''I know you told me your late husband's family members were tested on Annie's behalf and couldn't supply the bone marrow she needs,'' she said. ''But what about moral support? Surely they didn't just abandon you after his death.''

The look in Jess's eyes told her she'd hit a nerve.

''Actually, Annie's father and I were in the process of getting a divorce when he was killed in a car crash with his secretary,'' Jess confessed. ''He'd been having an affair with her, you see. It wasn't his first. The unfortunate girl was just the latest in a string of paramours that stretched back almost to our wedding day. His relatives didn't have a clue about his behavior, of course. When it came out in the inquest, they refused to give it any credence—blamed me, actually, for making it all up and besmirching his memory.''

The much-loved wife of an adoring husband who'd never given her the slightest reason to doubt his fidelity, Lindsay was appalled. Nothing in her experience—not even her grief over the deaths of her parents—could compare with the anguish of being treated that way. ''How awful, Jess!'' she exclaimed, reaching across the table to clasp her friend's hand. ''First a string of tragedies like that. And then Annie's illness. You've had so much to deal with!''

The sympathy and support of a relative and friend who truly cared eased a little more of Jess's pain. Her growing bond with Stephen had begun to do the same thing. Yet at times the uncertainty it generated outweighed the happiness.

As she sat there at the kitchen the table with Lindsay, she realized there were countless bridges to cross between that cool but sunny September morning and the hoped-for moment when Annie would be free of disease and ready to return to England or begin a new life in the United States. When the time came to decide on a future home, would she want to stay, or go? How would Annie feel? Were they putting down roots that would cause a painful wrench if they were pulled from the soil of a new extended family and a new country?

More importantly, would the man Jess had begun to love and trust, after doubting she'd ever experience those emotions again, turn out to be a steady beacon in their lives? Or would he abandon them? Having experienced her share of sorrow and disillusionment, she sensed that those emotions had marred his past, as well—stemming from some trauma or other that went deeper than the heartache of divorce and might make it difficult for him to commit to her. Though she hated to speculate along those lines, she couldn't help wondering if he felt safe in their relationship because it had a built-in cutoff date.

Only time would answer her question. Meanwhile, they were effectively prevented from making love by Annie's presence. The tension stemming from their abstinence was beginning to mount.

Annie and Chelsea chose that moment to troop into the kitchen, dollhouse residents in hand, and demand a snack. Obliging them with mugs of milk, bananas and homemade oatmeal-raisin cookies, Jess settled them at the table, while Lindsay refilled their teacups.

"Annie's temperature seems normal this morning," Lindsay noted, casually checking her young patient's forehead with the back of her wrist in a gesture more prevalent among mothers than among pediatricians. "No coughs or sniffles, I trust?"

Jess shook her head. "Smooth sailing so far."

"Stephen tells me the two of you haven't had any time to yourselves since Annie came home from the hospital. Do you think you might consider leaving her with a baby-sitter some evening, if I could recommend a trustworthy one?"

Jess got a warm feeling inside. Desperate to be alone with her, Stephen had approached Lindsay for help. "I've been thinking along the same lines," she acknowledged. "Both wanting to do what you're suggesting, and fearing it. If anything should happen..."

Lindsay patted her hand. "Your ambivalence is perfectly understandable," she said. "But Annie can manage without you for a few hours. Mrs. Larsen, who sits for Chelsea and Carter during the week, is often available in the evenings and on weekends. She's sixty-five years old. The grandmother of three. And an utter peach. Plus, Frank and I are just down the road for backup, in case of emergency. If Stephen asks you out again, I think you should accept.''

Stephen didn't let any grass grow under his feet. Advised by Lindsay that Jess hadn't turned down the babysitter idea, he phoned Mrs. Larsen and, assured of her availability, invited Jess to his house for dinner that very evening.

Aware that it would be dinner and lovemaking, she quickly accepted. She'd been aching for him, too. Besides, she longed to see his house. Mute glimpses of the private man and the past he never talked about might be available to her there.

He called for her around 7:00 p.m., after Annie had eaten her supper and settled down to have a pile of storybooks read to her by Mrs. Larsen on the living room couch. The air between them was electric with promise as she gave him a chaste hello kiss and stepped back to let Annie have a moment of his attention before they hurried out the door.

Due back at midnight, they'd have just five hours together. Jess wanted to make the most of them. She could feel Stephen's corresponding urgency in the possessive way his fingers gripped her waist through the lapis wool of her jacket as he helped her into his Mercedes.

"I hope you like plain old American steak and baked potatoes," he said in a low voice as he started up the engine. "Though it's fairly nippy out tonight, it won't be too cold to grill on the deck for quite a while yet."

Before long, the leaves would start changing color, metamorphosing from their one-note samba of summer green to a complex symphony of russet, gold and burgundy. In Minneapolis, Jess had heard, the snow flew early.

Though lacking any spoken assurances from him, she was ready to trust that they'd still be together when that moment came. "Steak sounds wonderful," she replied, snuggling against him.

His house was just five minutes away via the road that followed the lake's meandering shore. Dark and shuttered-looking when he'd driven her past it the night they came to inspect the cottage, his angular contemporary frame house glowed with light as they pulled into the drive.

Flashing her a grin that telegraphed both pleasure and possessiveness, Stephen raised the garage door with his electronic opener. A moment later, they were parking inside and he was ushering her up the quarry-tile steps that led to the kitchen. She noted a copper range hood, cherrywood cupboards and slate countertops—a Finnish table and chairs arranged before a two-way red-brick fireplace. A bottle of Bardolino and two tulip-shaped glasses stood in readiness. Aside from an automatic drip coffeepot, a set of steel canisters, a toaster and a microwave oven, the countertops were bare. Apparently his ex-wife had walked away with most of the kitchen gadgets and cookbooks.

"Would you like some wine?" he asked. "Or a tour first?"

Jess smiled. "The tour, then the wine, if that would suit. I can't deny I've been curious."

Like the kitchen, his living room was fairly Spartan, though the black leather sofa and love seat that faced the other side of the fireplace appeared quite comfortable. Their vertical blinds drawn back, a broad sweep of windows offered a panoramic view of tall oaks and the scattered lights that had begun to twinkle like stars on the opposite shore of the lake. She liked the jewel-toned Oriental rugs that softened the plank-style wooden floors, and the handful of carefully chosen contemporary paintings.

In her opinion, the low bookcase filled with art books and the rack of compact discs that waited beside the stereo were a step in the right direction. Yet the room lacked the softer, cozier touches an afghan might provide, or a jumble of throw pillows. It doesn't look as if a child has ever lived in this house, she thought. Or even spent much time here as a visitor.

Her surprise was that much greater, then, when she glanced into one of his guest bedrooms during their tour, to find herself gazing at child-size oak furniture and an extensive, boy-oriented collection of toys and books and pint-size sporting equipment. None of the things looked new. A rag-doll clown with a dirty face appeared to have been particularly loved. Yet the room was excessively tidy, as if no child had played or slept there for years.

"Whose room is this?" she asked, turning a puzzled face to him. "I thought you didn't have any children. Yet here's this absolutely perfect room for a little boy...."

He was gazing at the room's contents as if he'd temporarily forgotten about their existence and regretted showing them to her. "I don't," he told her. "Have any children, that is."

"Then... I don't understand."

"My, er, nephew stays over from time to time," he

muttered. To talk about David to her would inject the pain of his loss into their relationship. And he didn't want it there—yet. Besides, talking to her about a dead son when her daughter was so sick would hardly be kind.

Stephen hadn't mentioned having a nephew. Or family of any sort. There's a lot I don't know about him, she thought, deciding not to belabor the point. The fact that he'd furnish a room in his house with all these things for a nephew who only visits occasionally says a lot about his loneliness and his desire to be a parent. She wondered if his marriage had failed because his ex-wife hadn't wanted to give him a baby.

He seemed to relax a little as he showed her the master bedroom, which contained a leather chair, a matching hassock and a skinny, modern-looking reading lamp, as well as several smaller Oriental rugs and a suite of Danish teak furniture. By the time they'd returned to the kitchen and he was carrying the steaks out to the deck to grill them, most of the tension appeared to have eased from his shoulders. Instead of a man with secrets he refused to share and a hidden wound he didn't want to talk about, he was once again just Stephen, the tall, blond doctor she'd met at the zoo and learned to love.

It was chilly enough on the deck in the sunset's afterglow to bring a tingle of color to Jess's cheeks. But the cold didn't bother her that much. Nestled in the curve of Stephen's arm as he turned the steaks and pointed out various landmarks on the lake's opposite shore, she felt as warm as buttered toast. Whatever has hurt him in the past, he'll tell me about it eventually, she reassured herself. I can't expect him to divulge the secrets of his heart on a preset time schedule.

They ate off brown-and-black Arabia of Finland pottery at the Scandinavian-style table, in front of a crackling fire. In addition to the steak, he produced potatoes roasted amid the coals and a fresh-tasting salad made with tomatoes, onions, bits of Greek feta cheese and black olives. The rolls were French, from a local bakery. As they ate and sipped their wine by the fire's glow, they talked of Annie, the Todds, Jacob Fortune's tangled affairs—anything and everything but the impending lovemaking that was uppermost in both their thoughts.

Jess's latent arousal deepened when, after she refused dessert and offered to help with the dishes, Stephen responded with a husky "I'll wash them in the morning," and tugged her to her feet.

"What'll we do, then?" she asked breathlessly, imprisoned in his embrace.

The heritage of the Norwegian and English ancestors he'd told her about, his blue eyes took on their smoky look. "How about something we've been prevented from doing since Annie came home from the hospital?" he suggested.

She'd come to see his house and snatch a glimpse of the private man who lived there, and to make love to him most of all. "That suits me, Stephen," she whispered.

The moon was full, flooding his bedroom with its milky brilliance. They wouldn't need to switch on a lamp. Everything they yearned to see, touch and worship with eager hands and mouths would be clearly visible—her small but perfect breasts and softly parted lips, the glaze of lust in his eyes, his long, lean torso, culminating in the generous male attributes she ached to stroke and caress.

Throbbing with arousal, they couldn't get enough of looking at each other as they undid zippers and buttons. Moments later, the clothing that had separated them lay in a discarded heap on the floor as they lost themselves in each other's embrace.

"Jess... Jess...are you really here with me at last?" Stephen said wonderingly as he ran his hands down the creamy length of her back and grasped her buttocks, the better to position her against him. "You can't have any idea how much I've needed you...."

"Oh, *can't* I?"

So delicate and patrician-seeming, with her slender frame, naturally refined demeanor and upper-crust British accent, Jess was, for Stephen, that paragon among women, both an exquisite primrose to be gently plucked and a brazen temptress when they were in the throes of lovemaking. During their week of forbearance, her wild but oh-so-sweet behavior in front of the fire at her borrowed cottage had haunted his every waking moment. "Tell me," he demanded.

"Not a night has passed that I haven't dreamed of you sneaking in my bedroom window to claim me," she whispered.

The mental image of surprising Jess and pretending to overpower her as she lay rosy and warm from sleep beneath her coverlet was almost more than Stephen could take. Refusing for the moment to consider that fate could tear them apart if Annie's treatment didn't go well, he assumed protection and tugged her down on the bed so that they were face-to-face, with her on top, her shapely legs straddling him.

"I wish I'd known what you were thinking," he answered, lovingly caressing her nipples as he sought against her. "I'd have gone over the electric fence to get to you, sweetheart, if that's what it took."

During the course of the next two weeks, their "dinner dates" continued unabated, enriching both them and the benevolent Mrs. Larsen, who looked after Annie as if she were her very own granddaughter. Adrift in a romantic haze, Stephen was finishing up his office hours one afternoon in the professional building adjacent to the hospital when his secretary passed him a note. His ex-wife, Brenda, wanted a word with him.

I wonder what's on her mind, he thought apprehensively. "Ask her to hold, if she can," he instructed. "I'll be with her in just a moment."

Incredibly, for the second time in a row, the news from Brenda was good. "I just called to thank you for the advice you gave me the evening Tom and I had drinks with you at Gustino's," she informed him on an upbeat note.

Unable to recall giving her anything of the sort, Stephen said as much.

"How like you to forget!" she laughed good-naturedly. "I'll be happy to refresh your memory. When I told you Tom had asked me to marry him and confessed how afraid I was to let myself love again, let alone have another baby, you told me to 'go for it.' Well, we're getting married next week. And I'll share a little secret…I'm already pregnant!"

The news causing his head to swim with possible consequences for his own life, Stephen offered his heartfelt congratulations. As he left his office a short time later, he had to admit that Brenda seemed truly happy for the first time since David's diagnosis. Meanwhile, happiness had been sneaking up on him, as well.

Could he afford not to make a corresponding commitment?

Instead of heading home to change into casual clothes for dinner with Jess and Annie at the Fortunes' guest cottage, he pointed the Mercedes toward a jewelry store where he'd bought himself a new watch a few months earlier. By sheer happenstance, he was able to find a parking place a few doors away and enter the shop before it closed for the evening.

The owner, a man he knew slightly, happened to be behind the counter himself. "Looking for something special, Dr. Hunter?" he said with a smile.

An attack of cold feet didn't stop Stephen from asking to see the diamond engagement rings. "Something simple, with a decent-size stone, like that pear-shaped solitaire you have displayed on a velvet cushion," he elaborated, wondering if he'd lost his mind even to consider purchasing one.

According to the jeweler, the two-and-a-half-carat diamond set in platinum that he'd pointed out was one of the best-quality stones the small but exclusive shop had to offer. Though it was also one of the most expensive, Stephen could easily afford it, thanks to his income as one of the Twin Cities' top medical specialists. The question was whether he'd healed sufficiently from David's death to risk buying it for Jess and take on the risky emotional commitment that would entail. Loving her meant loving Annie, too, something he already did, to an extent that tore at his heart. What would happen if he couldn't save her? In addition to the profound personal grief and sense of failure he'd feel, would his relationship with Jess blow up in his face?

The shop owner was waiting politely for him to indicate his interest in the ring or ask to see something else. "No doubt you've guessed I'm marriage-minded," he acknowledged with some embarrassment. "Unfortunately, I haven't asked the lady yet. If I were to buy her this ring and she didn't like it, or no engagement actually took place, could I, uh, bring it back for a refund?"

An indulgent smile hinting he'd been asked that particular question a thousand times, the shop owner attempted to soothe Stephen's fears. The ring was fully returnable. "However, I think I should warn you, Dr. Hunter," he said with a twinkle. "Rings of this quality seldom come back to the store once they're purchased."

The ring was still in Stephen's possession on Sunday afternoon, when he, Jess and Annie reported to the Todds' lakefront home for a cookout. Though the weather was mild, the first hints of early fall color had begun to enliven the trees' canopy of green. Sunlight crosshatched the lake with diamonds.

Like the Viking Jess insisted he was, Stephen had called for her and Annie in his graceful Butterfly sailboat. Her downy blond head protected from the breeze by a tam that pulled down over her ears and a child-size flotation vest securely buckled about her too-slender frame, Annie watched him maneuver the little craft with obvious fascination.

"Will you teach me how to sail when I get well, Dr. Steve?" she said at last. "Pretty please, with sugar on top?"

She'd picked up the American expression from Lindsay's youngsters, he guessed. "I'll be happy to," he answered, giving her a fond smile as he tacked, preparatory to heading for the Todds' dock. "In fact, if it's okay with Mummy, you can help steer us toward Chelsea's backyard.''

With Jess's permission, Annie eagerly changed places to sit in the crook of Stephen's elbow and place her much smaller hands next to his on the tiller. How right they look together, Jess thought, noting the way his blond hair ruffled in the breeze and reflecting on the similarity in their coloring. She could be his daughter, instead of Ronald's. I wonder if, this time next year, the three of us will be healthy, happy, and still together.

Perhaps as an antidote to her uncertainty about where they stood with the man she loved and her constant worry over the outcome of Annie's illness, Jess teased Stephen about ''maneuvering the craft into the slot'' as they approached the Todds' dock. So innocent-sounding to the unsuspecting ear, the double entendre delighted him. What a delicate English rose she is, he thought. And what a bawdy, satisfying lover she can be! I don't want to lose her—or the precious little girl who's filling the empty spot David left in my heart at such a rapid pace.

Frank Todd and his son, Carter, were waiting on the dock to welcome them. ''They're here!'' Frank shouted at Lindsay and Chelsea, who could be seen waving from the kitchen window.

They'd eat in about an hour, Frank informed them. First, the adults would talk and enjoy the fine weather, while the children ran off some of their excess energy.

At least that was the plan. With both host and hostess on call at the hospital, it didn't work out that way. They'd just settled down in Adirondack chairs facing the water when Lindsay's cellular phone rang. She was needed in the Minn-Gen emergency room.

''Here's hoping I won't be gone too long,'' she said,

getting to her feet. "If I'm not back in an hour, start grilling without me. The side dishes are covered with plastic wrap in the refrigerator."

To everyone's surprise, Lindsay returned within forty-five minutes. "False alarm," she murmured, sliding into the empty chair beside her husband and slipping a hand into his.

So hesitant, yet clearly indicative of a strong need for his backup and support, the gesture caused him to give her a searching look. "What's up, babe?" he asked in his deep, gentle voice.

The glance she gave Jess prompted the latter to hold her breath. A moment later, she knew the reason.

"While I was at the hospital, I ran into one of the techs from hematology," Lindsay said. "The latest batch of blood tests was available. We've found a match for Annie. It's Chelsea."

Ten

"Oh, Lin..."

Her heart a bottomless well of joy and relief, Jess could imagine only too well how Lindsay felt. As much as the brown-haired pediatrician wanted to save Annie, she couldn't help but feel some reluctance over the prospect of causing her own sweet daughter the slightest discomfort.

Frank probably felt the same way.

No one spoke for a moment, as he and Lindsay looked at each other and then at Annie, Chelsea and Carter, who were playing in blissful ignorance of adult fears and the existence of fatal blood disorders. A study in restraint, though his emotions were deeply affected, too, Stephen lightly massaged Jess's shoulder.

We ought to go home and let them confer, she realized, a little sliver of fear that the Todds might not let Chelsea donate inserting itself in her consciousness. Knowing Lindsay as she did, she guessed her friend wouldn't hear of them leaving. "I think you and Frank ought to take a few minutes by yourselves, to talk over what's happened," she said at last. "Stephen and I can watch the children."

"Good idea," Stephen agreed. "Take a drive, if you want. We'll see that any scrapes get bandaged."

Exchanging a quick look and thanking them for their understanding, the Todds elected to walk hand in hand along the lakeshore. They settled on the dock, where they communed earnestly for a half hour or so, silhouetted against the lake's late-afternoon brilliance.

Unable to keep from glancing their way now and then, or stop herself from silently pleading with the spirit that ruled the universe that Annie would get the help she so desperately needed, Jess helped Stephen set up a children's croquet game and took her turn with the mallet.

At last Lindsay and Frank started back up the hill, their demeanor sober but unruffled, clearly united in the decision they'd reached. For Jess, the fate of the world hung on their answer. If Annie didn't receive an infusion of healthy bone marrow, she might not make it to her sixth birthday. Catching hold of Stephen's hand, Jess gripped it tightly, aware that she was all but holding her breath.

"I know how tough this has to be for you, and we won't keep you in suspense a moment longer than necessary," Lindsay said when they arrived, her brown eyes grave but compassionate. "What we've decided is this. While we want very much to help, the decision isn't solely ours to make. Young as she is, Chelsea should be consulted. We'll explain Annie's leukemia to her, and let her know what an important, unique contribution she can make. Of course, we won't minimize the need for her to be brave, or the fact that some discomfort will be involved."

"If Chelsea's willing to go ahead, once she understands these things," Frank chimed in, "then we're willing, too. We'll talk to her about it tonight, and let you know what she decided in the morning. I'm sure you know that, in our hearts, we hope her answer will be yes."

As a parent, Jess understood exactly where Frank and Lindsay were coming from. Her fears for Annie's welfare only partly eased, she murmured her understanding and assent. They would do their best for Annie as parents, friends and physicians—decent and caring members of the human race. It was the most anyone could expect.

With so much hanging in the balance, the cookout on the Todds' lawn turned out to be muted, at best. Jess barely tasted the American-style hamburger Frank grilled for her, or Lindsay's excellent potato salad. Try though she would to keep up her end of the conversation, she couldn't stop her gaze from resting on the blond baby fuzz of Annie's head and praying with all her might that the salvation that lay just out of reach would be made available to them.

Stephen suggested they call it an afternoon when the meal was finished and the paper cups and plates had been collected and dumped in the trash. Though Annie complained that she wanted to stay a while, Jess agreed with him. The sooner they left, the sooner Lindsay and Frank could talk to Chelsea. For her part, she doubted she could stand the strain of pretending she wasn't on needles and pins for another moment.

When they pulled up at her borrowed cottage's front steps a few minutes later, she asked Stephen to switch off the Mercedes's engine and come inside with them. "I hate to ask, because I know you have to be at the hospital very early in the morning," she confided, as her precious child wandered off down the hall to conduct a doll-size tea party in her room. "But I wish you'd stay the night. I'm not sure that, without you, I'll be able to stand the suspense."

Stephen didn't hide his surprise. "I thought that, with Annie here..." he began.

"We could sleep in our clothes, right here in the living room. If she wakes up, she won't be scandalized."

As their afternoon at the Todds' wore on, Stephen had begun to count the inherent complications in the situation for him. Though he'd bought Jess an engagement ring, he hadn't been able to overcome his scruples about giving it to her yet. Now, with stunning abruptness, the chance to secure a marrow donor for Annie hovered on the cusp of realization. Either the opportunity to do a transplant—and possibly fail in the attempt—would result, or the Todds would refuse and Jess would be plunged into a despair of unimaginable depths. Either way, he could lose the woman and child he cared deeply about.

I'm not sure I could survive a replay of what I endured when David died, he thought. It would kill me to lose Annie. Doubly so if, in the process, I failed Jess, the way Brenda accused me of failing her. Since he'd purchased the ring, it had occurred to him that Brenda had it easy with Tom McCaffrey. Unlike Jess, the Wayzata internist didn't have a sick child who might die and leave them tearing each other apart.

For the first time since Monica Malone had phoned so many months earlier and demanded he come by her house to discuss a matter of mutual interest, Jake's steady diet of calamity and mistakes was served with a side dish of good news. According to Aaron Silberman, who dropped by the jail to visit him, though there were plenty of fingerprints and bloodstains linking him to her murder—and none to incriminate anyone else—something curious had turned up. In going over the crime scene with their state-of-the-art equipment, the Minneapolis Police Department's physical evidence investigation unit had turned up some unidentified shoeprints in the dust of Monica's five-car garage. They'd found similar prints in the soft earth of a flower bed, together with several smudged examples of the same pattern, which was characteristic of a particular brand of running shoe.

"You own a pair of shoes like that?" the defense attorney asked. "Now or in the past?"

Jake shook his head. "I'm partial to Nikes. I doubt if I've bought another brand of athletic shoe in twenty years."

"What kind of shoes were you wearing when you went to Monica's house on the night of her murder?"

Stumped, Jake had to give the matter some thought. "My tasseled loafers, I guess," he said at last.

The attorney informed him with undisguised satisfaction that a print matching the loafers he'd been wearing when he was first arrested had been documented near where he'd told police he parked his car that night. The anomalous shoeprints hadn't matched any of the shoes investigators had found in his possession—or any footgear owned by Brandon Malone or any of the servants.

He quickly set Jake straight when the latter bemoaned the fact that the prints couldn't be used to incriminate Monica's son. "Don't you get it?" he asked. "Brandon Malone has witnesses who will swear he was in California that night. Provided they don't lead to your walk-in closet, prints that have no business being in Monica's garage, her flower beds, her living room...in other words, that don't belong to anyone with an established right to be there...*strengthen* our argument that an unknown killer waited for you to leave the house, then slipped inside to do his or her dirty work.''

Jake's head was reeling. Was it possible that he'd be exonerated by the evidence?

"In fact, there may have been *two* killers,'' Aaron Silberman speculated, his curly hair bristling atop his celebrated think tank as if it were drawing energy from favorable developments. "There's an unidentified partial in the garage that may have been originated around the same time, made by a woman. Like the athletic-shoe prints, it doesn't seem to belong to anyone known to be connected with Monica...or the murder case.''

For once, Jake wasn't bemoaning the depredations of an uncaring fate as he listened to his defense attorney. Instead, he was seeing light at the end of the tunnel. "How did you find out about all this?" he asked.

Aaron Silberman grinned outright. "A nifty little rule called discovery,'' he said. "The prosecution has to inform us in advance of the evidence they plan to use against you. That goes double for us, of course. We have to let them know if we uncover Monica's real killer first!''

Jake realized his whiz-kid counselor had made a little joke. "We'd damn well better,'' he replied, smiling for the first time since being returned to jail. "This place isn't exactly the Taj Mahal, you know.''

As he was about to leave, the defense attorney mentioned that he'd asked Gabe Devereax to redouble his efforts to find someone in Monica's neighborhood who might have seen someone else leave Monica's residence around the time of her murder.

"There has to be someone in the neighborhood who saw something, other than that crazy old broad with the dog who placed your sister near the scene. A description and a time frame from a credible witness might be enough to constitute reasonable doubt and get you off the hook.''

After a night of sleeping in a cramped, semierect position on one of the lattice-print sofas with her head pillowed on Stephen's shoulder, Jess was pacing the living room. If only he hadn't had to leave for the hospital so early, she thought. Just having him here made the waiting easier to bear. Without him, it's become excruciating.

Surely Lindsay would call soon!

With that thought, the phone rang and Jess snatched up the receiver. ''Hello?'' she said tremulously.

''Jess, it's Lindsay,'' the brown-haired pediatrician's sweet voice announced. ''I'm happy to report that the transplant's a go. Chelsea wouldn't hear of anything else once we'd explained the options. I'd have called last night but, given the fact that she's not quite eight, we insisted she sleep on it....''

Jess felt as if her feet were suddenly floating several inches above the ground. *Yessss!* Annie's going to be all right! she exulted in a torrent of relief. The fact that, by themselves, bone-marrow transplants could be fairly risky hadn't entered into her thinking yet.

''Dearest Lin...how can I ever thank you enough?'' she cried in a shaky voice, utterly frustrated by the inadequacy of language to express what she felt. ''Because of you and Frank and Chelsea—'' her voice broke ''—Annie won't be lost.''

If she was thinking of the remaining hurdles that had to be crossed, Lindsay didn't allude to them. ''I ought to mention that, though the transplant should be done as soon as possible, while Annie's still reaping the benefits of her recent treatment," she continued, "we want to wait until after Chelsea's birthday, which is coming up next week."

It was little enough to ask. "Lin, you know that's just *fine!*" Jess exclaimed. "I'm just so grateful I want to hug you until I crush your bones."

Lindsay laughed. "You can do it over an early dinner," she suggested. "I have abbreviated office hours today, while Frank has to work late. Rebecca and I decided to snatch the opportunity...meet, eat and brainstorm about what we can do for Jake. Since you're family, we'd like to have you join us. I've already arranged it with Mrs. Larsen...you can drop Annie off at our house on your way to meet us."

At Rebecca's suggestion, they got together at Lord Fletcher's, a Minnetonka lakefront establishment reminiscent of an old English tavern. Charmed by the British decor, the sweeping lake view and the crackling fire that warded off the evening chill as it lit a massive brick fireplace, Jess felt she was being treated to a glimpse of her native turf.

It didn't bother her that the fare was mostly steaks, chicken and seafood—typical of stateside menus. Thanks to Lindsay and Stephen, I'm becoming quite Americanized, she thought, and then frowned slightly. The only off note in what had been a strongly upbeat day for her had been Stephen's guarded optimism when he returned her call at midmorning. Undeniably happy as he'd been about the Todds' decision, he'd warned her that they weren't out of the woods yet. It's almost as if he thinks I should continue holding my breath instead of celebrating, she thought as she raised her glass for a toast Rebecca was about to propose.

"To Annie, with fond wishes for a quick recovery…and to Chelsea for helping save her life," Rebecca said, smiling at Jess and Lindsay in turn. "And to our brother, Jake…Jess's uncle, in my book, whoever his father was. Here's hoping we can hit on a plan to help him out of his current situation."

Unfortunately, try as they would over steak-and-shrimp combos, the best they could manage was to re-hash what they knew of the evidence to date.

"I know," Rebecca, who was well known in the family for her emphasis on right-brained thinking, exclaimed. "Why don't we hold a séance and and try to contact her? By coincidence, I have a medium lined up! Her name's Irina Ivanova, and she lives in St. Paul. I interviewed her about how séances work for one of my books, and she offered to let me sit in on one. I haven't had the time to take her up on it yet. We can have her do one for us as a group…contact Mom for us!"

When Lindsay, with her physician's pragmatism, pooh-poohed the notion, Rebecca dug in her heels. "It'll be fun, whatever happens," she said. "Jess…you must attend, too. We can hold it at Mom and Dad's former home on the lake, for atmosphere. Jake isn't there right now, so it should be available. I'm sure I can talk Sterling into it."

Though Jess wasn't related to Kate, and didn't put much stock in attempting to contact the spirit world, she was keen on seeing the Fortune mansion from the inside. After all, it had been built by her American grandfather. He'd lived there for many years. According to something Lindsay had let drop, it contained several fine portraits of him. "I'd be happy to come along for the ride," she answered, "if I wouldn't be in the way."

Approached by Rebecca about the proposed séance, Sterling turned to Kate for advice. He broached the topic during lunch at a small, out-of-the-way restaurant in the quaint Victorian town of Stillwater on the banks of the St. Croix River, after giving her a rundown on the latest evidence to surface in Jake's case.

"I suppose it couldn't hurt to indulge her in this foolishness," he grumbled, digging into his cheese-and-ham soufflé. "Yet I don't really like it. If word leaked out that Jake's sisters were attempting to contact you through a medium on his behalf, the press would have a field day. His trial hasn't even started yet. And it already rates as first runner-up to the Simpson case."

Her eyes unreadable behind the oversize sunglasses she'd adopted with gray wool slacks, a jewel-toned ruana handwoven in Peru and a slouchy felt hat, Kate was deeply touched. Quirky, precious Becky missed her and longed for her advice. So did sweet, levelheaded Lindsay, or she wouldn't have agreed to go along with such a scheme. How she longed to enfold them both and tell them of her narrow escape, confess that she'd been hiding out in Minneapolis all along—right under their noses.

To turn up among the living too hastily could prove disastrous, if Sterling was to be believed. Whoever had wanted her dead might try again if they realized their first attempt had failed. She could be putting herself in mortal danger.

Yet maybe there was a way for her to communicate with them.

Always a quick study, Kate put two and two together and came up with six, including several bonus points. According to Sterling, Jake's defense attorney believed that some footprints the police had found would turn out to be those of the real killer or killers. He'd charged Gabe Devereax with reinterviewing Monica's former neighbors, on the theory that one of them had seen the person or persons in question near Monica's property on the night of the murder.

Yet he hadn't thought of everything. Neither he nor anyone else seemed to have paid any attention to the one witness who claimed to have seen Lindsay in the area!

In a way, Kate could understand it. Lindsay had been able to offer an airtight alibi. However, if I'm not mistaken, Kate thought, that woman who claimed to be Lindsay's lost twin—wrong sex, but only I and the FBI know that—bore a striking if somewhat superficial resemblance to my beautiful, brainy daughter. With her designs on the Fortune money and her determination to force her way into the family at any cost, this Tracey Ducet, or whatever her name was, might have been intent on blackmailing Jake, too. It's altogether possible she went to Monica's house that night to steal the affidavits regarding his parentage, in order to use them as a club over him.

She could share her speculation with Sterling and let him pass it on to Aaron Silberman, Kate realized—if she could get him to take it seriously. Yet, with a séance in the works, it would be a whole lot more fun to reward Becky's initiative by contacting her in person, so to speak. Kate's thoughts flew to some twenty-something friends she'd made in her undercover role as benevolent, eccentric patron of the arts Kate Anderson. Several of them worked as sound and light technicians with a local theater company.

Across the table, her old friend and attorney had stopped eating to stare at her. "Say something," he demanded in his gravelly voice. "Your expression is making me nervous."

Her slow smile raised his hackles even further. "Contrary to your take on the situation, old dear, I approve wholeheartedly of Becky's plan," she informed him. "In fact, I've decided to reward her ingenuity by putting in a holographic appearance. Some technical people I know with the St. Paul Laser Theater have the know-how and the necessary equipment to pull it off. I'm certain I can count on their help and discretion."

Like Kate, Sterling knew that holography was a technique of producing moving, three-dimensional images by means of wavefront reconstruction—essentially a process of using lasers to record, on a photographic plate, a diffraction pattern from which such images could be projected at a distance. He didn't doubt for a moment that her scheme could succeed technically, greatly enlivening the proposed séance for everyone present.

It was the chance of her getting caught in the act that so disturbed him. "This is harebrained thinking, Kate," he chided her. "However successfully your friends carry out this plan of yours from a technical standpoint, the chance of your being caught red-handed is astronomical. For all her writer's dreaminess and right-brain activity, Rebecca's no fool. And Lindsay's sharp as a tack. Young Jessica Holmes will be there, too, and she has a good head on her shoulders. You might as well run an ad in the local newspaper, announcing a comeback!"

"You're wrong...I won't get caught," she contended. "These people are pros. They can project a talking, moving image of me and then make it vanish. I'll be in a completely different room. To make things easier, I know that house like the back of my hand...every exit, every hiding place."

Evincing a typical lawyerly skepticism, Sterling objected that, once they were aware of what was going on, the special effects people might demand a hefty price for their silence.

"Wrong again," she said, in a tone that told him his attempt to dissuade her would be a futile one. "They're decent, honest human beings. I'd stake my life on it. Besides, they don't know me as Kate Fortune. They'll just think I'm connected in some way with the medium...who, incidentally, is about to achieve her greatest career success ever, thanks to my help!"

Putting their heads together, Lindsay and Jess arranged a sleepover for Annie at the Todds' house, with Frank Todd acting as the children's baby-sitter while the séance was held. On the night in question, as their mothers headed for the Fortune mansion in Jess's MG and Frank did up the supper dishes with Carter's help, the two girls were playing quietly with Chelsea's doll collection.

"Know what?" Annie asked Chelsea as they set out the latter's collection of doll dishes for a tea party.

Chelsea shook her head.

"Mummy and Dr. Steve have been kissing. They don't know I saw them."

Chelsea thought over the revelation for a moment. "Do you think they'll get married?" she asked.

Annie confessed she had no idea. But she said, "I wish they would. He makes her happy. And I like him very much."

In response, Chelsea told her friend about her cousin Michael's wedding, during which she'd acted as one of several flower girls. "Maybe if they get married you'll get to be a flower girl, too," she speculated.

Her thoughts less concerned with pageantry than with the eventual outcome of such a merger, Annie wondered aloud whether Stephen and her mother would want to live in England or remain in Minnesota once her treatment was over.

"You'll stay here," Chelsea answered decisively. "That way, we can be best friends forever, and keep on playing together."

Arriving at the Fortune mansion a half hour early, Jess and Lindsay handed their purses and coats to the housekeeper. "C'mon," Lindsay suggested as they stood at loose ends in the spacious entry hall. "We've got a few minutes to spare. I'll take you on a tour."

Curious, but more ambivalent than she'd expected to be, about her dashing American grandfather, Jess found the likeness of him that hung in his former billiard room to be the most intriguing of the lot. Dressed for breaking horses or herding cattle on the ranch she knew the family still owned in Clear Springs, Wyoming, he stood brazen and seemingly half-amused at the thought of having his portrait painted.

Depicted in jeans and a faded denim shirt, he'd called attention to his less-than-youthful waist with an oversize turquoise-and-silver Indian belt buckle, as if to say that, despite his fifty-odd years and the moderate dissipation with which he'd indulged himself, he was still firmly convinced of his own attractiveness.

Several news accounts Jess had read about the Monica Malone murder case had suggested that the aging movie star might have gotten her first hint that Jake Fortune wasn't Ben's son during an affair she had with Ben when they were both in their heyday. Supposedly their liaison had been an open secret among the movers and shakers of Minneapolis.

It seems my grandmother wasn't his only affair, Jess thought. He must have had dozens of them. As a woman who'd been wronged in the same way Kate Fortune had, without being cherished to the same extent, she felt something less than liking for the genial but arrogant man who gazed back at her from the canvas. Yet she couldn't deny her fascination with him, or stop herself searching for some evidence of a family resemblance.

They'd just finished their tour, which had included the library and family room, when Rebecca arrived with Gabe Devereax in tow. Clearly at odds with the ultra-masculine, dark-haired detective, she whispered that she'd been unable to discourage him from coming, despite her best efforts. Stephen, who had also been invited to attend, joined them a few minutes later. Putting his arms around Jess, he scanned the mansion's interior with undisguised curiosity as they waited for Rebecca's medium to arrive.

The woman—plump, graying, with affected mannerisms and a clear preference for unmatched shades of purple when it came to her wardrobe—was deposited by her driver on the mansion's front steps on schedule. She looks like somebody's eccentric, somewhat affected great-aunt, Jess thought as Rebecca introduced her to everyone. But she's not the least bit exotic, unless you count her Russian accent.

After a quick consultation with Madame Ivanova to learn her pleasure, Rebecca announced that they'd hold the séance in the formal dining room. She sent the housekeeper, Mrs. Laughlin, in search of candles as they arranged themselves around the table.

They turned off the electric lights in the room, per

the medium's instructions, once the candles Mrs. Laughlin had fetched in a pair of heavy sterling candelabra had been lit with kitchen matches. With the drapes drawn and reflected candle flame puddling and dancing in its vermeil-framed mirrors and its polished wood surfaces, the big, ornate room took on an eerie, expectant look. Sighing in the huge oaks that surrounded the house, an unusually strong breeze off the lake caused creaks and sighs that added immeasurably to the spooky atmosphere.

Madame Ivanova glanced about her with satisfaction. "Have you provided something touched or owned by the deceased?" she asked Rebecca expectantly.

Her auburn hair and patrician features, so similar to those of Kate in a portrait Jess had seen of the Fortune matriarch in the mansion's living room as to be positively striking, Rebecca handed over a gold-and-diamond wristwatch Ben had given her mother a year before his death.

Holding it in her palm for a moment and then pressing it to her forehead so as to absorb unseen vibrations from it, the medium placed the watch on the table in front of her. "Are there any specific questions you wish to ask?" she said.

Again it was Rebecca who responded. "My sister and I long to hear our mother's voice. We're hoping she can suggest some means of helping our brother Jake get through his current difficulty."

The woman nodded. "Very good. Please to join hands, close your eyes and concentrate as we try to evoke Kate Fortune's presence," she requested, reaching out to Lindsay and Rebecca, who were seated closest to her.

Despite his obvious skepticism, Gabe Devereax

grudgingly went through the motions. However, when several minutes of highly dramatized concentration and repeated requests by the medium that Kate honor them with her presence had yielded no results, he began to squirm in his chair. Finally, he couldn't take it any more. "What do you say we give up, folks?" he demanded audibly. "And admit this séance stuff is a hoax?"

Rebecca was angrily shushing him when a wavering light appeared, coalescing into a luminous approximation of Kate's form. Concealed upstairs in a seldom-used bedroom with her theatrical accomplices, Kate could hear their gasps over the temporary audio system they'd installed, hiding the miniature microphones and speakers in an antique china cabinet.

"I'm here for you, children," she intoned on cue in her unmistakable, smoky voice, swaying slightly in a high-necked evening gown she was certain her daughters would recognize.

Downstairs, in the mansion's formal dining room, everyone was agog. When the medium fainted, sagging in her chair at the head of the table, none of the participants noticed, believing she was in a trance. Only Gabe seemed able to overcome his startled fascination sufficiently to express disbelief. "I don't know how she does this," he burst out in frustration. "But I know one thing. It's a hoax!"

Furious, Rebecca dug her nails into his arm. "Be quiet!" she whispered harshly. "Or, so help me God, I'll wring your neck!"

Usually so cool and levelheaded, Lindsay was trembling. "Mom...is that really you?" she whispered, her eyes filled with tears Kate couldn't see because of the imperfect resolution of the tiny video camera that fed a black-and-white image of the room upstairs.

The hologram of Kate wavered and strengthened. "Yes, it is. What do you want of me?" she asked, realizing for the first time how poignant seeing a lifelike image of her must be for the daughters she loved.

This time, Rebecca answered. "Jake's in such trouble," she said. "What can we do for him?"

Kate nodded wisely. "I know of his problem," she assured them. "My advice...don't forget the woman who looked like Lindsay."

Dimming again until it had faded completely, her image didn't reappear. Released from the vise of Rebecca's grip, Gabe switched on the lights, causing everyone to blink, and rushed into the adjoining service pantry to look for evidence of chicanery. To his disgust, he didn't find any. He returned to the dining room at Rebecca's cry of distress, in time to see Stephen bending over Madame Ivanova, who was moaning as she regained consciousness.

"I'm going to search the house," he announced to no one in particular.

"Search all you want," Rebecca snapped, "provided you help Stephen get Madame Ivanova to her car first."

Meanwhile, Lindsay was sobbing in Jess's arms. "It was Mom...I know it was," the brown-haired pediatrician wept against her friend's shoulder. "I'd know her voice...and that dress...anyplace. Why, oh, why, did she have to die and leave us?"

Eleven

As Stephen and Gabe helped Irina Ivanova to her car and Jess tried to comfort her friends, Kate and her accomplices quickly packed up their equipment and made a clandestine getaway in the rowboat they'd moored near the Fortune dock, in a thicket of willows.

Kate sat quietly on one of the plank seats in the full-length evening gown she'd worn to parties with Ben in the early eighties, as Patrick O'Malley and Jeff Söderquist, the two technicians from the St. Paul Magic Laser Theater who'd helped her pull off her spirit-world appearance, dipped their oars into the water. The laughter gone from her face, she brooded over what she'd accomplished. She'd gotten across her message about Lindsay's fake twin, at least. And had a scapegrace giggle or two about blowing away the phony medium.

In the process, she'd hurt her beloved daughters. You ought to listen to Sterling more, she reproached herself. Self-knowledge argued that it wasn't likely to happen to any great extent.

Back onshore, Gabe had bidden good riddance to the medium. The lights of the Fortune mansion winked on one by one, like those of a cathedral being lit for a midnight service, as he stormed from room to room, looking for evidence that Kate's appearance had been a hoax. Except for a few wires that appeared to have been

stuffed hastily into a closet and didn't seem to have any
specific purpose, he came up empty-handed.

Thoroughly bent out of shape, he returned downstairs, remaining just long enough to tell Rebecca what
a fake the whole performance had been. ''Why don't
you try hanging out in the real world for a change?''
he advised her sarcastically.

Aware that her companions were sizing up their relationship, she gave him a disparaging look. ''Why
don't you leave before you wear out your welcome?''

''Don't worry, I'm out of here!''

Meanwhile, Lindsay's preparations for Chelsea's
party were complete. Since Minnesota was enjoying unusually mild fall weather as the end of September approached, she decided to hold it outdoors. The clowns
she'd hired could cavort on the lawn to their hearts'
content without bumping into the host of school friends,
neighbors and relatives on both sides of the Fortune-
Todd family she'd invited to share the occasion with
them.

That year, Chelsea's birthday would fall on a Saturday. As if to bless the eight-year-old for agreeing to
help her friend, despite the personal discomfort it might
entail, the day proved mild and sunny—ideal for all the
treats that were in store. Lake Travis shimmered in the
background, an effective foil for the deeper shades of
crimson and gold the cooler nights had caused to high-
light the green canopy of leaves that rustled overhead
as the clowns blew up balloons and linked the trees with
crepe-paper streamers. Nearby, a magician and his assistant set up for their show. The caterers Lindsay had
hired unloaded birthday cake, ice cream and fruit punch

for the children, together with champagne and hors d'oeuvres for the adults.

A steady stream of guests began arriving as 1:00 p.m. approached. Having volunteered to help look after the younger set while Stephen helped Frank tend bar for the adults, Jess was in the thick of things, wiping noses, bandaging a not-so-skinned knee and helping settle disputes. Busy as she was, she had ample opportunity to meet quite a few Fortune relatives to whom she hadn't previously been introduced.

A tender, almost wistful expression on her pretty rich-girl face, Kristina Fortune came up to Jess and followed the children's excited play with her eyes for a moment. "That's Annie, isn't it?" she asked. "The one in the pale blue party dress and matching sweater, with the cropped halo of fuzzy pale blond hair?"

Jess nodded. "The hairstyle's courtesy of her recent chemotherapy. In a few days, even the fuzz will start falling out. They have to give her another course of it, you see, plus radiation, before they can do the transplant."

Kristina stared. "I'm so sorry," she said after a moment. "People get awfully sick from radiation and chemotherapy, don't they? A little kid like that...it must be tough."

Kristina had just headed for the house, murmuring something vague about powdering her nose, when Lindsay introduced Jess to Kristina's half brother, Grant McClure. "Like Kristina, Grant's here for Nate's and Barbara's silver wedding anniversary, which was yesterday," Lindsay said. "So you don't get confused, he's Barbara's son from her first marriage. He spends most of his time on his ranch in Wyoming, so we hardly ever get to see him."

Deeply tanned, with stunning blue eyes that looked as if they were used to gazing at wider horizons, the tall rancher grinned. "Hi, Jessica," he said. "I saw you talking to my sister, Kristina, a minute ago. Typically, she's wandered off again. I've been hanging around, waiting to take her to the airport."

Jess wasn't terribly surprised to catch a hint of indulgence in his tone. Kristina's family really *did* dote on her, it seemed. "I think she headed up to the house, to use the powder room," she supplied.

His grin broadened. "That'll take a while. You know, Jessica…I was very happy to hear Chelsea will be able to provide a match for your daughter. I'd have been tested myself if I'd thought it would do any good. Of course, since I'm not really a relative…"

As they chatted, a separate but linked chapter in the Fortune drama was unfolding on the small, somewhat overgrown lakefront estate that abutted the Todds' property on the opposite side from Stephen's. Empty for months, the house had long been home to a friend and client of Sterling's who was currently residing in Europe. Learning that the owner had given him a key in case of emergency, Kate had demanded he loan it to her.

"Haven't you been in enough trouble lately, appropriating the séance for your own ends and causing the medium to pass out, without fomenting a ruckus at the birthday party, too?" Sterling had protested, adding, when she stared, "You're damn right Gabe told me about her fainting spell!"

Determined to win his cooperation at all costs, she'd played on his sympathies. "It's to be held outdoors, and my whole *family* will be there," she'd wheedled. "And I do miss them so. I promise on my word of honor, old dear...I'll remain concealed, content myself with whatever I can see through a pair of binoculars. Or a telescope.'' She'd gotten her way, of course. Driving her over in his Lincoln, Sterling had unlocked the front door for her himself, promising to return in an hour. As Jess ended her conversation with Grant McClure to supervise a game and Lindsay stood exclaiming over her nephew Michael's baby, Kate was seated at one of the large, old-fashioned house's half-shuttered windows, observing to her heart's content. The telescope she trained on her relatives had come with the territory. Sterling's client had owned it for years, to watch the year-round parade of boaters and swimmers, skaters and ice fishermen.

Loving her large, extended family as she did, she found it a deeply pleasurable, if somewhat lonely, pursuit to spy on the host of new in-laws a bumper crop of romances had produced, and note the growth of the youngest family members. But it was her own children—Jake, Nate, Lindsay and Rebecca—whom she missed the most. I hate being separated from them, she acknowledged. Though I try my best to keep up with what's going on in their lives, I'm falling so short it's criminal.

Attempting to put a rein on her emotions, she reviewed her reasons for going underground. They were still valid. The necessity for keeping up this masquerade had damn well better end soon, she thought. Yet she knew that, if it didn't, she was tough enough to let events take their course for a while longer, before making her reappearance.

Predictably, when Sterling showed up to collect the key and drive her home, she wasn't ready to go. Granting her a little more time, he took a seat opposite hers.

As she turned the telescope this way and that, focusing on different family members, they discussed the progress that had been made by her children and grandchildren as a result of keepsakes or property she'd left them in her will.

"You were right...my absence has let them take full credit for the changes they've made in their lives," she admitted, stroking him a little in exchange for the favor he'd done her. "Too often, in the past, they looked to me for guidance. Of course, Lindsay's always fine. Rebecca, too, though I wish she had a man in her life. After twenty-five years, Nate's still happy with Barbara. Or would be, if it weren't for his constant clashes with Jake."

Deeply fond of Kate, despite his grumbling, Sterling knew how concerned she was about her oldest son. In his opinion, she had good reason to feel as she did. "What *about* Jake?" he asked. "Will getting through the mess he's in without you help strengthen his character, too?"

Like clouds scudding across the sky in advance of a stiff breeze, sadness and worry flitted across her expressive face. Jake was in the most jeopardy, and might seem to need her intervention the most. Yet she sensed that its absence might benefit him most, as well. "Without even knowing who his real father was, he always felt at a disadvantage in the family, and he leaned on me psychologically," she pointed out. "Now he can't. He'll have to sink or swim on his own. I'm betting it'll be the latter."

Sterling regarded her with admiration. "You're a strong old broad, did you know that, Kate?" he asked.

"So I've been told," she answered with a grin.

Her longtime friend and attorney wasn't finished

speaking his piece. "What you need is a man to settle you down...and shake you up once in a while," he allowed. "One of these days, I might take on the task myself."

Kate's grin broadened. Though she remained in her chair, separate from him and fully in charge of her own space, she wasn't totally unavailable. At the right time and place, she admitted to herself, *I might be open to what he's proposing.*

"Who knows? One of these days I might let you...if you're sure you've still got the kind of fire it takes to please a woman under that snowcapped chimney of yours," she shot back before returning her gaze to the telescope's eyepiece.

Back at the party, Lindsay frowned slightly as she spoke to Natalie and her new husband. A tiny flash of reflected sunlight from one of the dining room windows in the empty house next door had caused her to squint. *It's as if someone's in there, training a pair of binoculars in our direction...watching us,* she thought. *Yet I know for a fact that Bernice McDermott's still in Europe. We got a postcard from her just last week.*

It occurred to her that a supermarket tabloid might have invaded their privacy from a distance to augment an exposé its editors were planning on the Fortune family because of Jake's involvement in the Monica Malone murder case. Maybe they'd dispatched a photographer to take pictures of her daughter's birthday party with a telephoto lens. If so, whether or not they had permission to use her neighbor's house, their paparazzilike behavior wouldn't go unchallenged!

Excusing herself, she cut across the yard without pausing to tell Frank where she was going and brushed through a hedge to emerge in Bernice McDermott's drive. To her amazement, Sterling's Lincoln was parked there. She recognized the license plate.

A few more determined steps brought her to the front door, where she leaned on the buzzer, completely unaware of the fright she was giving her supposedly deceased parent.

Following a brief delay, the family attorney appeared.

"What's up, Sterling?" she demanded with a skeptical edge to her voice. "Did you go to the wrong house by mistake? The party's next door!"

Thinking on his feet with his customary agility, the silver-haired attorney explained that his client, her neighbor, was weighing a sale of the property. He'd agreed to show it to an extremely private potential purchaser on her behalf.

Forcing herself to remain hidden in the dining room, Kate was overcome with a second, more powerful wave of nostalgia for her old life as she listened to Lindsay's sweet voice. Still, she remained steadfast in her agreement that it wasn't yet time to show herself. Some of her children and grandchildren still had a lot to learn. Her attempted murder—and the murder of her archrival, which had been laid at Jake's door—needed to be resolved, as well.

Still convinced something fishy was in the works, as Bernice McDermott hadn't mentioned anything about putting the house on the market and Sterling had seemed so determined to block her entry, Lindsay quizzed him a little further. Citing attorney-client privilege, he was anything but forthcoming. Eventually, she had to return to the party. She was the hostess, after all. Plus, Chelsea would soon be opening her presents. Yet she continued to keep an eye on the house, curious about her potential neighbor and the need for so much secrecy. When Kate came out, heavily veiled, something hauntingly familiar about her carriage resonated, causing the brown-haired pediatrician to stare.

I wonder what faded but fabled movie star might be moving in next door to us, she thought, wishing she could button down the sense of déjà vu she felt. At least it wouldn't be the evil Monica Malone. On balance, she decided to be grateful.

The night before Annie was scheduled to return to the hospital for her radiation and chemotherapy, Jess and Stephen took her to see a popular children's movie about a klutzy dog's misadventures. Despite the hilarity it evoked, as they laughed together over popcorn and sodas, an underlying edge of tension haunted them.

Carefully, in tandem, they'd explained to Annie what the treatment would entail. The rest of her hair would fall out and she'd be very sick—maybe even sicker than she'd been during her original treatment. Afterward, of course, she'd get better. Once she was well, she probably wouldn't have to return to the hospital as an in-patient again.

"Will Chelsea and I get to share a room?" she'd asked doubtfully, aware that her friend would be going to the hospital too, though Jess wasn't sure she fully comprehended the connection.

"Because of the danger of infection before your new immune system takes hold," Stephen had explained, "you'll have to stay under a laminar-flow hood in one of the 'clean rooms,' the way you did last time. Despite its role in keeping you free of germs, visitors have to be limited, because they can bring infection with them. Though Chelsea will be on the same floor, you and she won't be able to see each other."

The memory of her first hospital stay still vivid in her mind, Annie had begun to weep. "I'm fine, Mummy," she'd pleaded. "Tell him. My head hasn't been hot for a long, long time. I don't *need* to take any more of the nasty medicine!"

When morning came, it was as they'd feared. Tears streaming down her cheeks, Annie balked. She tried to pull away and run back to the cottage when Jess attempted to fasten her into Stephen's Mercedes for the trip to the hospital. Stephen watched helplessly as she corraled and calmed her daughter, having been through a similar incident with David.

Ultimately, because she was such a well-behaved child, they didn't have to drag her in kicking and screaming. Yet the ache of reproach in her eyes nearly killed Jess as she helped her precious daughter don a hospital gown preparatory to being wheeled downstairs to radiology for her first total-body irradiation treatment.

Her anguish only increased when, late that afternoon, the IV nurse arrived in Annie's room to insert a catheter needle in one of the large veins in her chest. The catheter would function like an access road for the chemotherapy that would kill off diseased cells, antibiotic treatment, the ongoing administration of needed blood products and the infusion of her donated marrow. Because her immune system had to be a blank slate for the new marrow to engraft and give her a healthy, fresh start in life, no diseased cells could remain to reinfect it. This time, her dose of chemotherapy would be a heavy one.

Already placed on electronic heart-monitoring equipment because chemotherapy sometimes weakened the heart muscle, Annie lay mostly still, though she whimpered softly when the needle bit into her vein. Her protests used up, she was behaving like a model victim.

As the toxic but ultimately healing chemicals began dripping into her body, causing her usually bright eyes to glaze over with lassitude and her fuzzy blond head to loll weakly on her pillow, Jess thought her heart would break. If only I could go through this in her place, she thought, scrambling to retrieve a kidney-shaped metal basin from Annie's bedside table as her vomiting started. I'd change places with her in a hot second.

Stephen's reaction to the situation was, naturally, somewhat different from Jess's. As a physician, he'd learned to keep his fears and worries locked up inside. However, he loved Annie, too. Her misery cut him deeply, even as it recalled his own little boy's suffering and sparked his fear of sustaining another devastating loss.

Coupled with his fears for Annie was his soul-deep anxiety that he'd fail Jess emotionally when the chips were down. Each time she let herself lean on him, after first glancing toward the hall to make sure none of his colleagues would catch her in the act, his terror renewed itself. He'd failed his ex-wife, hadn't he? Where was the guarantee that, on the second go-round, he'd behave any differently?

Frightful as it was, Annie's nausea had subsided somewhat by the third day following her chemotherapy, when Lindsay dropped by to check on her and relay a report from Rebecca.

It seemed that Detective Harbing was a bit skeptical about Kate's spirit giving them clues. However, his department had begun investigating the leads she'd provided. It was just possible that Tracey Ducet and her odious boyfriend would soon find themselves answering investigators' questions.

In a related development that had cheered Jake and given Aaron Silberman additional ammunition for his defense, several hairs found at the murder scene and analyzed by the crime lab didn't fit Jake's DNA pattern, or Monica's. Neither did they match any belonging to other persons known to have lawfully spent time at her house. At least one of them, a natural strawberry-blond color, had been dyed a medium-to-dark-brown shade that closely matched Lindsay's—and the Ducet woman's—tresses.

"Jake's immensely heartened by the news," Lindsay reported. "According to Rebecca, he would have taken the trouble to be tested if he'd thought there was even a remote chance he could provide a match. But you know, the most incredible thing is the way he phoned Nate from jail to apologize for his part in past conflicts. He even admitted that he can see the wisdom of Nate taking his place at the helm of Fortune Industries for the time being! He's promised to do whatever he can to cooperate!"

Having hung out with the Fortunes for the better part of two and a half months, Jess knew of the rivalry between the brothers, and the fact that it caused their sisters a good deal of distress, in addition to being detrimental for business. "That's great, Lin," she answered with as much enthusiasm as she could muster. "I know how much their cooperation and friendship means to you. Now, if only we can get through the next couple of weeks in one piece..."

As if it had been waiting for just such an opening to

emerge, the anxiety Lindsay felt over the donor procedure Chelsea would have to undergo showed its face.

"Stephen mentioned at lunch that it would probably be appropriate to harvest Chelsea's bone marrow the day after tomorrow," she said. "As you know, we've been able to wait this long because, with an incredible five out of six antigens matching, Stephen didn't have to check her marrow before giving the procedure the green light. Though at first I was relieved about that, the waiting has made things fairly intense for us. I know you have far greater fears than mine wrapped up in this, Jess. And I feel for you…more than words can express. But I can't deny that I'm a little apprehensive over what my baby will have to go through."

Twelve

Taking some time off from their busy his-and-hers careers, Chelsea's parents brought her to the hospital as arranged. Sedated and wheeled into the operating room so that the donor process could get under way, she was prepped and on the table when Stephen entered from the scrub area in pale blue surgical garments and sterile gloves. The operating room crew waited in readiness as he gazed down at his eight-year-old neighbor for a moment.

It wasn't often that the bone-marrow donor for a leukemia patient was a child of such tender years. Because of Chelsea's courage and generosity, Annie would have a chance to grow up and marry someday, though her chemotherapy had already made it likely that she'd never have children of her own. He vowed to do what he could to make her procedure go as smoothly as possible—for her sake and that of her parents.

You're a brave girl, Chelsea, he told the unconscious child silently as he held out his hand for the proper instrument to make four or five minute incisions in her pelvic area. *Your parents are raising a magnificent little person.*

Having harvested bone marrow for transplanting too many times to count, Stephen was able to draw out the necessary pint of precious marrow in less than forty minutes. Giving Chelsea a pat on the shoulder that she might or might not register in her unconscious state, he sent her to recovery, with orders for an infusion of antibiotics, plus a pint of blood she'd had drawn and stored in the hospital blood bank the day after her decision was made.

A minute later, still in his scrubs, though he'd peeled off his surgical gloves, he was reassuring Frank and Lindsay in the family waiting room. "Your daughter's quite a trooper," he told them. "I stopped to see her before the nurse sedated her, and she didn't seem particularly awed by the hospital. Maybe she'll grow up to be a doctor, poor kid."

Relieved though she was that Chelsea's part in the effort to save Annie was over, Lindsay was still slightly tremulous. "At the moment, she's thinking of becoming a ballerina," she said with a shaky smile. "She asked me to ask you...how soon can she return to her ballet classes?"

Before Annie's transplant could take place, Chelsea's bone marrow had to be strained repeatedly through a series of fine screens to remove blood and bone fragments. It was thoroughly purified by the time an IV nurse brought it to her bedside in a sterile plastic pouch and hooked it up to her catheter while Stephen watched.

Jess couldn't stop tears of worry and jubilation from flowing as she observed in the mask, gown and gloves she'd be required to wear whenever she spent time with Annie in the special "clean room" that was designed to keep her free of infection. It was finally happening! And it seemed so simple, after all the begging and pleading she'd done to bring it about. The plastic pouch containing Chelsea's priceless gift seemed just one more addition to the metal IV stand that was already hung with similar pouches like some high-tech Christmas tree.

The fact that Annie would never make her a grandmother without adopting, and the possibility that, at some point in the future, she might need cataract surgery, seemed like a small price to pay for the opportunity to grow up, choose a career, fall in love and marry. Of course, Jess knew they weren't out of the woods yet. Despite all Stephen's precautions, an infection could crop up and ravage her body before her new immune system was ready to deal with it.

The specter of graft-versus-host disease also lingered to worry them. Because of the single antigen in Chelsea's marrow that *hadn't* matched Annie's, there was always the possibility that the girl's borrowed immune system would recognize certain of her tissues as "an invader" and launch an attack. If that happened, Stephen had warned, it would be regarded as a serious, possibly life-threatening complication. Hugging herself, she prayed that their trip through the valley of the shadows would result in her beloved child's survival.

Chelsea was discharged in the morning. Though she couldn't enter Annie's room, she was allowed to wave to her from the hall. As the day after that dawned, and the next, ushering in the end of Annie's first week in the hospital, it looked as if her transplant would be successful. Her appetite spoiled by the chemotherapy, which had made her mouth sore and caused extensive gastrointestinal upset, she willingly took small sips of water and gave her mother an occasional wan smile before drifting into another of the naps Stephen said would prove restorative. No fever or chills developed.

Strung out as a result of her inability to snatch much

restful sleep in the reclining lounger beside Annie's bed, Jess noticed Stephen had dark circles beneath his eyes. Perhaps he was suffering from a similar problem. She was also aware that he'd begun staying later at the hospital, as if he were determined to be on hand if any problems arose. Despite Annie's progress, he continued to list her condition as "guarded."

So cautious and ambivalent, the word seemed an apt description of his emotional commitment to them. He's just worried, as I am, Jess told herself, attempting to explain his somehow tentative manner whenever they had a moment to embrace.

Nine days after the infusion of Annie's new bone marrow, Stephen did an aspiration test, and informed Jess that it was beginning to function. Exhausted and relieved, though he'd cautioned that this was the point in her treatment where graft-versus-host disease would be mostly likely to rear its ugly head, Jess let herself fall into a relatively sound sleep that night in her imitation-leather lounger beside Annie's bed. A slight sound shortly after 3:00 a.m. awakened her. Two nurses with a flashlight were bending over her daughter.

"Her temperature's gone up," the older of the two women whispered with a frown. "And she has a skin rash. We'd better call Dr. Hunter."

No amount of terrified pleading could get them to say anything further. Jess would have to speak to her daughter's physician if she wanted more information.

It was like being thrown a lifeline when she learned that Stephen would come in to the hospital in person instead of issuing orders by phone. Her relief soon sagged, however, when she saw the look on his face as he entered her daughter's room.

"Stephen..." she cried, a universe of hope and fear contained in the single word.

"Give me a moment to look her over, Jess," he requested, holding her at arm's length.

Retreating with difficulty until he'd finished examining Annie and scanning the chart her nurses were keeping on her, she suppressed the question that lay like a weight against her chest until he'd issued orders for Annie's treatment.

At that point, he summoned her out into the hall.

"Is this the graft-versus-host thing you were talking about?" she asked before he could speak.

Heartsore, Stephen nodded in the affirmative. "She has all the symptoms, I'm afraid. There are three sites the donor immune system usually chooses to attack...the skin, the liver, and the gastrointestinal tract. She's already having skin problems. I suspect her digestive system will be involved, too, irritated as it was by her chemotherapy. Though there's no sign of jaundice yet, I've ordered a liver-function test."

"I was hoping that, with five of six antigens matching, she wouldn't have to worry about this," Jess protested.

"Five out of six is very good...far better than we could reasonably have expected to find, given that the donor wasn't an identical twin. Unfortunately, the unmatched antigen set is the one doctors refer to as D, for want of a better label. It determines the level of immune response and rejection of foreign tissue."

She didn't want a scientific explanation. What she craved was some form of reassurance and comfort from him. "You said some people *die* from this kind of thing, if the reaction is severe enough," she reminded him, silently begging him to contradict himself.

He had to be honest with her, no matter how much he'd have preferred to deliver the promises she wanted to hear. "Some do," he agreed, his heart breaking. "Annie has her youth and the five matched antigen sets going for her. If it's any comfort, studies have shown that patients who survive this kind of episode have the strongest remissions."

The way he was talking scared her to death.

"Stephen!" she cried. "I don't want to lose her...."

It's here. It's happened, he thought in anguish. Annie could die in my care, though I'll do my damnedest not to let her, with every imperfect treatment currently available to us. He couldn't help it if seeing her so gravely ill beneath her sterile hospital coverlet with seven or eight plastic-packs hooked to her IV stand, dripping fluid into her catheter, brought David's battle back to him and made him want to retreat to save himself.

"Nearly half of all allogeneic transplant patients get graft-versus-host complications, and most of them don't die," he said, retreating a little farther behind the mask he'd donned to avoid spreading germs to his young patient. "We're giving her a battery of drugs to prevent it, and I've asked that the dosage be increased. Why don't you walk down to the family lounge area and stretch out for a while, Jess? One of the orderlies can get you a blanket."

"I want to be with Annie!"

His husky, Minnesota-inflected voice, which had whispered so many love words to her, took on a gentle but almost impersonal note. "I've asked one of the nurses to bathe her every ten minutes to bring down her fever," he said. "You'd only be in the way."

Aware that he was withdrawing from her emotionally, and unwilling to do anything that would be detrimental to Annie's care, Jess followed his suggestion with great reluctance. Emerging half an hour later, she asked the head nurse where Dr. Hunter had gone.

"Back home to get some more sleep, I imagine," the middle-aged woman answered. "Try to do the same if you can, Mrs. Holmes. We'll take good care of your daughter."

Short of checking the physicians' parking lot, or paging him, Jess was forced to accept the woman's response. Stephen's the man I love—the man I thought loved me—and he's left me in the lurch just when I need him most, she thought. It's as if we'd never dated, never been intimate. He seemed warmer, friendlier, the day I brought Annie to the emergency room.

Neither she nor the head nurse on the hematology floor had any idea that Stephen was still in the building, stretched out in the doctor's lounge, with his beeper at his elbow.

When she overheard her parents discussing the news about Annie, Chelsea was distraught. "I thought what I did would help her, not *hurt* her," she protested tearfully, scrambling onto her father's lap.

It was all Frank could do to comfort her, explaining that what had happened to Annie happened to quite a few transplant recipients—nearly half of those who didn't have an identical twin to donate. "Once she gets better, this graft-versus-host thing could turn out to be a blessing," he said, hoping he wasn't sugarcoating the situation too much. "That's because it usually gets rid of any remaining cancer cells the chemotherapy didn't wipe away."

A few miles away, having heard via the family grapevine about Jake's more reasonable attitude toward Nate, Erica was paying another visit to the jail. In a tender, unguarded moment, she told her estranged husband that she'd always be there for him, whether they returned to their marriage or not.

"After five children and nearly thirty-three years together, we ought to remain good friends, at least," she said.

The pressure he'd felt for years to live up to some idealized notion of him that she carried around in her head seemed to fall away, and suddenly Jake felt tenderness. If she could see him sunk so low, yet still care about him, there might be hope for them.

"Maybe even more than that, huh?" he asked, wishing he could kiss her pretty mouth. The see-through barrier that separated them was in the way. "The way you've stood by me, come to see me...I've really appreciated it."

After she'd gone, matching her palms to his in a parody of touch that was a substitute for the embrace they both coveted, he sat quietly, thinking over his life and future more calmly than he had in years. If I can prove my innocence and get out of this mess, he promised himself, I'm going to make some changes. I'll appreciate my family more. And do what I can to realize the dreams I had as a boy—at least those aspects of them that are still open to a man of my age.

Frantic when Annie didn't seem to be getting any better and Stephen seemed to be avoiding her, Jess unburdened herself to Lindsay one afternoon. "He acts as if he'd prefer to forget that we were ever intimate," she said miserably. "Whenever I try to talk to him about Annie, his answers are highly technical. I feel more awkward talking to him than I would to a physician I barely knew. What on earth did I do to make him treat me this way?''

To her surprise, a look of understanding appeared in Lindsay's sympathetic brown eyes. "It seems to me that the way Stephen's behaving is only natural," she responded, "given the fact that he lost his eight-year-old son, David, to an inoperable brain tumor two years ago, then suffered through a divorce over conflicts that resulted from his death. Letting you and Annie past the wall he built around his heart at that time must have seemed a tremendous risk to him. Yet he took it for your sake. The fact that Annie's so sick and he's responsible for helping her get better... Well, you see what I mean.''

Stunned, Jess couldn't hide the fact that she'd known nothing whatever about Stephen's loss. "He never breathed a word to me about it," she confessed. "And I never guessed. My God, Lindsay. Imagine how difficult this must be for him...like losing his son all over again! I've got to find him...let him know that I understand.''

Scouring the halls for Stephen, Jess came up empty-handed. She'd decided to seek out one of the hospital chaplains instead, for advice, when she spotted him on one of the curving benches in Minn-Gen's small nondenominational chapel. His head was bent as if he were praying. Courage helped her walk softly to him and place a gentle hand on his shoulder.

His pain was evident as he turned to her. "I've done all I can, Jess," he said with a catch in his voice. "Maybe someone else will agree to take a hand.''

The chapel was empty except for them, and she slid onto the bench beside him, facing the artist-designed brass basin, with a bubbling fountain, that was the chapel's centerpiece. It seemed the most natural thing in the world to rest one hand on his knee, establishing a bridge of touch.

"Lindsay told me everything...about David, the way he died, and the reasons Brenda gave for divorcing you," she whispered. "It's helped me understand a lot of things. Whatever happens, I want you to know that I realize you've done everything possible for Annie. And that I'll always care about you just as much."

Murmuring something about being grateful for friends like Lindsay, Stephen couldn't seem to overcome his reluctance to bare his feelings to her. He hated to confess what he still regarded as his failure to be there for Brenda when she'd needed him. He didn't want to seek Jess's sympathy for his own unresolved loss, when she already had so much to deal with.

Yet he didn't want to lose her, either. Or to push her away emotionally, as Brenda had claimed he'd pushed her. Succumbing to instinct, he put his arms around her in a bone-crushing hug.

"I want you, Jess," he confessed. "I want to make a life with you and Annie. You'll never know how much. I'm just not sure I can be a good husband to you and the kind of father Annie needs. I doubt if my ex-wife would think so. There's no guarantee I won't clam up...pull away from you whenever the going gets rough. Or that you'll be able to put up with the demands of my profession."

A little knowledge can make for an awful lot of wisdom, Jess thought. Instead of pushing him to make a commitment he wasn't ready to make, she told him that, for the time being, his arms around her would be enough. "I'm going to need them as I continue to hold my breath and pray for Annie's recovery," she said.

Stephen tightened his embrace, grateful for her restraint and open-mindedness. "That doesn't seem like much to ask."

They rode the elevator up to the hematology floor together a short time later. In light of what she'd learned, Jess hung back, giving the professional man in him sufficient space to conduct his examination of her daughter.

His blue eyes seemed lighter, freer of torment, than they had in quite a while when he finished and turned to her. "The change in her condition is slight," he said with cautious elation. "But I think I see some improvement."

By morning, that improvement was even more evident. Propped up slightly in her bed, Annie was asking one of the nurses for something to drink when Jess awoke after another restless night spent in the chair beside her bed. *My baby's going to be all right!* she exulted, getting to her feet and bending over to place a relieved kiss through her mask on Annie's rapidly balding head. *For the first time in what seems an eternity, her prognosis is close to that of an ordinary child.*

Afraid to let herself relax and believe at an emotional level that Annie was really out of danger—that she'd grow up to be a strong, healthy woman someday—despite her obvious progress, Jess refused to be pried from her bedside, even for sleep.

With other patients to care for, some of them quite ill, Stephen couldn't be with her as much as he wanted to. Nor did he feel free to suggest that she spend a night with him at his house. At the moment, Annie had to be her first priority.

It was a perfect example of the tug-of-war that had existed in his marriage—between his responsibility for his patients and his personal life. It had been a serious problem even before David became ill, and only worsened thereafter. Though he'd told her a little more about how it had been since their talk in the chapel, he didn't know how she really felt.

After everything she'd been through, including Annie's illness and her unhappy first marriage, which she'd finally discussed with him in one of the few private moments they'd had together, was it fair to ask her understanding of his predicament—to hold meals and cancel plans, do most of the parenting herself, in deference to his work?

I'd like to have a child with her, a little brother or sister for Annie, he thought. But it might add to the already heavy burden she'd have to shoulder.

Kate was prowling the confines of her penthouse that evening, after her maid went to bed, when Sterling paid her an unexpected call.

"Turn on your TV," he directed without preamble. "We've just had another break in the Monica Malone murder case...one you'll definitely want to hear about."

Breathless with anticipation in her red silk oriental pajamas and matching satin mules, she switched on the set with the remote control while he poured them each a Scotch from her liquor cabinet. The local news came on a minute or two later. To her amazement, the top story concerned the vial of Secret Youth Formula that had been stolen from Fortune Cosmetics in one of a series of mysterious break-ins at the lab many months earlier.

The missing vial, still tagged with a Fortune Cos-

metics label that bore several scrawled notations in the
all-but-illegible handwriting of the company's chief
chemist and director of research, Nick Valkov, her
granddaughter Caroline's husband, had been found in
the late Monica Malone's residence by none other than
the police. Apparently thrown for a loop by the random
bits of evidence that continued to surface in the case,
pointing to the possibility that they might have arrested
the wrong man, they'd secured a search warrant and
given the mansion another thorough going-over.

Exchanging a split-second look of incredulity with
Sterling, Kate returned her gaze to the screen.

"The vial, reported stolen last year, was jumbled in
a shoe box with various other bottles of brand-name
perfumes and skin lotions," the TV news anchor was
saying. "It had been shoved under a bathroom sink.
Police won't say what, if any, bearing its recovery
might have on the trial of Jacob Fortune, CEO of the
cosmetics firm's parent company, Fortune Industries,
for Miss Malone's murder."

"Amazing!" Kate exclaimed with a little shudder,
pressing the mute button as the newscast moved on to
a wrangle over zoning. "Monica was behind those
break-ins! Obviously she wanted to stop us from suc-
ceeding with the formula. Maybe she was behind my
plane crash, too. If she'd commit burglary, why should
she stop at murder?"

"I shouldn't wonder if you're right," Sterling agreed,
"though we can't be sure without a thorough investigation. The other big question is—"

"What this will mean to Jake." Having remained
standing throughout the news segment on the vial's recovery, Kate came over and perched on the edge of an
easy chair, facing him. "Does it give him another mo-

tive for killing Monica?'' she asked. ''Or point in another direction?''

In Sterling's opinion, the effect of this latest discovery was still up for grabs. Identifying Monica as the thief would go a long way toward establishing her as a determined enemy who wanted to ruin the Fortunes and bring down Fortune Industries. Unfortunately, that didn't exculpate Jake from killing her—perhaps in retaliation for blackmailing him.

''I plan to initiate a civil suit to recover the vial, which the police will almost certainly want to retain as evidence,'' he added. ''If nothing else, it'll help establish our side as the aggrieved party.''

Day by day, Annie was improving as, outside her hospital room window, the brilliant foliage that was Minneapolis's annual glory reached its peak and began to drift downward, to rustle on the sidewalk. Sitting up in bed for short periods of time, she graduated from intravenous nourishment to soup and gelatin and then to a regular diet, which to her delight, one sunny day, included a cheeseburger. She began to show a renewed interest in coloring books, the plastic toys Stephen had given her and her favorite cartoons on television, and to nag Jess about returning to the cottage, which had become a second home to her.

The results of her aspiration tests were everything they could have hoped. After causing her so much risk and discomfort, her new immune system had settled down to allow a solid graft to form. Her chances for a complete and permanent remission were excellent.

Compelled by her elation to give Stephen a grateful hug when he outlined Annie's prognosis and said that, if her progress continued, she could go home by Halloween, Jess kept the embrace light. Though they'd reached an understanding the day she discovered him agonizing over Annie and their situation in the hospital chapel, she realized it was a tentative one. He'd confessed to wanting a life with them. Yet instinct told her he was still grappling with his concern that he wouldn't measure up as a stepfather and husband.

Since Annie's admission to the hospital, they hadn't made love or spent much private time together, despite the fact that, once her daughter was on the mend, Jess had begun driving home to the cottage each night for a shower and a good night's sleep. In part, that was because she'd decided to give Stephen as much room as he needed. Annie's recovery from leukemia and her bout with graft-versus-host disease had restored a place of calm that usually existed in her soul. If Stephen's love and trust could grow organically, in a similar place, things might work out for them the way she wanted.

She'd come to another decision, as well. Having insisted she didn't want anything from the Fortunes but bone marrow for her daughter, she'd traded on their hospitality long enough. Though she'd remain in Minneapolis until Annie's follow-up care was complete and she knew where she and Stephen were headed, she'd rent a place of her own. A charming two-bedroom apartment had just become available for sublease near the hospital, where, for the next six months, at least, Annie would be going for tests on a regular basis. Putting down a deposit of one month's rent, she told the landlord they'd move in by the eighth of November.

Except for the pin oaks, which would retain their brown, withered leaves for most of the winter, the trees were bare, and the weather had turned decidedly nippy by Halloween. Walking on air because her little girl would be coming home with her later that morning, Jess had planned a quiet dinner celebration to take place that evening, when Annie had settled in and taken a lengthy nap. Just the Todds, Stephen and Rebecca had been invited. Chelsea and Carter would have ample time for after-school trick-or-treating first.

Before driving to the hospital to collect Annie, Jess hung the cottage's living room with crepe-paper streamers, balloons and a giant Welcome Home! sign she'd had made at a local print shop. The theme was orange and black, as befitted the American holiday.

Tears prickled her eyelids when Stephen came to Annie's room to do her final inpatient assessment. "You're as good as new, sweetheart," he told the five-year-old finally, smiling as he lowered his stethoscope.

Aware that her departure was imminent, a number of the nurses who'd cared for the plucky little girl and grown fond of her had crowded into her room for the occasion. "Don't forget us!" and "Come visit us anytime!" were two of the injunctions Jess heard as the head nurse presented her daughter with an enormous stuffed dog.

"This doggie can stand in for the one you left in England, until you see him again," the woman explained as Annie gave him a hug and Jess recorded the moment with her camera.

Understandably tired by the time they reached the cottage and she saw her welcome-home sign, Annie didn't object to being tucked beneath the covers. Jess had plenty of time to make chili and chocolate cake for the party, and pack a few boxes with the belongings they'd collected for their move.

Annie was up, reclining on one of the lattice-print couches with an afghan over her knees, when the Todds and their children, who were dressed for Halloween as an Indian princess and a pirate, came over around 6:00 p.m.

Rebecca showed up a few minutes later, bearing picture books for Annie and a loaf of homemade bread. But there was still no sign of Stephen, who'd phoned to say he was running late. I wonder if he's busy with a patient—or still keeping his distance, though the biggest stumbling block to our relationship has been removed, Jess thought.

Caught up in dealing with a newly admitted thalassemia patient, Stephen finally managed to leave the hospital around the time Jess, Annie and their guests were sitting down to dinner in the cottage's kitchen. This is a perfect example of what Jess will face if she agrees to spend her life with me, he thought with a rueful shake of his head. Still, he planned to ask. If she could forgive the way he'd waited out the rigors of Annie's treatment before proposing, maybe he could forgive himself.

They'd almost finished eating by the time he arrived, after stopping at his house to collect the diamond he'd bought for Jess nearly a month earlier. She greeted him with a hug—light and undemanding, the way all her hugs had been since their talk during the darkest days of Annie's allergic reaction. I want more than that from her. A lot more, he thought, the ferocity of his longing bursting through the fetters he'd placed on it. I want to make love to her all night long, until we're both gasping for breath.

Doing his best to push down the tumult of emotions in him until the proper moment came for him to reveal them, he planted a kiss on Annie's forehead and greeted the Todds and Rebecca before disappearing to use the washroom. About to return to the kitchen and partake of the meal Jess had prepared, he happened to glance into her bedroom. And saw the boxes she'd packed for the move he knew nothing about.

As a result of his vacillation, she'd decided to return to England without a word to him!

Jess could tell something was wrong the moment he returned to the kitchen and took his place at the table. Ostensibly hungry, and in an agreeable if somewhat keyed-up mood when he'd arrived, he refused her excellent chili to brood over a mug of black coffee and take very little part in the conversation.

Even Annie noticed it. "Are you all right, Dr. Steve?" she asked with something of her customary verve. "Or do you want Mummy to take your temperature?"

Clearly aware of the undercurrent that had developed between Jess and Stephen, Rebecca and the Todds bade them a premature good-night as soon as the meal was over and they'd helped clear the table, despite Chelsea's and Carter's objections. Yet Stephen wasn't able to accost Jess about his discovery just yet. First she had to help Annie brush her teeth, change into pajamas and get back into bed for some quiet time with one of the books Rebecca had brought her.

"All right, let's have it," she demanded, returning to the living room. "You've been glowering at me like a thundercloud since you arrived."

She looked so beautiful standing there with her hands on her hips, in her lapis wool slacks and matching sweater, with fire glinting in her big brown eyes and roses blazing in her cheeks—like some spirited English damsel of old, confronting her angry Viking lover. He longed to sweep her up in his arms and tell her exactly how it would be with them. They'd marry the moment they could get a license. She and Annie would come to live with him. Herkie would be shipped from London by air express.

"Not quite since then," he pointed out.

"So...tell me."

"You might say I'm a little upset by the prospect of you and Annie returning to England," he growled. "When I saw those boxes in your bedroom—"

Jess's eyes widened. "Actually—" she suddenly sounded very cool and British "—I've rented an apartment near the hospital. Though Lindsay and Rebecca urged me to, it didn't seem right to stay here indefinitely after assuring the Fortune family I wanted nothing but bone marrow for my daughter. You ought to know I have the good sense not to take Annie away from you and Minn-Gen so soon after her transplant."

As she spoke, Jess was fully aware that she wasn't telling him the whole story. Another very important reason she planned to stay was related to her feelings for him. With some of their problems resolved, she was hoping he'd ask her to marry him.

It's now or never, Stephen realized. If I hesitate, I'll lose her. The amazing thing was, he didn't want to hesitate. Or procrastinate for any reason. In essence, his grief over the breakup of his first marriage was history. He loved Jess and Annie with all his heart. Though he'd never be entirely healed of his son's death, restricting his life to work and sleep was hardly a fitting memorial to David.

Annie needs a dad, he thought. Jess needs a husband. And, oh, how I need them! Confronting the possibility that he might lose them had conjured up the image of a desert in his head.

His voice husky with emotion, he speculated that she

might not need the apartment. "I hope you didn't put down a big deposit," he said.

Jess got extremely quiet at that. "Why?" she ventured after a moment.

"Because you're going to marry me. You and Annie will live with me, at *our* house. I've got a ring for you in my pocket, and a heart full of love for you and your precious daughter...."

With a little rush of relief and happiness, Jess threw herself into his arms. "There's nothing I'd like better," she confessed. "Are you sure you mean it?"

"Ah, darlin'..." Feeling as if he owned the earth, the moon and the stars, Stephen tugged her close. Just to hold her that way, and know they belonged together, was like water after thirst, balm for what had wounded him.

"Let's get the license tomorrow," he proposed, his head filled with a cavalcade of images: the three of them playing in the snow, him and Jess making love by the fire, waking up in the same bed with the woman he loved all warm and smooth next to him under the covers. He wanted to give her everything he had. Everything he was. A child, maybe even soon. He or she would be David and Annie's little sister or brother.

Though he couldn't know it, he sensed that Jess was thinking similar thoughts. "I wish you could have known my son," he said, adding in a complete non sequitur, "I want to give you a baby."

The idea suited her to perfection. "I'd love to have your child," she answered. "And to get the license tomorrow, though not necessarily in that order. There's just one thing..."

Secure in her affection, Stephen invited her to name it.

Her voice was soft and dreamy. Yet it resonated with a lusty note. "I'd like to postpone the ceremony until Annie can walk down the aisle with us," she said. "But I don't want to wait that long to make love to you. Got any ideas?"

Epilogue

As Stephen dialed Mrs. Larsen's number with the objective of asking her to stay with Annie for an hour or two while he and Jess "ran some errands," Nate was stopping by the jail so that Jake could sign some papers. To the brothers' amazement, they were getting along better than they had in years. When Nate produced the necessary documents, handing them to a bailiff to be checked and passed through, Jake signed on the dotted line without a ruckus.

"Maybe we've just needed a wall of glass between us," Jake quipped when Nate remarked on it.

To his surprise, his sibling responded by confessing how worried he'd been about him. "You've been a thorn in my side for years," he admitted. "And yet I love your ornery hide."

The reward for his honesty was a wry smile. "That goes double for me, little brother," Jake said. "Sitting in my cell, I've had plenty of time to think about things. And I've decided you should take a bigger role in managing the executive affairs of Fortune Industries, the way you've always wanted. If I manage to get out of this mess, I plan to spend more of my time doing something related to the medical career I wanted and gave up so long ago. I've decided to found a children's medical mission to third-world countries."

Impressed with Jake's humanitarian plans and relieved that they'd be able to cooperate more fully over the business, Nate congratulated him. "You really have grown in this situation," he said with a shake of his head. "I hope I can do your confidence in me justice."

The moment was bittersweet. Both brothers knew that Jake was facing the fight of his life to prove his innocence.

When he returned home, Nate phoned Sterling and told him of their conversation. "I never thought I'd be saying this," he conceded. "But I think things are going to flow a little more smoothly between us."

As always, Sterling reported his words to Kate, who had invited him for a late supper at her penthouse apartment. Holding hands afterward as they gazed at the crazy quilt of lights spread out below against the velvet of Minneapolis, they speculated softly about what the future might hold.

"It'll be touch and go. But I think Jake will get off and the mystery of my attacker will be solved," Kate predicted. "It's a matter of accretion. Too many clues that point elsewhere are piling up."

With all his heart, Sterling wished he could make that outcome happen for her—that he wasn't such a pessimist.

"I hope you're right, kitten," he said, leaning his head against hers. "Nothing would make me happier than to see you happily ensconced in the heart of your family again."

Still as beautiful as a girl to him in the subtly irridescent lounge coat she'd worn for their tête-à-tête, Kate tossed him one of her more mischievous looks. "Are you sure about that, old dear?" she asked.

Her need to remain hidden, yet have an agent in the sphere of her family to do her bidding, had brought them closer than he'd ever dared hope. Yet he realized that, for the time being, nothing earthshaking would come of it. Maybe when Jake was free and they'd found the real murderer...

"You know me...I'm never sure of anything," he answered, giving her a little squeeze. "Let's just say it's my most *selfless* wish. As for the selfish ones, we needn't talk about them yet."

* * * * *

FORTUNE'S CHILDREN

continues with

THE WRANGLER'S BRIDE

by Justine Davis

Available in April

Here's an exciting preview...

The Wrangler's Bride

Was she really that good, or was he just that much of a pushover?

Grant McClure shook his head ruefully as he walked out to the main barn. It was probably a little of both; he'd always fallen in with Kristina Fortune's maneuvers, even when he'd seen right through them. But his half sister was such a charmer, more full of high spirits than any real maliciousness, it was hard to say no to her.

So he hadn't. And in the process had saddled himself with an unwanted guest for the foreseeable future. And at the worst possible time for him, and the ranch.

The sound of the ranch's truck returning cut in on his thoughts.

"Here goes," he muttered to himself, reversing his steps to go greet his visitor.

He saw Chipper first. Standing beside the driver's door of the mud-spattered blue pickup, the young man looked utterly dazzled. Grant frowned. And then he saw the obvious reason for the hand's expression: the woman who had scrambled without help from the high truck's passenger seat. Long blond hair pulled back in a ponytail bounced as she walked around the front of the truck. She was wearing jeans and a heavy sheepskin jacket and seemed unbothered by the briskness of the air.

She came to a halt when she spotted him, her eyes widening slightly. Grant knew he was staring, but he couldn't help himself; he hadn't expected this.

Meredith Baxter was small, at least from Grant's six-foot viewpoint, and not just in height; from her pixiesh face to a pair of very small feet encased in tan lace-up boots every inch of her looked delicate, almost fragile. And the dark circles that shadowed her eyes only added to the overall air of fragility. She looked tired. More than tired, weary, a weariness that went far beyond the physical. Grant felt an odd tug somewhere deep inside.

She was looking at him, that fatigue dimming eyes that should be vivid green into a flat dullness.

"Hello, Grant."

Her voice was soft, husky, and held an undertone matching what he'd seen in her eyes.

"Hell, Mercy," he said quietly.

She smiled at the old nickname, but the smile didn't reach those haunted eyes. "No one's called me that since you quit coming home summers."

"Minneapolis was never home. It was just where my mother was."

She glanced around, as if trying to take in the vastness of the wild landscape with eyes used to the steel-and-concrete towers of the city, not the granite-and-snow towers of Wyoming's portion of the Rocky Mountains.

"No, this was always home for you, wasn't it?" she said.

"Always."

His voice rang with a fervency he didn't try to hide. He'd known as a child that this place was a deep, inseparable part of him, that its wild, elemental beauty called to something so intrinsic in him that he would never be able to or want to resist.

"So this is what you always had to go back to. I think I understand now."

She sighed. It was a tiny sound, more visible than audible. He'd thought, when Kristina had told him Meredith had become, of all things, a cop, that she must have grown a lot since that last summer, when she'd been a pesky fourteen-year-old. She hadn't. If she'd gained more than an inch in the twelve years since, he'd be surprised.

"You've...changed," he said. And it was true; he remembered her as a live-wire girl with a lot of energy but not much stature. The stature hadn't changed, but the energy had; it seemed nowhere in evidence now.

"Changed, but not grown, is that it?" she said, sounding rueful.

"Well," he said reasonably, "you haven't. Much. I remember you as a tomboy chasing around me everywhere I went."

"And you were my white knight," she returned softly. "Ever since you rescued me from those bullies." A shadow flew across her face, almost wistful.

Grant winced; he wasn't hero material, not even for an impressionable child.

"Oh, don't worry," she said as if in answer to his expression. She smiled widely, one that almost brightened her eyes to the vivid green he remembered. "I got over it long ago. Once I realized I'd fallen for a pretty face without knowing the man behind it, I recovered quite nicely."

"Oh."

It came out rather flatly, and Grant's mouth quirked again. Was he feeling flattered that she'd admitted to the long-ago crush? Or miffed that she'd gotten over it so thoroughly? He nearly laughed; hadn't he had enough of women enamored purely of his looks?

But Mercy wanted something different from him—a place to rest and recover. He just wasn't sure he knew the first thing about providing sanctuary for a heart as wounded as Mercy's seemed to be. He knew about the pain of loss, he'd known about it for a long time, ever since his mother had left his father and the ranch. And he'd had it pounded home again when his father had died, a long, slow death that had been agony to watch.

He'd found nothing to ease the pain he'd felt then. So how could he hope to provide it for someone else? He wouldn't even know where to begin. Kristina had said Mercy wanted only a place to hide, to heal, to find peace. While he had found these things himself in the wild reaches of this Wyoming country, he had little hope that a city girl would find the same kind of relief. Especially since she was dealing with such a brutal, unexpected death. The death of someone, judging from that look in her eyes, she had loved very much.

He wasn't sure there was any relief for that kind of pain.

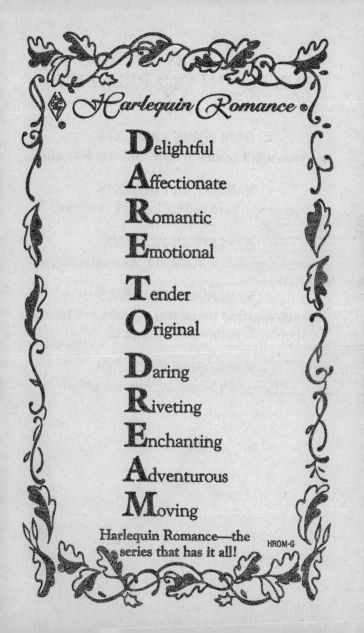

Harlequin Romance ®

Delightful
Affectionate
Romantic
Emotional
Tender
Original
Daring
Riveting
Enchanting
Adventurous
Moving

Harlequin Romance—the
series that has it all!

HROM-G

HARLEQUIN ✦ PRESENTS®

HARLEQUIN PRESENTS
men you won't be able to resist falling in love with...

HARLEQUIN PRESENTS
women who have feelings just like your own...

HARLEQUIN PRESENTS
powerful passion in exotic international settings...

HARLEQUIN PRESENTS
intense, dramatic stories that will keep you turning
to the very last page...

HARLEQUIN PRESENTS
The world's bestselling romance series!

Harlequin® Historical

If you're a serious fan of historical romance,
then you're in luck!

Harlequin Historicals brings you
stories by bestselling authors, rising new stars
and talented first-timers.

Ruth Langan & Theresa Michaels
Mary McBride & Cheryl St.John
Margaret Moore & Merline Lovelace
Julie Tetel & Nina Beaumont
Susan Amarillas & Ana Seymour
Deborah Simmons & Linda Castle
Cassandra Austin & Emily French
Miranda Jarrett & Suzanne Barclay
DeLoras Scott & Laurie Grant...

You'll never run out of favorites.

Harlequin Historicals...they're too good to miss!

HH-GEN

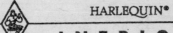

HARLEQUIN®

I N T R I G U E®

THAT'S INTRIGUE—DYNAMIC ROMANCE AT ITS BEST!

Harlequin Intrigue is now bringing you more—more men and mystery, more desire and danger. If you've been looking for thrilling tales of contemporary passion and sensuous love stories with taut, edge-of-the-seat suspense—then you'll *love* Harlequin Intrigue!

Every month, you'll meet four new heroes who are guaranteed to make your spine tingle and your pulse pound. With them you'll enter into the exciting world of Harlequin Intrigue—where your life is on the line and so is your heart!

Harlequin Intrigue—we'll leave you breathless!

LOOK FOR OUR FOUR FABULOUS MEN!

Each month some of today's bestselling authors bring
four new fabulous men to Harlequin American Romance.
Whether they're rebel ranchers, millionaire power brokers
or sexy single dads, they're all gallant princes—and
they're all ready to sweep you into lighthearted fantasies
and contemporary fairy tales where anything is possible
and where all your dreams come true!

You don't even have to make a wish...Harlequin American
Romance will grant your every desire!

Look for Harlequin American Romance wherever Harlequin
books are sold!

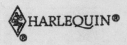

Not The Same Old Story!

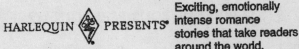

Exciting, emotionally intense romance stories that take readers around the world.

Vibrant stories of captivating women and irresistible men experiencing the magic of falling in love!

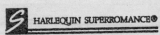

Bold and adventurous—Temptation is strong women, bad boys, great sex!

Provocative, passionate, contemporary stories that celebrate life and love.

AMERICAN ROMANCE

Romantic adventure where anything is possible and where dreams come true.

HARLEQUIN
INTRIGUE

Heart-stopping, suspenseful adventures that combine the best of romance and mystery.

Entertaining and fun, humorous and romantic—stories that capture the lighter side of love.